Timber Ridge

A PORT PROMISE NOVEL

KELLY COLLINS

Copyright © 2024 by Kelly Collins
All rights reserved.
No part of this publication may be reproduced, distributed, or transmitted in any form or by any means, including photocopying, recording, or other electronic or mechanical methods, without the prior written permission of the publisher, except as permitted by U.S. copyright law. For permission requests, contact kelly@authorkellycollins.com.
The story, all names, characters, and incidents portrayed in this production are fictitious. No identification with actual persons (living or deceased), places, buildings, and products is intended or should be inferred. All products or brand names are trademarks of their respective owners.

Chapter One
TIMBER

"Are we going down?" I shout over the engine's roar as the tiny plane bucks wildly. I grip the edge of the seat and eye the bushy-bearded pilot with a mix of terror and disbelief.

Hank offers me a grin that's more alarming than comforting. "This is as routine as a surprise test on a Monday, Teach!"

His hands are steady on the controls while I send a prayer to the universe—surely it didn't line all of this up to watch me do a swan dive into the Alaskan wilderness. I followed the breadcrumbs here. I mean, the job opening might as well have had my name on it. Coincidence isn't part of my vocabulary. Everything happens for a reason.

"Just think of it as a field trip ... with a touch more turbulence." Hank's laughter is lost in the sound of the wind that slams against the fuselage as we narrowly skim a craggy mountain peak.

"Field trips usually have permission slips, signed for safety, not ... near-death experiences!" I laugh because, at this point, it's laugh or cry, and I'm not about to give in to tears.

"Alright, brace yourself, Timber, we're coming in hot!" His tone is oddly casual for our precarious descent.

"Fabulous," I mutter, my voice trembling despite the sarcasm, but I sit up tall because if this is how I bow out, I'm doing it with my spine straight and chin up.

The plane splashes down and skitters across the water as if it's gliding on my just-released breath, before coasting toward the dock.

"Welcome to Port Promise!" he says cheerfully. The engine dies with a final cough. He tosses off his safety belt and swings the door wide open. He wastes no time tossing my duffle bag onto the wooden planks, followed by the mailbag, and he gently places a box of chirping chicks next to everything.

I'm hit with a sense of unease when I step onto the dock. The chicks inside the crate seem to sense it, too, as they peep anxiously through the air holes. Above, an eagle watches us from atop a lamppost, and for a second, I wonder if it's waiting for us to make a move or a mistake.

"You're all set," Hank says with a hint of worry as he eyes the brewing storm clouds.

I scan the deserted dock, and despite the sinking sensation, I say to the wind, "Well, who needs 24-hour doughnut shops when you've got ... endless ocean views?" I let out a sigh, louder than expected, and turn to him. "I was supposed to meet someone here."

He gives me a knowing nod as he climbs into the plane. "That would be Kane," he says. "He's on his way. Kane operates on island time—it's like waiting for paint to dry or dough to rise. It'll happen, just not on a schedule. You'll adapt. You might even find you prefer it to the pace of city life."

"Island time," I say with a wry laugh that vaporizes in the biting air. The phrase always conjures images of balmy beaches and drinks garnished with flowers and paper umbrellas. I come here with no such illusions, fully expecting this brisk, secluded reality. Yet the irony isn't lost on me that they still call it "island time" when the only thing slow here is the sun's crawl to warm the day. Hugging my coat closer as the wind whips with a frigid frenzy, I ask, "So, what's the game plan while I wait for this 'island time' to bring Kane around?"

"Guard duty," he answers, nodding toward the nearby box of birds. "Kane would have a fit if he found even one feather out of place."

"I came here to teach, not be a pet sitter."

"We all do what we have to," He says.

I hoist the box of chicks high on my hip, scanning the desolate dock for shelter. "Alright, little ones," I say with false confidence. "Time for your first lesson: Survival."

"Sarah? Is that you?" An older woman approaches from the direction of a quaint, weather-beaten cafe. She walks with unhurried steps, her silver hair peeking out from under a blue knit hat, glasses as thick as the bottom of a wine glass perched low on her nose. Despite the chill in the air, her smile is warm as she stops before me and leans forward. She squints in my direction, before shaking her head and taking a step back. "Of course, you're not Sarah."

"Uh, no, I'm Timber. Timber Moore, the new summer-school teacher," I say, but she's already waving a dismissive hand.

"I can see that now. My Sarah was a slip of a thing, and here you are, all sturdy with light hair and blue eyes." She pats my arm, her eyes twinkling. "You can't fault an old woman for wishing. I'm May Sweeney. Welcome to Port Promise."

"Thank you," I say, unsure if she means sturdy as a compliment or a jab. "Do you happen to know where Kane might be?"

May exhales a cloud of breath and gives a slight, knowing shake of her head. "Kane will make his entrance from that direction," she says with a casual tilt of her chin. In the distance, the trees give way to a peek at the ocean. "In the meantime"—she nods to a building whose neon "Open" sign blinks against the salt-sprayed window—"why not take refuge in my café? The coffee's hot, and it'll chase away the chill."

"Appreciate it, May, but first"—I glance down at the chirping box—"I gotta do something with these guys." I tilt my head skyward and nod toward the bird still eyeing them for his next meal.

"Ah, always looking out for the young'uns," she

says. "You'll fit right in." She points up the dock and to the right. "The storage room is just over yonder. That should do for now. Just prop open the door a smidge for air." May turns and walks back up the dock to her café.

"Thank you," I call after her. I lug the box of chicks to the room, setting them carefully inside. "There you go, fluff balls. You won't be eagle snacks today."

As the chicks settle, I step back onto the dock, taking in the sights and sounds around me. Waves lap gently at the pilings, and gulls squawk overhead, their cries echoing against the backdrop of dense forest.

From where I stand, I spot the only street in town— the essentials with their weather-beaten storefronts. From my research, there's May's Café, a bar, and a secondhand store. Right next to the community center is a place to do laundry and get drinkable water. The central hub seems to be the dock with a fueling station for boats, a bait and tackle shop, and a small grocery store. It's not much, but it's what I have to work with.

"You signed up for this," I remind myself, taking one last look at the water. "Warmth first," I say, as the incoming storm settles in my bones. "Everything else can wait." As I head toward the building, a creaking and groaning sound draws my attention to the inlet.

May pops her head out of the café door and points to a large, imposing boat as it cuts through the choppy waters. "Looks like your man is here."

"Oh, he's not my man." The words claw their way out, each syllable a shard of glass in my throat. The ghost of my ex-husband lingers in a sharp presence that still cuts deep.

"Kane's a good man. You could do worse," May says.

I meet her gaze, the weight of every letdown in my life hanging heavily. "I'm not looking," I say flatly, the words a shield against expectations I can no longer bear.

May's lips curve up with a hint of knowing. "That's when love finds ya."

I shoot her a cynical look. "Right, because I need love like a case of the pox—itchy, irritating, and leaves you scarred for life."

May shakes her head before entering the café and closing the door.

The boat nears the dock, and at the helm is a man with sharp angles and rough edges, from his waxed, weathered jacket to the set of his bearded jaw.

He slides his boat next to the dock with the ease of a seasoned professional and secures it with a rope before turning to acknowledge me.

"Timber Moore?" His voice is like gravel, the words barely making it over the wind.

"Yep, that's me," I say, trying to sound more confident than I am.

He hoists a bin onto the dock and steps back toward the boat, pausing. "Apologies for the delay. Had an argument with the engine earlier." He nods at the vessel, which bobs gently in the water as if in agreement. "You're a long way from home. Why Alaska?"

"I could use the extra money, plus it seems like it will be an adventure." The truth is, I inherited my mother's tiny one-bedroom home when she died, and everything from the plumbing to the air conditioner needs fixing. Summer jobs are hard to find, and this one landed in my lap.

"The quicker I get these fish offloaded, the faster your adventure begins. We need to get the salmon on ice before the storm hits. Will you give me a hand?"

"What do I have to do?"

"Start loading the bin with fish."

Before I can process his words, he tosses a shiny, slippery body. I dodge it with a yelp. "Wait, I'm not ready."

"Salmon waits for no one. These fish are paying your salary," he states flatly, making it clear that complaining is not an option. I catch the next glistening fish, but it slips through my fingers and hits the dock with a thud.

"Fish are friends, not projectiles!" I say, snagging one mid-air and dropping it into the bin, a flash of pride washing over me until another smacks into my chest and falls to the dock. "Woah, hold on a second."

"Storm's about ready to break. We need to hurry."

After delivering what seems like an entire school of salmon to a plastic holding cell, Kane jumps to the dock and tosses several sanitizing wipes to me.

"Good job." He hoists the mailbag over his shoulder and disappears briefly into one of the old shanty-style buildings while I attempt to remove the scales and slime from my hands and jacket. When he returns, I follow as he drags the salmon bin to the top of the dock and fills it with ice from a nearby machine. He stops and looks around. "Have you seen a box of birds?"

I point to the storage closet. "May said to put them in there."

With a grunt of acknowledgment, he strides over, retrieves the box, and for a moment, his gaze softens as he looks inside.

"Will they be family pets?" I ask.

He chuckles, closing the container with care. "Nope, they're Sunday dinner in about three or four months."

"Ah," I say, the reality of my new life settling in. In an environment like this, sentimentality has no place. As a teacher, I've learned to accept the reality of raising animals for food, understanding the necessity of it for survival.

"Ready to see your new home?"

"Yes." The word is a whisper, my chest hammering against my ribs, nerves simmering beneath the surface.

"Then let's go." He takes off at a double-time pace.

I race down the dock to grab my duffle and rush behind him along the wooden walkway that seems to go on forever.

"How far does this go?" I call out as I race to catch up.

"It connects most of the houses in town. It's our version of a superhighway, but built for ATV's, snowmobiles, and foot traffic."

"That's awesome."

"It's convenient."

Rain falls from the sky, and I pull my jacket tighter, cursing myself for not dressing warmer. I should have splurged on the higher-rated down coat, but all my research suggested that what I bought was appropriate. I suppose they didn't consider I was from Phoenix, which often has temperatures equaling the fiery pits of hell.

We walk for what seems like an eternity, but likely only ten minutes.

"We're here," he says as he stops before a log cabin.

I take a moment to absorb the sight: weathered wood logs forming the walls, a pitched roof covered with green shingles or maybe moss. There's a small porch adorned with a set of antlers over the door. Off to the side is a quaint water pump, which I find oddly charming. It would look adorable with a pot of flowers planted beneath it. The cabin is nestled in a small clearing, surrounded by towering trees that create a picturesque backdrop. I'm awestruck by how perfect it is.

"Let me show you the inside." Kane pushes open the unlocked door and leads me into the one-room cabin.

"Cozy," I say, trying to mask my disappointment. Inside, the reality is far from the fairytale image I had conjured. There are no rocking chairs flanking a stone fireplace. No quilts hanging on the walls. It's more utilitarian than charming. The room is sparse, with just a bed, a table, and chairs. The far wall is lined with shelves, and below them is something that resembles a sink. This isn't the retreat I had envisioned. It's a stark reminder of the bare-bones functionality required to live here. I look back at the door.

"No locks?"

"Not necessary," he says. "You'll find you have everything you need. There are battery-operated lanterns around the room." He points out three. "You'll need to start a fire." He nods toward a wood stove in the corner, which looks like it belongs in a museum.

"Right." I stare at it, willing it to ignite by sheer force of will.

Kane sighs and moves past me. "The first one is on me." He expertly stacks the kindling and wood, lights it, and for a moment, there's the comforting crackle of flame—then smoke billows out, surrounding us in a choking fog.

"Awesome," I cough, waving my hands futilely.

"Damned flue." He gives the stovepipe a rattle, there's a clank, and suddenly, bits of charred who-knows-what rain down, but the smoke clears.

"Thank you," I manage between coughs.

"Don't burn the place down. It's been in the family for a hundred years."

I want to point out that I wasn't the one who nearly set years of history ablaze just now, but I keep quiet.

"My sister Eliza should've mentioned that it's a dry cabin with no running water. There's a water pump just outside to the right, and you'll find the outhouse by the forest's edge straight ahead," he says.

I pause, taken aback. Eliza said it was a rustic cabin but had all the amenities I'd need. "Outhouse?" I took it for granted that all the amenities I needed included running water and a bathroom.

One of his eyebrows lifts, and I notice how his eyes are not quite blue or gray. They are the color of the storm churning outside, beautiful but dangerous.

"Welcome to the wild. Cell phone service is not good. It's spotty at best. Food is in the kitchen." He nods at the far end of the cabin before striding toward the door.

The food turns out to be jars lining the shelves, the contents looking back at me like pickled science experiments. My stomach churns at labels proudly proclaiming Squirrel Stew and Beaver Bolognese.

"Is there anything here that wasn't living in my yard last week?" I call after him.

"Check the bottom shelf," he shouts back, his voice fading with distance.

Relief floods me as I see more recognizable fare, such as salmon and fruit compote, lined up five jars deep.

The door slams shut as the wind lashes against the small windowpanes, leaving me with the echo of its bang. I stand alone, center stage in a one-woman play called *Timber Takes the Tundra*.

"Okay, this is it," I say, rolling my shoulders back. "This will be a fabulous experience or a spectacularly poor decision."

I toe off my boots and pad over to the solitary bed, pressing down on the lumpy mattress. The springs groan beneath the comforter like they're telling tales of past guests. I laugh. It's a sharp sound that's more nerves than humor, and I peel back the cover to see the sheets. They're cold but new looking. I sit on the side of the bed and reach inside my pocket for the familiar edges of the postcard that led me here. Pulling it out, I hold it up to the last remnants of light filtering through the window. It was postmarked over three decades ago, but the scene on the front looks the same: the dock, the water, and the pristine mountains in the background.

I turn it over. Almost nothing is legible. No addressee, no name for return, only a faded message.

Please come back. I love you. We can work it out.

I trace the worn corners and realize there's so much I don't know.

Chapter Two

KANE

WALKING the forest path to Eliza's, the chicks nestling in the box under my arm chirp quietly, almost lost beneath the whisper of the wind. Serenity Cove is just half a mile away, but the weather isn't keen on making my trek easy.

I think of Timber, the Phoenix transplant. It's quite the switch—scorching desert to unpredictable Alaskan skies. I imagine her gazing out the cabin window at the brooding clouds with that city-bred blend of wonder and worry, bundled up against a chill she rarely sees in Arizona.

I don't know what I expected, but it wasn't her. Instead of looking every bit the city girl lost in the wilds, with heels sinking between the gaps in the dock and a flimsy coat that wouldn't ward off the winds, I came across a woman in jeans, sturdy boots, and a jacket that looked warm enough to laugh in the face of Alaska. It's impressive, to be honest. It could be she is more prepared for this place than I give her credit for, or my sister has been more thorough in explaining the rugged realities of life here. Eliza always has a way of vividly describing things to make anyone listen, even a city girl like Timber. But the look on her face when I mentioned the outhouse leads me to believe that she doesn't quite have the entire story. However, she seems to be rolling with the punches pretty well.

Despite her looking the part, it's better to not judge a person's staying power by the clothes they wear, the gear they carry, or the original determined set of their shoulders. You can buy the warmest boots and the thickest jacket, but the grit within counts out here. I've seen enough people come and go, bright-eyed and bushy-tailed, only to find that the relentless wilderness isn't for them. The women, especially those not born in this land, often find the solitude too lonely and the nights too long. Many come, but few choose to stay. But then again, Timber isn't here for the long haul. She's here for a check and the adventure. She's a temporary fixture, a brief brushstroke in the broader canvas of Port Promise. Yet, a part of me wonders if she'll defy expectations and see the full stretch of her eight-week tenure.

She's the answer to a problem I wish I didn't have. I need someone to keep an eye on Hailey so I can pull in enough salmon to buy my new boat. My livelihood depends on her. She's unknowingly more a caretaker than an educator, which is a deception of convenience, and I tell myself it's for the good of everyone. My daughter needs looking after. Without Timber Moore, the fishermen and women with small children, are unable to fish.

Sadly, we need her more than she probably needs us. I just hope she stays, but my experience with outsiders keeping their word hasn't been great.

A thunderclap sounds sharp and close, and I pick up the pace on the wooden walkway. The forest becomes a streak of green and gray as I hurry, the familiar scent of damp earth filling the air—a scent that, to me, means home.

Serenity Cove's lights twinkle through the trees in the distance. Knowing my sister, she'll have a pot of something on the stove. Hailey will be sipping cocoa while watching a DVD of *Frozen* for the zillionth time. Thoughts of my daughter are all I need to move faster. The storm can do its worst, but it won't stop me from getting to where I'm headed.

As the path opens up to Serenity Cove, I see Eliza's house perched like a watchful guardian over the waters.

I step onto her property. Her house, a sturdy structure of logs and stone, seems to embrace the rugged charm of the cove. The windows glow with a welcoming light against the dusk, and a well-worn dock juts into the water, its planks bearing the scars of countless storms. The house and the dock stand firm, like everything here in Alaska—built to face the elements, to endure.

The chicks, previously peeping companions on my trek, have fallen silent in their box, perhaps lulled by the rhythmic patter of rain. I set them gently on the bench beside the door, under the small awning that offers shelter from the storm. As I scrape my boots on the worn mat that says, "Wipe your paws," I knock on the door before I open it.

The heat of the house wraps around me like a much-needed embrace. I take off my jacket and hang it on the hook next to the door. The scent of something rich and hearty—stew or chowder—fills the air, a clear evidence of Eliza's culinary skills.

Before I can call out a greeting, a blur of energy vaults over the back of the couch. "Daddy!" Hailey's voice, the sweetest sound, cuts through the day's heaviness. She's all flying hair and wide, bright eyes as she races toward me.

I scoop her up into my arms, her small frame as light as a feather, her grip firm and sure. "Hey there, Noodle," I say, the nickname slipping out with all the affection I've stored up while away. "How was your day?"

"I got to hear the baby's heartbeat, and I got an ice cream for being good." Her eyes turn to the TV but come straight back to me.

As I hold her close, I realize that, in my daughter's eyes, I rate higher than Elsa and Olaf. That alone is enough to lighten the load of any storm I might face, both the one raging outside and the quieter, more persistent one that sometimes stirs in my heart.

I glance down at her and realize that time has slipped by so fast. If it keeps going like this, she'll be eighteen before I know it, off to college or chasing some dream. And then, like everyone does eventually, she'll move on to her own life. The thought twists my gut.

As I set Hailey down, Eliza turns from the stove, her

pregnant belly pronounced against the kitchen backdrop. "Hailey was a trooper today," she says. There's a tiredness around Eliza's eyes that speaks to the weight she carries. Not just the baby but being alone in all of this. No husband nearby to help and no mother to give her advice.

"Looks like you're ready to pop. Are you sure you have a few weeks left?" I say, my voice filled with concern.

Eliza laughs, a hand resting on her curved abdomen. "It could be any minute now," she says, but her smile doesn't quite reach her eyes. I imagine she's thinking about Matt, her husband, out on the oil rig, the timing of his return uncertain.

I glance out the window, hoping Matt can make it off that rig and through the weather's wrath. He should be here, standing where I am, soaking in the cozy atmosphere, the smells of a home-cooked meal, the laughter of family. He should be here to see his son come into the world.

I wish for that for her as well as our father returning to the island in time to see his first grandson born. I've wished for a lot of things over the years, and that's exactly what they are ... wishes. They're breaths of air that get lost in the wind and never come true.

Hailey tugs at my hand, bringing me back from my thoughts. "Uncle Matt will be home soon," she says with confidence, and she's right. My brother-in-law wouldn't miss this for the world.

Eliza glances over from where she's filling bowls with whatever she's made. "Grab a seat, will you? I've made crab and corn chowder," she says. "Figured I'd feed you both before you head out. Save you a bit of hassle tonight."

I nod, appreciating her thoughtfulness. If not for this chowder, we'd be eating grilled cheese sandwiches and a bag of chips tonight.

"How was your appointment?" I ask, taking a seat at the kitchen table.

"Everything is right on track," she answers. "We had a good check-up in Craig. But, honestly, I'm glad to be back. The noise there was getting to me." She sets three bowls of chowder on the table and joins us.

I chuckle as I get Hailey settled beside me. With little more than a thousand people, Craig barely qualifies as a town, nonetheless an actual city. "Yeah, the city life," I tease. "So loud. Coming from Phoenix, the new teacher, Timber, might find our noise level too low for her taste."

Eliza's face brightens up at the mention of Timber. "Tell me about her," she begins, a spark of enthusiasm in her voice that I haven't seen in a while. "Is she pretty?"

"Didn't notice," I lie, giving my sister a shrug that I hope will end the conversation. Eliza raises an eyebrow, clearly not buying it, but thankfully, she lets it slide.

Inside, though, I must admit I did notice a few things about Timber, just not what Eliza's fishing for. After the shock of me tossing fish her way on the dock, she found her rhythm, packing the bin with surprising efficiency. And when I set a quick pace to the cabin, she kept up without complaint.

It's clear she's not afraid of a little hard work or

getting her hands dirty. But I won't give my sister the satisfaction of knowing that. She has a way of taking an inch of information and stretching it into a mile of matchmaking schemes. I don't need her playing Cupid, especially with someone like Timber, who's not planning to stick around. I've been there and done that. Nope, some thoughts are better kept under wraps.

"Kane, were you at least nice to her?" Eliza asks with a knowing look, the corners of her mouth twitching up in amusement.

"I'm nice to everyone," I say, trying to keep my expression neutral as I spoon the chowder into my mouth.

At that, Eliza laughs, the sound filling the room and bouncing off the walls. She shakes her head. "Oh, brother, your reputation precedes you. Around here, you're known to be as gruff as a bear woken up in winter."

"Daddy's a grumpy grizzly bear," Hailey says.

I grunt in response. I'm aware of the image I project, and sure, maybe it's warranted, but it gets things done and keeps the overly curious at bay, and that's the way I like it.

"I was nicer than you," I say, giving her a bit of a stern look. "I told her about the outhouse and the dry cabin. I thought you would've at least mentioned the living conditions."

Eliza's cheeks redden, a touch of something that looks like guilt flashing across her features as she takes a spoonful of chowder. "I might have left out some of the

... finer details," she confesses. "But Kane, she was the only one who applied, and you saw the cabin—I made sure it was well-stocked, and there are even new sheets." She looks up, her eyes earnest and a little defensive. "And I'll go over first thing tomorrow to check on her. Make sure she's settled in and has everything she needs before she starts Monday."

I nod, recalling the cabin's interior. Despite its basic setup, Eliza had indeed made it as welcoming as a dry cabin can be. The thought of her going out there, especially in her condition, to ensure Timber's comfort is like her—always looking out for others, even with a baby of her own nearly here.

"I can check on her," I say.

Eliza shakes her head. "She's probably already had enough of you. Besides, I want to meet her and tell her about the kids."

Hailey's spoon hovers mid-air, loaded with the last bite of chowder. "Auntie Eliza, when your baby comes, will you be its mommy forever, or will you leave too?" she asks with curiosity.

A tightness grips my chest as Hailey's question hangs in the air.

Eliza sets down her spoon and offers Hailey a reassuring look. "Yes, my little love, I'll be here with my baby forever, just like I'll always be here for you."

Hailey doesn't often bring up her mother, but Amanda's absence weighs heavily on her little mind. Postcards with foreign stamps clutter a drawer, and the phone rings once a month—Amanda's way of reaching out. It's not the life I had in mind, and damn sure not what Hailey deserves. Since Amanda's departure, she's only been back a few times, and those times were because Amanda was between projects and had no place else to go. Poor Hailey's got that gap in her life, the kind you can't plaster over, and I see her trying to make sense of it with every new photo of a place she hasn't been and a voice that's more distant than the miles it travels.

Hailey eats the last bite of chowder with a contented sigh. The day will come when she asks more questions, but Eliza's reassurance is enough for now.

"Dinner's done, Noodle. Time to pack up your things," I say, standing up from the table. "We need to get back. I've got a box of chicks that would prefer the coop."

Hailey scrambles from her chair. "Can we go to May's tomorrow for pancakes?" she asks, her eyes lighting up with the prospect of a treat.

"If you're quick about it, we'll swing by for those chocolate chip smiley-face ones you love before we run our errands." She dashes off with enough energy to power the town's lighthouse on the darkest of nights.

As I clear the table and wash up, Eliza watches me. "You'd make quite the catch for the right woman," she says, leaning back in her chair.

I shake my head, focusing on the soapy water. "I'm done with all that. My heart's got room for two—just you and Hailey."

When I turn to her, I see sadness in her eyes. It's been just us kids for a while now, especially since Mom passed away a few months back. The absence of Mom's laughter is a silence that still echoes in the corners of every room. It's why Dad is gone, too. He can't sit in the quiet and not wish for something different. Damned wishes.

I finish up with the dishes, dry my hands, and glance back at my sister, who's now gently rocking in her chair. "Let's keep it just us," I add, more to myself than to her, a quiet commitment to trust the family I have in place.

With a parting hug, Hailey and I put on our coats and walk outside. I secure the chicks and Hailey into the ATV I left for Eliza to use that morning. Hers is in the shop, making getting around difficult when you're pregnant. The town isn't car friendly. ATVs and snowmobiles reign here, and my Polaris four-seater has been a lifesaver over the years.

The rain has dwindled to a mist that barely whispers against our faces as we wave to Eliza's silhouette in the window and start up the mountain. The vehicle's lights cut through the dark, and as we ascend, my thoughts drift back to Timber, and I wonder how she is getting along on her first night in town.

Chapter Three
TIMBER

After setting down the postcard, a fleeting shiver reminds me of the practicalities of frontier life. My socked feet curl against the cool wooden floor as I reach for the battery-operated lantern, its switch sounding with a soft click. Instantly, a warm light floods the room, pushing the darkness into the corners where shadows linger.

Despite the unease of solitude, a grin crosses my lips. The lantern brings modern comfort to the rustic space. It's a blend of old and new here, much like the postcard's history meeting my present. The lantern has a socket—a small yet significant amenity. I rummage through my bag, retrieving my phone cord. While a phone call might be optimistic with the spotty service, I can at least set an alarm. I pull out my phone, seeing the battery's charge holding on, though the signal is barely a whisper of a bar.

With day turning to night, it's time to prioritize sustenance over sentiment and cell phones. Kane left a fire smoldering in the wood stove, a welcome luxury I'm not keen to squander. I kneel before it and wonder if all I'm supposed to do is add a log? Surely it can't be much different from the firepit in Mom's backyard. Once lit, all it requires is consistent feeding. The logical choice is to add a piece of wood and pray that it coaxes the fire back to life. When I do, the fire grows and heat seeps into the room, making up for the lack of amenities. Maybe Eliza is right after all. Perhaps this is all I need.

I'm convinced of that until my stomach grumbles with a complaint that it, too, needs feeding, so I search for something to cook with. The lantern light guides me to a cupboard, filled with mismatched items, each with its own story. My fingers close around a plate, its porcelain edge chipped—a slight imperfection that hints at a long history. I wonder about the meals it has held, the laughter or conversations it has witnessed, all here in the quiet seclusion of the cabin.

I locate a pot next, its bottom blackened from the many fires it has sat above. I realize that all my cooking here will depend on the wood stove, a challenge I accept with a mix of apprehension and excitement. There's a romance to the idea of this cabin, this simplified way of life that I will experience. Love it or hate it, it's what I have for the next eight weeks, and I can do anything for that long.

With a sigh, I place the chipped plate on the countertop alongside a small jar of salmon—less daunting, more familiar than squirrel or beaver. Beside it, I place single serving jars of preserved vegetables and a fruit compote, their colors vibrant even in the lantern's artificial glow. It's a balanced meal—simple, yet nourishing.

I set a small pot for the vegetables and salmon on top of the stove, the heat welcoming and ready. Once cooked, the salmon will be warmed through and the vegetables tender. This is cooking stripped back to its essence. I glance at the plate again. Its chip is now a feature I admire. It's a mark of endurance and resilience—qualities I hope to embody here.

At the small table, I eat and look around the cabin. The wood stove is the heart of the cabin and sits in the corner, its matte black surface a stark contrast against the warm glow of the flames within. A pile of wood is stacked neatly beside it. Everything here has a purpose. The plate in my hand is not just a container for food but a piece of the cabin's soul, and now, a part of my story, too.

After finishing, I spy a plastic bin tucked beneath the sink. It seems like the likely candidate for water collection. This task, in theory, should be simple, but in practice, it seems like an initiation into a life I've only read about in adventure novels.

I don my jacket and tug my hood over my head. With the bin in hand, I step outside and into the dwindling rain. The cool air is a brisk reminder of my new reality. The water pump stands a few yards away, looking like a relic from a bygone era. I approach it with a mix of determination and the kind of trepidation one might experience when meeting a legend. The pump handle is foreign, but water gushes out in a rhythmic beat soon enough, a sound oddly satisfying.

Water sloshes over the rim as I carry the bin back inside. I tread carefully to avoid more spills. This simple act is so different from turning on a tap, and it leaves me feeling accomplished and utterly out of my element. But I'm here to embrace it all—each small victory and every new challenge.

I heat the water on the stovetop, carefully pouring it into the tub to wash the dishes. Each plate and cup is like a small victory as I scrub them clean. Even a simple task like washing dishes becomes complicated without plumbing.

With the night deepening, I cast a wary glance toward the outhouse. The wooden structure stands ominously in the darkness, its weathered door hinting at untold secrets. I imagine what horrors might await me behind that door—spiders, ghosts, or perhaps something even more sinister. As I gather my courage, the realization hits me that living here will be full of unexpected challenges.

I grab a lantern as I step outside. Shadows stretch and play tricks on my eyes. The rain has stopped, and the cool, moist air of the night is scented with pine and damp soil. It fills my senses, leaving me exhilarated and slightly on edge. Droplets fall rhythmically from the pine needles, punctuating the stillness. The forest seems to hold its breath, observing me. My boots press into the soft earth, the quiet so complete around me that each step echoes between the trees. I'm wrapped in solitude, yet the rustle of leaves and the soft creaks tell me I'm far from being alone.

I reach the outhouse door and pull it open with a trembling hand, half expecting a rush of nightmarish critters to burst forth. Instead, I'm met with the startling civility of cleanliness. The toilet paper is stacked with military precision, and a box of wipes sits next to a bottle of hand sanitizer. On the wall is a poster of a squirrel with its eyes covered as if to say, "No peeking!" It's absurd, it's hilarious, and for a moment, I forget to be afraid.

With a sigh of relief, I do what nature demands while trying to ignore the chorus of 'what-ifs' my mind comes up with. Something at that moment releases a haunting screech into the night, and I'm convinced it's the dinner bell for every creature with teeth or claws.

I finish up, shaking slightly as I pull my pants up and slather my hands in sanitizer. I'm ready to bolt when another shriek pierces the air, sending a shiver down my spine. Is it an owl, some small furry woodland creature, or something scarier? I'm trapped in the tiniest room of my life, and suddenly, it's a fortress against the vast, unknown wilderness.

What will I face on the other side of the door? A bear? A pack of wolves? Should I go or stay? I chastise myself for my fear of the unknown and for even thinking for a second that I could sleep in the outhouse. With a deep breath, I fling the door open and practically leap out. The darkness has transformed every bush into a lurking predator, every innocent shadow into a hungry hunter. My mind is a Hollywood director of horror films, casting each rustling leaf as a potential ravenous beast.

Heart sprinting, I sprint too. The 20-yard dash back to the cabin is like a marathon through a gauntlet of imagined monsters. I burst through the door, half expecting applause for escaping the clutches of the night, but I'm met with only the crackling of the fire.

Slamming the door shut, I lean against it, panting and laughing at my wild imagination. As the adrenaline fades and I settle into the cabin's embrace, my phone, which had struggled to cling to a solitary bar of signal earlier, lights up with the arrival of a message. Surprise washes over me. Messages are rare for me in my usual world. I'd expect them to be non-existent here.

I cross the room, wondering who texted. Back at school, my phone is purely practical—always a colleague asking for a favor, a last-minute substitution, or a reminder about a deadline. Social invites, the kind that hint at inclusion and camaraderie, like happy hours or a Bunco night, never show up on my screen. Those are for the tenured teachers who have firmly established their place within the faculty's inner circles. There would be no calls from my best friend because that was always Mom, and she's no longer here. When she passed, it was like losing a piece of myself. It would have been different if she'd passed after a long illness. I would have been almost happy in that scenario to not see her suffer, but Mom was healthy and vibrant when she was struck by a car on a morning run. That's what makes it so much harder. Mom had so much life left in her.

I swipe the screen and find a message from Eliza telling me she'll pick me up at nine to show me around.

I text back, but the message fails to send because my whisper of a bar has turned to none. I set the phone down, and my attention shifts to the duffle bag lying open. It's time to make this space mine.

I work quickly, pulling out the essentials. First, my Kindle. Its library of unread books is a lifeline, a comfort I'm not willing to do without.

Next comes the hefty bag of Jelly Belly candies, a colorful splash against the cabin's muted tones. I hope they'll last the duration of my stay, but my sweet tooth might have other plans. I think about May's comment and laugh. You don't maintain a sturdy frame like mine without a few indulgences.

I dig deeper, finding the framed photo of my mother. It's a candid shot, her laugh frozen in time. I place it on the small bedside table, a piece of home, of her, to watch over me.

"I can't imagine you being here." I glance around the cabin and look out the window into the inky night. "Is this why you hated the cold so much?"

There are so many unanswered questions. The only time my mother ever mentioned my father was when I asked about him, and she told me he left her—left us. She didn't know how to find him. She told me the past is the past, the future is the future, and all we have is here and now—the present. She'd insisted it was a gift, meant to be unwrapped with care and lived with joy, not with eyes fixed backward or gazing too far ahead. I never thought about him again until that postcard dropped out of my mother's herbal medicine journal. One of my parents is dead, but the other is around, and I'm curious about a lot of things. I have so many questions that need answers. Like, why did he leave? What does he look like? What parts of me are like him? I hope to find the answers while I'm here.

I refocus my energy on unpacking, and a few other treasures emerge, like a soft, well-worn hoodie that's seen better days, and a beanie baby. Cubby the Bear has been with me for as long as I can remember. There is no way I'd leave him behind on this adventure when he's been here through every major event in my life. I set him on the nightstand beside Mom. Lastly, I take out a soft fleece blanket. It's comforting and warm to hold on to during the lonely nights ahead. I lay it across the bed, ready to be my cozy hug in this new, quiet place.

My makeshift home now holds the small but significant imprints of my life. I stand and step back, surveying the cabin, sensing a thread of connection to everything within it. This is home, for now. With little left to do, I change into flannel pajamas and climb between the sheets to read.

The morning light filters in, and I wake ready to conquer the day. My morning routine is easy, and the trip to the outhouse doesn't seem as scary in the full light of day. Just as I'm finishing a bowl of jarred peaches, the unmistakable sound of an ATV approaches. I peek through the window, my breath catching at the sight of who could only be Eliza, steering the vehicle with one hand while the other rests on her pregnant belly. A mix of emotions tugs at me. I'm struck by the excitement of meeting her and the concern that she's forced to come out and help me in her condition.

I push the door open as the sound of the engine cuts off.

"Morning, Timber!" Eliza's voice, bright and clear, breaks the stillness around me. She vibrates with energy. "Looks like you've survived your first night!" she says.

"Survived is one way to put it," I say, stepping into the crisp morning air. "A heads-up about the outhouse could've been part of the welcome package."

Eliza's laugh is full and unapologetic. "I guess I could've, but then I might have risked you changing your mind. And we can't have that," she says, her tone light but sincere.

"Well, I'm here now."

Inwardly, I know the truth of it. Even if Eliza had sent a list of every hardship and every challenge that awaited me, it wouldn't have deterred me. I would've come regardless, even if it meant sleeping in a tent. I need the money, and I have a mystery to solve.

Eliza slides off the ATV and walks to me. Her stomach reaches me a full second before she does. "Are you ready to see what we have to offer?"

"Absolutely." I look around, seeing my temporary home in the light of day, and I find it enchanting. If everything else in town is half as captivating, I'll be in for a treat. "I'm quite happy to be here."

Eliza's belly pushes against mine without notice, and her arms wrap around my shoulders. "I just knew in our few conversations that you'd be perfect for the job."

The hug is surprising, but not unwelcome. It has been a long time since anyone hugged me, and I hold on a few seconds longer than I should.

"I'll do my best to fill your shoes while you're busy."

"You'll be great. Let's get on with the tour." Eliza climbs back on the ATV and pats the seat beside her. "Just got this baby back this morning."

I climb onto the contraption that looks more like a souped-up golf cart.

"Is this the normal mode of travel?" I look at her stomach and wonder how she'll get around once the baby is born.

"It's this, the snowmobile in the winter, or walking." She points to the back seat. "I can strap him in for safety."

"You're having a boy. That's wonderful."

Eliza laughs. "Yes, much to the disappointment of the entire town. Women are outnumbered here at least four to one. But I'm happy to have a son. We're naming him Cody."

"That's a wonderful name. Now, tell me about Port Promise. I mean, the things I couldn't learn from an internet search."

"We have a small community. We've dwindled to less than a hundred from about four hundred a few years ago.

And trust me, it seems like most of them are related to me!"

As we ride, her words mix with the ATV's buzz. She talks about the trees and wildlife and asks me if I'd like to accomplish anything while I'm here.

I think about all the woodland sounds that kept me sleeping with one eye open last night. "I'd like to stay alive." I keep my real mission under wraps—finding the mysterious postcard sender. I'm not sure I'm ready to share that just yet. It seems too personal to share that with someone I don't know. Besides, how do you ask about a man you know nothing about? I don't even have a name.

"We'd like you to stay alive too," she says as she winds around the wooden path I walked yesterday. "You started well. You survived Kane, who can come across as a bit rough around the edges. Was he alright to you?"

I offer a noncommittal smile. I couldn't tell her that he was like a welcome wagon and showed up with gifts, but then again, I couldn't say anything negative either. He was direct and to the point. "He was ... efficient," I say, which is true enough.

She laughs, a sound that seems to understand the unsaid. "Efficiency is a virtue with that one. He's had to be on top of things, being the oldest of us. Port Promise isn't without its challenges. My brother has faced many," she says. "I'm the youngest, the last attempt for a daughter. And let me tell you, growing up with all those boys ... you learn to stand your ground. Thankfully, I had a good role model in my mother. May God rest her soul."

"I'm sorry for your loss," I say. We share the understanding and experience of grief. "I lost my mother recently, too. It seems we have a lot in common."

Eliza's face shows a blend of empathy and sisterhood. "I'm sorry to hear that," she says.

She looks down at her stomach. "I miss my mother always, but I wish I had her now. Thankfully, she was here when we got the news that I was pregnant, and we were able to celebrate. I just wish she could have held on so she could meet the baby. I never imagined having a child without her here to guide me," she says.

"That must be so hard." I can't imagine having to be a mother without my mother's support. For the first time, I'm grateful that I'll never have to face that.

With a knowing nod, Eliza adds, "I bet we'll be fast friends, you and me. And who knows? The town might grow on you, and you'll want to stay. Lord knows we don't have enough people like you here."

"You mean women?"

She nods. "They come, sure, but stick around? That's rare, which goes back to my four to one ratio," she says, eyeing the endless stretch of wilderness.

It gets me thinking. Alaska? Mom never breathed a word about this place. With her shivering at anything below sweater weather, it just doesn't add up. The postcard's "come back" haunts me. Could she have braved the cold here for love? The pieces don't fit.

While I'm not comfortable asking about a man I don't know, I certainly don't mind asking about a woman I do. "Do you ever remember meeting anyone besides me with the last name Moore? Like an Aspen Moore?" I ask, hoping for a speck of recognition. "I think my mother may have visited here in her youth."

She furrows her brow, steering the ATV around a particularly stubborn rock before answering. "Moore? I can't say I recall anyone by that name. But you have to understand that we don't always get to know the short-term visitors. Especially if they stick to themselves, and if it was your mother, she would have come long before my time. The person to ask is May. She's always in the know."

"Thank you. I'll consider that. I met her on the dock yesterday. She seems nice."

"May's the wisdom of the town—she's seen seven decades come and go. If your mother was here for anything longer than a weekend visit, May would remember. That woman's got the memory of an elephant. She's the backbone of this town. We don't have a doctor close by. I have to travel to Craig for my appointments, so May's the one we turn to for the less serious things. She's got a remedy for every cough and a potion for every ache, all from the plants she tends like her own kids. She's our gem, and without her, well, we'd be a bit lost."

As the trees begin to thin and the dense woods open up to the expanse of the water, the dock comes into view, signaling the edge of town. Eliza guides the ATV onto a clearer path.

"We're headed to her place now," she announces as we approach the center of the town. "Best pancakes in town, and you'll get to meet some of the locals."

Chapter Four

KANE

THE JINGLE of the café door chimes like a warning, and I lift my gaze. It's them—Eliza, who could outshine the Northern Lights, and Timber, the newcomer, her presence a stark reminder of how fast things can change. Just yesterday, she was an unfamiliar face, and today, she's the linchpin in my carefully balanced life during salmon season. I don't know her, yet I'm tethered to her by necessity, a fact that irks me more than the cold bite of the morning.

Hailey's squeal cuts through my brooding thoughts. "Daddy, Auntie Eliza's here!" Her little hands clap in excitement, chocolate chip pancakes forgotten. "And the new teacher! Can they sit with us?"

I hesitate, preferring to enjoy my breakfast in peace, but that hasn't happened since Hailey was born. I try to find an excuse to say no, but Hailey's looking at me with those big, hopeful eyes, and I know I don't stand a chance against her, not for the first time, and certainly not the last.

"Yeah, Noodle," I say, masking my reluctance with a half-hearted grin for her sake. "Invite 'em over."

Eliza doesn't need an invitation. She leads Timber straight to our table. "Kane, I hope you don't mind us crashing your breakfast." Her voice carries the same ease it always does, but I catch a glint of something else in her eye—something hopeful.

Timber trails behind, eyes scanning the café like she's casing the joint. There's a determination in her posture that I begrudgingly respect. She meets my gaze, and I glance down at my plate which is filled with eggs, bacon, sausages, and hash browns.

"We'd be happy to share our table," I say, and it's true, for Hailey's sake. Timber sits down across from me. Our eyes meet again. Hers are the color of the sky that peeks through the trees of my ridge.

Hailey's voice cuts through the hum of the café like a knife through butter. "Daddy, you said she wasn't pretty, but she is."

Heat crawls up my neck, and I swear even the old jukebox in the corner skips a beat as her statement hangs in the air. "No, Noodle," I correct quickly, the words stumbling out in my rush. "I said I hadn't noticed." It's a feeble save, and from the way Timber's eyebrow arches, I'm unsure if she's offended or entertained.

May, bless her, slides into the fray with the grace of a seasoned diplomat. "Well, I notice everything, and I say we've got a room full of pretty people here today," she declares with a grin that's seen its share of awkward moments. She winks at Hailey, who giggles, thankfully moving on from her earlier conversation.

"So, what can I get you ladies?" May asks, pulling out her notepad, the professional in her effortlessly smoothing over the crinkles of our morning.

"Before we order," Eliza says, "Timber wants to know if you've heard of someone named Aspen Moore, who might have come through here years ago."

May taps her chin with her pen. "That name doesn't ring a bell."

"Do you think you have ties here?" I ask, probing deeper than I'd intended.

"No, not at all," Timber replies with a quick shake of her head. "I had this thought that my mom might have passed through, but she hated the cold. She would've never considered staying here, especially when the temperatures fall so low."

"Folks drift in, but few drop anchor and stay," I say. The wheels turn inside my head. Could my mom have brushed paths with her mother had she graced Port Promise with her presence? I hate that I can't pick up the phone to ask her.

"That's the truth of it. Many drift past but few plant roots. Sorry, I can't help," May says, positioning her pen on the order pad. "But I can feed ya."

Eliza orders her usual corned-beef hash and eggs, and Timber hesitates just a moment before requesting coffee and pancakes.

I keep my eyes on my plate, focusing on the ooze of

the egg yolks rather than the weight of Timber's gaze. The silence is comfortable for no one, filled only by May's scribbling on her notepad. As she walks away, I risk a glance up, meeting Timber's eyes, and I clear my throat. "So, what's on the agenda for today?"

Eliza perks up, always the organizer. "I'm going to give Timber the grand tour of town, which should take twenty minutes, and then head over to the community center to get her familiarized in the classroom for tomorrow."

"Sounds like a good idea." I'm relieved that I have no place in these plans. That means Hailey and I can run our errands and get home. There's work to be done on the chicken coop.

"What time do you need me there tomorrow?" Timber asks, her hands wrapped around the warm mug of coffee May just delivered.

I pause, a spoonful of hash browns hovering in mid-air. "No later than six," I reply, the words landing on the table with a thud.

The shock on Timber's face would be comical if the situation wasn't so dire. "Six in the morning?" she echoes, and it's clear this wasn't in the job description Eliza provided. "When does the day end?"

Eliza winces, her shoulders hunching up around her ears. "I might have, um, forgotten to mention that the days are long. Most people will be by to pick up their kids by four, but you usually will have extra days off because the weather mucks up so many schedules."

Timber's head cocks to one side and then the other

before she shrugs. "So, it's a forty-hour week. Sounds about normal."

"Give or take," Eliza says and rushes on. "But think of all the time you'll save! I've got the first week's lesson plans ready for you. We're bringing firewood straight to your door, and you won't have to worry about meals—"

I watch as the information sinks in. I half expect Timber to stand and declare that she quits before she starts. Instead, she takes another drink of coffee and says, "If anyone is taking orders, I'll pass on the squirrel."

"Squirrel tastes just like chicken!" Ever the innocent commentator, Hailey pipes up with the earnestness only a child can muster. She's beaming and proud to share.

A burst of laughter escapes me that seems to lighten the morning load. "Well, you heard the expert," I manage between chuckles, grateful for the break in tension. "Who needs chicken when you have squirrels?"

"If squirrels taste just like chickens, why did you need to mail order a whole flock?" Timber asks with a playful tilt of her head.

I wait for Eliza to answer, but she stares at me.

"Well, you see," I start, leaning back in the booth, "the squirrels here are a part of the local charm. It wouldn't do to have them all disappear into stews and pies. Plus, chickens lay eggs, and as far as I know, no one's managed to get a decent omelet out of a squirrel. Besides, the closest fried chicken joint is in Anchorage, and DoorDash doesn't deliver here."

"You'll have to give it a try. It's far better than it sounds," Eliza says.

Timber shakes her head. "Between you and me, I'd rather eat my boots than a bowl of bushy-tailed stew. I'm fairly certain of where my boots have been."

After a hearty laugh, we fall into a comfortable silence. May delivers their food, and our breakfasts disappear while conversations weave around bites of food and sips of coffee. Hailey's stories about her kindergarten adventures serve as our soundtrack.

The meal progresses smoothly until Eliza suddenly stills, her hand reaching for the top of her belly. She winces, a low groan escaping her lips.

Timber's head snaps up, concern etching her features. "Eliza, are you okay?"

Eliza takes a deep breath. "It's just heartburn," she assures us, though her eyes are tight at the corners. "It happens all the time lately, but I think ... I might have to pass the town tour torch to you, Kane."

That look in her eyes, and the slight tilt of her head—it's Eliza's way of saying "I'm sorry, but you know you're the only one who can," without words.

I run a hand down my face, a catalog of excuses racing through my mind, each flimsier than the last. I can't let Eliza down, not with her in this state, or in front of Timber, who's watching the whole exchange with worry and curiosity.

But there's a nagging suspicion in my mind, a thought that this might be too convenient. I narrow my eyes at Eliza, who meets my gaze with an apologetic expression. I give her a look that I hope conveys "I'm onto you," but the resolve in her eyes tells me she's not faking.

"All right," I say, pushing back from the table and standing up. "Hailey and I are your tour guides for the day."

Eliza's relief is palpable, and she squeezes my hand. "You're the best, Kane. I owe you one."

I give her hand a reassuring squeeze back, my role as the protective big brother never fading, no matter how much I grumble. "Just take care of yourself, okay?"

With a plan reluctantly in place, I turn to Timber and say in my friendliest tone, "Ready to see the town?"

I reach for the check while Eliza gathers her things, still pressing a hand to her belly. "Remember to call if you need anything," I tell her.

Eliza gives me a slight nod. "I will."

"I'll pay for mine," Timber says.

I shake my head. "I've got it. It's the least I can do since I was late yesterday."

I sense that she wants to argue, but she doesn't. She nods and says, "Thank you."

After paying, we say goodbye to May and step outside. The brisk air hits us with the subtle bite of reality. Eliza heads to the ATV, her steps slow but steady. I watch for a moment, making sure she's settled before turning to Timber, who's looking up at the blue sky with a tourist's wonder.

There's an awkward silence. I shove my hands into my pockets, sensing the weight of what lies ahead.

"I didn't tell her you weren't pretty," I whisper, almost against my will, as we start walking.

Timber turns in my direction with a teasing sparkle in her eyes. "Oh, so you think I am?"

The corner of my mouth twitches up despite my efforts. "You're okay for a city girl."

We walk side by side now, with Hailey skipping ahead as if she's the tour guide. I let it happen because when Hailey thinks she's helpful, she's happy, and I only want her to be happy.

Hailey's chatter is as constant as the waves lapping the shore, filling the space between us with innocent observations and questions. Her small hand finds mine, tugging me along as she skips toward town.

"Uncle Rhys runs everything on the dock, and when I'm super good, he gives me a lollipop!" Her voice is full of pride, eyes wide with the importance of this grown-up transaction.

"Is that so?" Timber engages her with a warm expression, clearly charmed. "I'd love to meet this generous uncle of yours."

Hailey beams at the prospect, but I'm quick to temper her enthusiasm. "Not today, Noodle. We've got a job to do."

Hailey's shoulders slump briefly before she's off again, resilient as only a child can be, skipping ahead to the next point of interest.

"You call her Noodle. Why that nickname?"

"From the second she was born, she was all floppy, just a wriggly little thing in my arms," I explain.

"Couldn't hold her head up, limbs waving around ... I called her Noodle right then and there. And it stuck."

"I see that it's just you and Hailey today. Will I have a chance to meet Hailey's mother? Will she be dropping off or picking Hailey up from school?"

Timber asks in a way I imagine a teacher would at a conference when a parent is missing, but it still irks me. I hate making excuses for Amanda. "No, she doesn't live here."

Timber nods, but she doesn't press for more information and walks forward.

Hailey points to the communal showers by the water station. "Since you're staying in Grandpa's old cabin, you'll have to shower here. Or you could come to our house?"

Before Timber can respond, I'm shaking my head. "No, no, these showers are closer and more convenient for you," I say too quickly. I don't need Timber looking all ... well, looking like she does, showing up at my doorstep for a shower. The thought lingers, unbidden and unsettling. I stare at her, taking in the way she's talking with Hailey, the easy set of her shoulders, the softness of her laugh.

And that's when it hits me—against all my resistance, I find her ... nice looking. It's more than nice looking, if I'm honest. It's a realization that clings like a snagged net, something I can't quite shake free of.

I tuck the thought away, somewhere deep and out of sight, and focus on the path ahead. For now, the showers by the water station are just showers, and Timber is just the woman who will help us through the summer. That's all.

We round a corner, and Hailey races ahead to a weathered sign standing guard at the entrance of the town. The wood has turned silver with age, but the words are still legible, carved deeply and backfilled with black paint that resists the relentless kiss of the sun and the bite of winter's chill.

"The port's promise," Hailey reads aloud, her fingers tracing the carved letters. "We vow to create a community where every hand is extended in support, and no one stands alone."

"Good job, Hailey," Timber says.

I laugh. While Hailey can read, she's made me recite that every time we visit town. "She's got it memorized. She's a Dr. Seuss junkie, though."

"That's still amazing."

Pride swells in my chest. "Yes, I agree." Hailey is amazing. While her hair is never right, and her clothes are a mismatch of whatever I can throw together in the morning, she's thriving, primarily due to her time with my mother and Eliza. But things change. Mom's gone, and Eliza will have her own child to watch after. I've technically always been a single parent, but I never had to do it on my own until now.

Timber's gaze lingers on the sign, a hint of curiosity in her eyes. "Is it true?" she asks, looking at me for confirmation.

I offer a half-grin, a mix of nostalgia and skepticism

in my glance. "It used to be," I admit. "These days, everyone's caught up in their lives."

Our stroll takes us by the familiar landmarks of the town. There's Yeti's Tavern with its window signs promising cold beer and warm company. All I've ever found there were stale chips and a hangover. Second Chance Consignment is like a hospice center—a place where you bring the things that have a little life left in them.

The community center stands before us, its facade a patchwork of maintenance and neglect. "This place was once the heart of it all," I tell Timber. "We had Sunday potlucks here as a kid, movie nights, too. But things have changed."

I push open the door to the center, the creak of the hinges echoing through the quiet building. "Now, it's mostly just for school and the occasional town meeting. The community ... we don't gather like we used to."

As I lead Timber inside, the heaviness of Port Promise's promise weighs on my shoulders—the pledge of neighborliness that's grown threadbare with time. But who has time for all that?

"And that ends our tour."

She walks into the room and slides her fingers across the tables. I can't gauge what she's thinking. On the other side of the room, she turns to face me. "Six in the morning ... really?"

I sigh. "I'm sorry Eliza wasn't transparent. Hank is only a call away if this isn't your cup of tea." I offer her an out, but I'm praying she doesn't take it.

She looks at me like she might ask me to make the call and then shakes her head. "It isn't exactly what I expected, but some of the best things come from surprises. I'll give it a shot."

"I appreciate that. Should we walk you back to your cabin?"

"No, I'll stick around here for a bit and try to find those lesson plans Eliza made for me." She points to the cabinets. "I should get familiar with what I have to work with."

"Sounds good." I glance over and find Hailey drawing flowers on the chalkboard. "Time to go, Noodle."

"Aww, I want to stay."

I kind of want to stay too, but there's work to do. "We need to take care of the chicks. You'll see Miss Moore tomorrow." It's also the first Sunday of the month, and while I hate to bring it up in case it doesn't happen, I remind her anyway, because I know it will get Hailey moving. "It's your mom's Sunday to call."

At the mention of the call, Hailey is by my side and waving goodbye.

Chapter Five

TIMBER

IT'S A CRISP, quiet morning as I leave my cabin at 5:15 and head to the community center. The air is still as I walk the ten minutes to town. The path reminds me I'm far from the heat and dryness of Phoenix. Here, the air is thick with moisture, and the trees are heavy with dew.

As I step out of the woods, the dock's hustle greets me as fishermen ready their boats. I pause, take in the scene, and think about Kane, who will show up within the hour to drop off Hailey. What is his morning routine? How early does he have to rise to be ready to work at six? Since Hailey's mom doesn't live there, he does it all. In the short time I've been here, he's shown so much about himself. He fishes for a living, raises a daughter on his own, and is the backbone of his family. He has a lot on his plate.

The community center door stands open. I was certain I'd shut it, but the latch must not have caught.

Maybe I can get Kane to look at it. I dismiss the thought immediately. I don't want to add to his workload.

Inside, it's quiet now, but it won't be long before the place fills with a few lively children. Eliza's notes said that it could be between three to five kids this week. Some are on vacation and many of the town's children work during the summer.

Just before six, a boy barrels through the door. "Hi, I'm Lucas," he says. His dad follows, a grin lighting up his face. "I'm Eric, and this bundle of energy is mine. He's heading toward twelve but has the attitude of a well-seasoned teenager. I hope you're ready for him."

"I can't wait to get started." That is true. I love teaching, and doing it here is no doubt going to be a learning experience for everyone.

"We're grateful to have you here."

A sweet sensation bubbles up inside me.

With Eric and his son looking at me like I'm actually here and seen, I experience a spark of something special. It's just for the summer, I remind myself, but this short season can be the one where I make a lasting impression, where I matter. I offer my hand. "Good morning. I'm Timber Moore, and I'm thrilled to be here."

Then, a burst of energy rounds the doorway—a little boy with a spring in his step that could rival the liveliness of the waves crashing on the port's shores. But the moment his mother follows him inside, this live wire retreats behind her, suddenly more of a cautious kitten than a bounding tiger. The only thing I see is his hand trying to grasp his mother's jeans but can't because of the plastic Thor in his hand.

"Hi there, I'm Theresa, and this shy guy here is Tommy," she says, her strong voice contrasting with the delicate touch of her handshake.

Tommy peers out from behind Theresa's legs, his earlier enthusiasm now tempered by a bashful silence.

"Hey there, Tommy!" I say, kneeling before him. "You know, Thor's pretty cool, isn't he? He's all about bravery and strength, just like you showed when you walked in here. I bet you and Thor would make an unstoppable team, taking on any adventure together." I offer him my hand. "Are you ready to start the day?"

Tommy's eyes, bright and curious beneath the fringe of his bangs, meet mine for just a moment. He inches forward, a small victory as he tentatively places his hand in mine. His grip is light, a whisper of connection, but it's enough.

I stand, looking back at Theresa. "He'll be fine. By the end of the day, he'll likely be as happy as when he first came bouncing in."

Lastly, Kane walks in with Hailey, dressed in jeans and a flannel shirt, and my stomach somersaults. How do denim and wool look so good on him? He's the kind of man who could easily be on the cover of a men's fashion magazine. The Off the Grid edition, if one existed. Beside him is Hailey, who sports an outfit of many colors and patterns. Her hair is in pigtails that seem to have been styled during a game of tag. "Fashion by Hailey," Kane says, his eyes lit with humor.

Hailey's tiny face is a thundercloud, a contrast to her vibrant attire.

Kane leans in, and the scent of his cologne wraps around me. He smells like pine, and leather, and temptation. I'm so caught up in it that I barely hear him whisper, "Amanda, her mother, forgot to call yesterday." The words crawl into my mind, each one heavy with meaning. As they sink in, my heart aches for the vulnerable girl in front of me. With newfound determination, I nod in response.

"We'll have such a fun day that it'll be just a distant memory soon." I turn to the parents, who stand in a line looking like they are waiting to be dismissed. "I'll take it from here."

They file out one by one with a wave or a nod, and I walk to the front of the classroom with Kane's cologne still tickling my senses.

The kids hang up their jackets and put away their lunch boxes while I wait a few more minutes to see if anyone else shows up. When they don't by five minutes past the hour, I start the day.

"Good morning, everyone! Come and take a seat." I point at the table in front of me. "I'm Ms. Moore, your teacher for the summer," I start, my voice filling the quiet of the community center. "I've come all the way from Phoenix, Arizona." I look at them and find it funny how they sit in order of age. "Now, I'd love to learn something about each of you. How about we go around, and everyone can share one thing about themselves? Who wants to go first?"

The room seems bigger without the parents, the air charged with excitement and nerves. Lucas raises his hand before he stands. "I like building model ships," he says with a hint of pride. "And I've got three dogs named after sea monsters. They are Kraken, Leviathan, and Cetus."

"That's wonderful, Lucas. In a place like Port Promise, I would imagine boats are important." I think about Kane again and how he was late to greet me because of boat problems. "And three dogs are a lot. Do you help take care of them?"

"I feed them, but they poop in the woods." At the mention of poop, all the kids laugh.

"Thank you for sharing, Lucas." I turn to the little superhero. "What about you, Tommy?"

Still clutching the action figure, Tommy looks up. His voice is small but clear. "I like to draw," he says, "and I make the best mud pies."

"It sounds like you're an artist through and through. There is an art to baking pies, too." I think about my mother's lattice-top pies and how she'd cut the dough into shapes to add something special to her holiday treats. They were always a work of art.

"Now it's Hailey's turn."

"I collect rocks," she says, a glimmer of enthusiasm breaking through her clouds. "I've got a bunch from the beach. And I can skip stones on the water really well." She pulls a handful from her pocket and sets them on the table.

"Wonderful, Hailey. There is so much to learn from

rocks, and they are pretty, too." I pick up a black one and think it may be coal.

All eyes are on me. I clap my hands together. "Wow, we have a shipwright, an artist, and a geologist here! This will be an exciting summer," I say, thrilled at what these little personalities will bring to our days ahead.

With the parents gone and the kids' introductions warming the room, I glance at the lesson plans Eliza left behind to make sure I didn't miss anything yesterday when I went over them. There is no strict curriculum to adhere to, no tests overshadowing the joy of learning—just pure, imaginative education. Eliza's lessons are infused with fun, with room for creativity and exploration. Today's lesson plan is about geography. About Alaska, its landscape, climate, and industry. I can already tell I'm going to like it here.

Knowing Hailey needs a pick-me-up and remembering how much she likes to lead and help, I say, "Hailey is going to be my teacher's aide for the day. Would you like that, Hailey?"

Her pigtails bob as she nods her head.

"Great. Can you get the crayons and butcher paper out of the closet? It's the big roll of white paper."

Hailey jumps from her seat and dashes to the closet with enough excitement to rival a puppy chasing a ball. When she struggles with the weight of the roll, Lucas jumps up to help. It would seem that the community motto might still be alive.

I roll out the paper and empty the box of crayons on the table. How do I integrate five-year-old Hailey, and six-year-old Tommy, with the budding complexity of eleven-year-old Lucas? I sketch a quick diagram—the sea for Lucas, a blank slate for Tommy's artistic endeavors, and a rocky shoreline for Hailey's collection.

I glance at the expectant faces before me—Lucas, Tommy, and Hailey—and an idea blossoms. "Alright, crew," I announce, "today, we're going to create our own sea adventure. Lucas, you're the captain of our ship. Tommy, you'll draw the maps and landscapes we'll explore. And Hailey, with your rock collection, you'll help us navigate and find treasures. We'll be sailing the coast of Alaska."

The morning passes in a flurry of activity. Lucas sketches a formidable vessel, his fingers smudging the pencil lines into the waves. Tommy's crayons move across the paper, bringing to life the worlds of our imagined voyage. Hailey arranges her stones, assigning stories to each one, transforming them into a navigator's most prized possessions.

By lunchtime, the room is alive with the energy of creation. Hailey talks of smooth stones that could guide us through treacherous waters. She points out her favorite, a white stone that she sets on the paper. Tommy describes an island off the Prince of Wales Island where his parents take him to collect clams. He swears the ground is as soft as his mud pies. Lucas entertains us with tales of how our ship could stand up to the fiercest storms—storms his father has fought on the sea. My mind goes straight to Kane. What dangers does he face when he sails out of the cove? Has he ever been stuck in a storm? I read about the dangers of whales breaching beside boats. Has he ever experienced something so majestic, and yet terrifying?

As they share their tales, I'm thankful for this space where I can teach in color and dimension, where a child's imagination is the curriculum. The joy of discovery is the outcome. I'm excited about what we covered as we tidy up for the afternoon. It was more than geography. For Lucas, it was a lesson in physics and engineering as he constructed a paper ship. He learned about the forces that keep a boat afloat and the science behind sailing, all while believing he was just playing captain.

Tommy's drawings did more than decorate our imaginary world. They were a lesson in art and environmental science. As he sketched our provisions, we explored where food came from, dipping our toes into biology and the life cycle of plants native to Alaska.

Hailey's rocks were more than just playthings. They were the foundation for a beginner's course in geology. We talked about the different types of rocks and how they form, and I watched her get excited as she realized that her collection told the story of Earth itself.

This morning was education disguised as a day of play. If teaching was like this every day, I wouldn't have accepted that testing coordinator job for next year, but the raise was too hard to pass up.

Lunchtime sneaks up on us, and the kids unwrap their meals with the seriousness of pirates uncovering treasure. I retrieve my lunch from my bag—a jar of homemade chicken noodle soup that I found on the shelf of recognizable foods.

Staring into the jar, I wonder about the chicken—could it be a relative of Kane's mail-order flock? My imagination paints a comical lineage of chickens raised here, destined for mason jars and the mouths of hungry people.

My gaze drifts over to Lucas, who's unwrapping a bologna sandwich with an air of satisfaction. Then there's Tommy, tackling a tuna salad sandwich with the enthusiasm of a six-year-old gourmet. Lastly, there's Hailey, halfway through her peanut butter and jelly sandwich, the quintessential staple of childhood lunches. And once again, my thoughts are on Kane. Are mornings chaos in the Hollister household or does he run his home like a tight ship, ensuring everything is organized and prepared in advance? If Hailey's appearance is an indicator, I'm going with chaos.

I glance at the kids' lunches, and a smirk tugs at my lips. While I'm grateful for the soup, I would kill for one of those sandwiches. Staring at Hailey's peanut butter and grape jelly, the soup seems more like a sentence than sustenance.

I unscrew the lid and microwave it for a minute. The ease at which it heats is not lost on me, and I remind myself to never take a microwave or a light switch for granted again.

The metallic clink of my spoon against the jar of soup is almost melodic in the quiet that falls as the children eat. Just as I'm about to take another delicious spoonful, the door swings open, and Eliza walks in, carrying what looks unmistakably like a small picnic basket. The kids' heads pop up, eyes wide, like meerkats on alert. They shout a loving hello to her as if they haven't seen her in weeks.

"Thought you might want something a little less ... jarred," Eliza says with a wink, handing me a wrapped ham sandwich.

"The soup is delicious."

"I know, but it can't beat all that bread and mayonnaise. Let's not forget the cheese and ham."

"Thank you for being so thoughtful." I swap the jar for the sandwich. She reaches into her small basket like Mary Poppins' carpet bag and pulls out a baggie of cookies for each of the kids and one for me. It feels like winning the lottery, as the kids squeal with delight and start counting the chocolate chips to see who has more.

"How's the first day going?" Eliza asks.

"It's been great." I take a bite and savor the salty ham, the cheese, the lettuce, and the fresh-baked bread. As I chew, a couple of questions come to mind. "Eliza, why didn't I need an emergency license for this summer gig?" When I emailed her about it, she said it wasn't necessary and then said something about summer programs being less strict.

She leans against a desk, her expression a mixture of amusement and conspiracy. "Well, this isn't exactly a Board of Education-sanctioned program. It's more informal than that."

I cock my head to the side, processing another half-truth in the job description. "So, I'm essentially a summer camp counselor?"

"You could say that," Eliza says. "But think about it—have you ever wanted to teach without constraints? This is your chance to make a real impact."

I take a bite of the sandwich, and I can't deny the truth in her words. "That does sound wonderful." I glimpse at the children who are digging into their cookie bags. "Why would you hire me when I have so few children to work with? I would imagine someone in town could fill in."

Eliza explains how summers work in Alaska. "The kids over twelve are working with their parents." She points to Lucas. "This will be his last summer in the classroom. He'll get a different education on his father's boat. Those who aren't working to support their families during salmon season have jobs, like May or Rhys. If you're not working on a boat or running a business, then you're probably too old to help." She looks down at her stomach. "Or you're pregnant and need someone who's willing to step in for you. Thank you for being that someone."

"You're welcome." I'm reminded once more that life operates on a different wavelength compared to Arizona.

"I should get going. I need to stop by May's to make sure she's ready to deliver my boy."

"May's delivering your baby?" I knew she helped with simple things like coughs and colds, but she delivers babies too?

Eliza nods. "Yes, she's delivered most of the children

here. Any complicated pregnancies force the mother to stay in Craig. The only way there is by float plane, or a boat around the island to where you clear the ridge. I certainly don't want to be on a boat when I'm about to deliver."

I had not thought about how remote this place is. Even though it's a part of the Prince of Wales Island, the population is locked in a small piece of land surrounded by a mountain range. There is no way in or out unless you travel by air or sea.

"I'm off. Have fun, everyone."

The kids rush to give her a hug.

With a wink and a wave, Eliza leaves me to my newfound freedom and the kids' afternoon of adventure.

The rest of the day passes in a blur of activities and laughter. Four o'clock rolls around, and the boys' parents arrive to pick them up, leaving Hailey and me to tidy up the remnants of the day's creative storm.

Kane runs in at 4:30. He's late and looking harried. "I'm sorry. The boat's giving me trouble again," he says, scooping up Hailey in a hug. "I'm pushing it hard because this season's important—I'm close to getting a new troller."

I can see the stress in his eyes, the weight of his dreams on his shoulders. Something has shifted since I last saw him. He no longer smells like pine and leather. Instead, the scent of salt and sea air clings to him. His hair is windswept, tousled by the coastal breeze, and the sleeves of his flannel are rolled up, revealing strong forearms weathered by hard work.

As I watch him, a fleeting thought crosses my mind: what would it be like to be wrapped in those arms? I continue to observe him embracing Hailey. I can't deny the growing curiosity, the subtle pull of attraction that seems to linger in the air when he's nearby.

"Not to worry, it's not like I have a hot date or anything. Hailey and I took the time to clean up. She's been my teacher's aide today."

He looks up. "We're heading to May's for dinner. Would you like to join us?"

"No, it's okay. I don't want to intrude."

"Inviting you to dinner is the least I can do since I was late again."

I hesitate, thinking of my quiet cabin and the evening ahead. The idea of sharing a meal with Hailey and her dad, who has become more intriguing with each passing moment, appeals to me.

"I'd like that," I say, neatly wrapping up my day of "camp counseling."

Chapter Six

KANE

I TRAIL behind Timber and Hailey as we walk to May's Café. It's been a long day, and my muscles remind me of every line I hauled in. But as I glance at Timber, walking beside Hailey, who's chattering away, a tug of something warms in my chest.

We arrive at the café, and Hailey immediately declares she wants to sit next to Ms. Moore. I appreciate her enthusiasm, even though a quiet voice in my head warns me not to get too comfortable. People come and go, and I worry about the connection Hailey's already forming with Timber. My poor little girl will have to face another unavoidable goodbye, but I suppose it's better to learn early that nothing is permanent than live with the fantasy that everyone stays.

As we settle into our booth, May approaches with her usual blend of motherly affection and bustling efficiency.

"Welcome back," she says. "Are you here for the fish fry? Eric dropped off about fifty pounds of halibut."

"That sounds good to me," I say.

"I'll have the same," Timber replies.

"Daddy, I want chocolate chip pancakes!" Hailey's declaration is firm, her eyes gleaming with the unyielding determination of a five-year-old.

"But Hailey, it's dinnertime, and the halibut here is the best around. Eric caught it fresh. You love fish."

"No, I want pancakes!" she says, crossing her arms, her resolve setting like concrete.

"Hailey, while pancakes are great, halibut is the food of adventurers," Timber chimes in, her voice as smooth as the calm sea. "Why don't you order the fish and then tell your dad about your day as my special helper."

I glance at May to see if she's going to add her two cents, but she holds her pad and pen, watching the exchange with an amused look.

"Alright, I'll have the halibut, even though I want pancakes." Hailey says.

I send a silent thank-you to Timber for stepping in.

Timber laughs, a sound that's quickly becoming familiar and welcome. "Maybe if you're lucky, your dad will take you for chocolate chip pancakes on the weekend." She looks at me, her eyes asking if it's possible.

I nod. "We can have pancakes on Sunday. Deal?"

Hailey nods. "Deal!"

May jots down our orders. "One adventurous halibut for the young explorer, and two more for the table. Coming right up."

As May heads back to the kitchen, a sense of peace settles over me, and I turn my attention to Hailey. "Tell me about this special assignment."

Hailey talks non-stop for the next five minutes about everything she helped Ms. Moore with. I dropped off a kid that was all doom and gloom and picked up a ray of sunshine. Normally, when Amanda doesn't call, it's a minimum of two days before Hailey finds her joy again. I'm grateful for the reduced sentence.

When Hailey finishes, I turn to Timber. "How was your day at the center?"

Timber's face lights up much like my daughter's. "It was wonderful," she begins. "The kids were so engaged. We learned about buoyancy, ecosystems ... Lucas even built a little ship from paper! And Hailey, she categorized her rock collection by age and type—did you know she has a piece of quartz she found on the beach?"

"Is that the white one?" I ask.

"Yes, it's white with lots of sparkle."

"This one," Hailey says and places the rock on the table.

I pick it up and turn it over in my hand. "She likes the sparkly ones." I remember the day she found it. We were picnicking with my mom at the lighthouse. The day was uncharacteristically warm for early spring, and my mom was in good spirits. A month later, she passed. I give the rock back to Hailey, and she puts it back in her pocket.

"Tomorrow, we're going on a little trek to gather herbs and learn about local plants." Timber talks with her hands, painting a picture in the air of a classroom alive with discovery and laughter. "There's so much you can learn just from the surrounding nature."

She sounds so much like my mom and sister, getting excited about the silliest things, like a weed with a yellow flower. Mom always said there wasn't anything called a weed. They were merely unappreciated flowers. A wave of memories washes over me. "Sounds like you made the most of the day."

"It was a good day, considering I found out that I'm essentially a summer camp counselor and not a summer schoolteacher." She laughs, shaking her head slightly. "But I'm okay with it. It's liberating, actually. It takes all the pressure off."

A twinge of guilt pulls at me as I internally wade through my own sea of half-truths and omissions. I'm with the murkiness of not being completely honest with her about the job.

But seeing her take it all in stride, focusing on the positives, eases the weight of my conscience.

I'm grateful that Timber views life as a glass half full. She sees the unexpected turn as an adventure rather than a misstep, a quality that's rare and, frankly, needed in a place like Port Promise.

As I watch her interacting with Hailey, her laughter mingling with the soft light of the café, I make a silent agreement with myself to be more transparent going forward. Because someone who can find joy in the unexpected deserves nothing less than the whole truth.

"And what about you? How was the sea today?" she asks, shifting the spotlight.

I let out a half-laugh, rubbing the back of my neck. "Brought in a decent haul, but on the way back, the engine decided to quit on me. It took some coaxing to get her going again. She's old, and I can't wait to get a new boat—one that isn't held together by spit and prayers." I look at my little girl and think about the plans I have for us. "I need a summer of abundance before I can make that kind of investment. A new boat's not just a purchase. It's a commitment to a better future." A future I can't imagine without a new troller. It's not just a dream. It's a necessity. Without it, I don't know if I can count on next year's salmon season to support Hailey and me through the leaner months.

Before the conversation can drift in another direction, May arrives with a tray laden with steaming dishes. As she sets the plates on the table, the golden and flaky halibut is a mouthwatering sight.

Hailey squeals with delight when she looks at hers. The cook has shaped her halibut into a small boat with sails made from thinly sliced cucumbers. Everything is riding atop a sea of green vegetables and colorful bell pepper buoys. On the edge of the plate, a tiny flag made from a toothpick and a piece of carrot stands proudly, as if marking the start of a voyage.

"Daddy! My fish is sailing!" she says, her voice bubbling with excitement.

"Healthy food doesn't have to be boring." May gives a knowing wink. She turns to Timber. "Did I hear you say you were going on a trek tomorrow?" May tells us about Old Danny, who's been troubled by arthritis, and her plans to collect Devil's Club for him. "That plant's a bear to handle, being all prickly."

Timber leans forward. "Devil's Club is tough to harvest, but it's an effective remedy. My mother often tried herbal treatments before she turned to modern medicine. She always had a jar of Devil's Club salve on hand."

"Is that so?" May asks. "What about you?"

"I've dabbled a bit in herbalism myself," Timber says.

"Well, you'll have to share some of your knowledge with me," May says. "It's nice to find someone else who believes in the healing power of nature."

As they talk about herbs, I dig into my meal. Here's Timber, fitting into our town like she's always been part of it. And me? I'm just a fisherman trying to keep my head above water.

As I watch my daughter eat, I think maybe this summer won't be so bad after all.

"If you happen to come across some Devil's Club on your adventure, and you're not too afraid to harvest it, Old Danny and I would appreciate it."

"I'm happy to get you some if it presents itself."

May nods and walks away.

Timber takes her first bite, and the sound that escapes her lips is a soft, contented hum. It's a small noise, barely audible over the chatter of the restaurant, but to me, it's like music. It makes me wonder what other sounds she's capable of making, what she sounds like when she's...

I stop that train of thought immediately, though it's hard to shake off the image of her lips parting with that small, delightful sound. Clearing my throat, I divert the conversation. "Tell me about life in Arizona."

She sets down her fork, her gaze meeting mine. "Life in Arizona ... well, it's definitely different from here in Alaska. For one, it's about 80 degrees warmer most days and requires fewer clothes."

Her words ignite a fire in me as I imagine Timber wearing much less. Swallowing hard, I redirect the conversation once again.

"Have you ever been fishing?"

She nods. "A lot. I could fish the pants off most people."

I stare at her and wonder if she's going out of her way to torture me.

"You fish?" I imagine her with a pole in her hand and a lake before her. That's all I allow my imagination to see because where this conversation is headed in my head will do neither of us any good.

"Yes." She takes another bite.

"Amazing. We'll have to take you fishing and see if you can fish the pants off me." I hadn't meant to say that, but once it's out, the heat coils in my groin and rushes to my cheeks. "I mean, not like literally, but if you like to fish, I'd love to be your guide." I take my last bite and another thought enters my mind. When I swallow, I ask,

"I know you haven't been here long, but is Alaska everything you imagined it would be?"

She looks down at her almost empty plate. I can't see her expression, but I sense some resistance to answering. Finally, she sighs and shrugs her shoulders.

"It's definitely not what I was led to believe, but I like it. As much as I've been a city girl, my mother raised me with common sense and an outdoorsy flair."

"She must have if you know what Devil's Club is."

"My mother was a big believer in being self-sufficient. Sadly, she passed away several months ago. It's left a hole in my heart." Her shoulders sag forward slightly. "I understand yours did, too. I'm sorry for your loss."

Something is different when she says it as opposed to someone whose mom is still alive. Timber understands the profound loss and has experienced the devastation. "I still can't fathom that my mom is gone. I miss her every day."

Hailey chimes in. "Grandma is in heaven. I bet she's with your mom."

"Wouldn't that be great?" Timber says.

"What about your father?" I ask. "Is he in Arizona?"

Timber sits up. "I never met him. When I was little, my mother used to tell me a stork brought me. As I got older, I had questions." She looks down at Hailey, who's playing with the vegetable flag and bell pepper buoys. "He went MIA before the big day."

"That has to be hard." There are so many parallels between Timber's life and mine. Both of our mothers are gone. And Timber has experienced what Hailey is going through, only different.

She shrugs. "You can't miss what you never had. What about your father?"

I rub my chin. "He's off the island for now, visiting friends and family."

"I bet the change of scenery is good for him. It's hard to be someplace where there are so many memories."

I wonder if losing her mom is part of the reason she jumped at the chance to come to Alaska.

May swings by and drops off the bill before moving to another table.

Timber reaches for the check. "I got this. You paid for breakfast last time."

"Because I was late, and I was late again today, so I'm happy to pick up your dinner."

"I don't expect you to pay for my meal each time you're late."

After a bit of back-and-forth, I relent and let her pay for hers, but I lay down the cash for mine and Hailey's.

We say goodbye to May and exit the café and step into the cooler evening air. The idea of walking Timber home floats through my mind, but before the offer can leave my lips, she asks, "Do you think the store is still open? I need some staples. A girl can't live off of squirrel stew and beaver bolognaise alone." She appears to shudder. "What I really want is a loaf of white bread and a jar of Nutella."

"I'm not sure you'll find the Nutella, but Rhys is sure to have bread and a few other options."

Hailey's already bouncing. "Can we take her, Daddy? Please? I'm her helper for the day, and she's going to need me in there. Besides, Uncle Rhys always gives me a sucker."

"Alright, let's make a quick trip out of it." I tell myself it's the neighborly thing to do, but that's a lie. I wouldn't offer to take anyone else to the store. The truth is, I wouldn't mind spending a few more minutes with Timber.

The store on the dock is quiet, a gentle buzz of fluorescent lights welcoming us inside.

Behind the counter stands my brother Rhys. He folds up a magazine and tucks it into his back pocket. If it were anyone else, I'd guess it was this month's *Hustler* with how quickly he hid it, but knowing Rhys, it's probably a bait and tackle catalogue. Everyone has their thing, and my brother's passion is flies called Dolly Llamas and Wooly Buggers.

"Welcome," he says. "I'm Rhys." He pulls a sucker from a basket and hands it to Hailey before offering one to Timber, who declines.

"He's my little brother." I don't know why I need to make a point that he's younger than me, but I do.

"Hello, Rhys," Timber says. "I'm Timber Moore."

"Welcome."

"Thank you." She grabs a basket and starts down the closest aisle.

I try to see everything through her eyes. The first thing I notice is Rhys is wearing jeans and the same flannel shirt as mine. It strikes me as funny that we are wearing what would seem like a uniform. I turn to look at the store, which has been in my family since the beginning. Rhys took it over when he was eighteen. To an outsider, it probably doesn't seem like much. There are only seven aisles to the store with everything vying for space on the shelves, but it's a lifeline for most.

Timber starts with the basics: bread and peanut butter. When she turns the corner, she picks up a few pieces of fruit. I notice each item she chooses requires no refrigeration, a reminder of her new off-the-grid lifestyle. It's easy to forget how out of her element she might be, yet in the couple of days I've known her, she's never voiced a complaint. "It's not like a big-chain supermarket," I say as I catch up to her. "But we make do with what we have. If you want something special, Rhys can order it."

"Something special like Nutella?"

"Let's see if he can get that for you. It's important to have the things that comfort you—things that remind you of home."

She laughs. "Currently, home is about 130 degrees, and it seems like your skin melts off your bones every time you step outside. I'm happy to be here, but the Nutella would be a bonus."

Hailey tags behind her with the sucker from Rhys in her palm. "Can I help?"

"Do you know where the hot cocoa is?" Timber asks.

Hailey nods and races to the front of the store and points to where two boxes of cocoa remain. Timber takes one.

"That should do me for now." As we reach the counter, Timber stops at a postcard display. She pulls out one with an image of the dock.

"Those have been here for decades," Rhys says. "You're welcome to take whatever you like. I don't have the heart to throw them away, but people don't mail postcards these days."

"I imagine they don't, but there's an old-world sweetness to them. Imagine getting this card from the one you love? It's kind of romantic."

"What do we know about romance?" Rhys says.

"You know a little more than you did a few minutes ago." She slides the postcard of the dock away and pulls out one of the ridge and sets it on the counter. "This is beautiful."

What Timber doesn't know is that the image is of my land.

"I forgot instant coffee. What aisle is that on?"

Rhys tells her aisle three, and as soon as she's out of sight, he lets out a low whistle. "My teacher never looked like that. Mrs. Miller had less hair than Dad and she was missing her front two teeth. She used to spit when she talked."

"This isn't Mrs. Miller."

"I can see that. She's pretty."

There was no doubt in my mind that every dude in town was going to have the same reaction as Rhys, and I'm not sure how to process that. Young, pretty women are a rarity here.

"She's here for the summer. She's not staying."

"I know, but she's here now. Not everything has to be forever. You can enjoy her company while she's here. You don't have to marry her."

I absorb my brother's advice. It's a reminder to appreciate the here and now without getting lost in dreams of forever. But deep down, I can't shake the longing for something more permanent, something enduring like the love my parents shared. Only death made my mother leave my father's side. Thinking about them makes me wonder if it's better to face the loneliness because love never found you or face it because it did and it left you.

Timber returns with a jar of Folger's Classic Roast.

"This is like a jar of gold when you have to get up at four in the morning." She reaches for a pack of gum and places it on the counter. "I think that's all I need."

Rhys rings her up. "Did I hear something about Nutella?"

Timber sighs. "Today, I could have killed for a bologna sandwich. I can't imagine what I'd do for chocolate."

"I'll put it on the next order."

"I'd hate for you to go to the trouble, but I'd be lying if I said I didn't want it. I brought my number one vice, which is Jelly Bellies, but I don't think they'll last the entire eight weeks."

I give my brother an "I told you so" look at the mention of eight weeks, and he shakes his head.

"I get weekly deliveries. You'll have your Nutella soon."

As Timber pays, I instinctively step forward, my hand reaching out to gather the bags before she even has a chance to reach for them. It's a reflex honed by my upbringing, a reminder of the lessons my mother instilled in me.

"It would appear chivalry isn't dead."

"Not among the Hollisters," I say. I turn to my brother. "See you tomorrow, Rhys."

Rhys nods and smiles. "It's a pleasure to meet you, Timber."

"You had coffee in stock and you're ordering me Nutella. The pleasure is all mine."

I put my back to the door and push it open. Hailey skips ahead, sucker unwrapped and in her mouth. Timber walks through and smiles at me, and my chest tightens as if the weight of my brother's words is sitting there. "You can enjoy her company while she's here." He's probably right.

We reach the edge of the forest. "We're happy to walk you home, or I can get the ATV and we can drive you."

She shakes her head. There's a pleasant look on her face. "Thanks, but I could use the walk after that dinner. Besides, I need to get used to making it on my own here."

I hand her the bags. They aren't heavy, but her words carry weight. Why is someone like Timber, clearly smart, capable, and beautiful, on her own here? My eyes drop to her hands. I hadn't noticed a ring before, and there's no glint of gold or flash of diamond.

It's not my place to ask, and yet the question burns in

my mind. It seems she's carved out a space for herself in the world without anyone else's help.

"Alright, but the offer stands," I say. "Anytime you need help, just ask."

She sets down the bags and gets on her knees, opening her arms to Hailey. "Thank you for being the best helper ever."

Hailey falls into her arms for a squeeze, and when Timber stands, she hesitates for only a second before wrapping her arms around me in a brief hug.

"Thank you for making my first day great." She picks up the bags. "See you both tomorrow."

And as she walks away, I'm left wishing that the hug didn't end so quickly.

Chapter Seven
TIMBER

As I part ways with Kane and Hailey at the dock, the golden hue of the evening sun drapes over Prince of Wales Island like a warm shawl. It's nearing 6 PM, yet the June sky is bright, its light a lingering hint of the summer's longer days.

The wooden walkway thuds under my steps, a steady rhythm that marks my journey toward solitude. The cabin, my temporary home, waits nestled in the forest, promising quiet. In Phoenix, I never got to unwind after a busy day. The relentless hum of the city reverberated like a never-ending echo, which is so different from the tranquil hush here where only the sound of nature exists.

With each step, memories of my first day on the job fill my mind. The laughter of the children, the look of discovery in their eyes, the sense of accomplishment—it's more than I ever expected. The job description that brought me here suggested a different scenario from the reality. They needed someone adaptable, resilient, capable of turning the tide of young minds. Yet, they never said it would be creativity and chaos. And it's perfect.

It would take a special kind of person to thrive in such an environment, wouldn't it? And as the forest welcomes me, the cool whispers of the trees seem to affirm that I am, indeed, that person. Serendipity, it seems, has a sense of humor. Every false note, every twist in my path, has led me to this moment, this place, where I am exactly where I'm meant to be.

Each step I take deeper into the woods seems to plunge me further into darkness. The sunlight filters through the leaves above like golden thread, lighting patches of moss and ferns but leaving much of the forest in a mysterious twilight.

An owl hoots, a sound that two days ago sent a shiver down my spine, but now it's merely the evening song of the woods. "You don't scare me anymore," I say as a declaration of newfound courage.

But then, there's a rustle. A shadow flits between the trees, a silhouette that slices through the comfort I've just wrapped around myself. My heart skips a beat, no longer a calm drum, but a wild, frantic banging against my ribs.

"But that does."

Adrenaline surges and I race along the wooden walkway, the rhythmic thud of my footsteps mingling with the soft rustle of leaves in the breeze. I should have taken Kane up on his offer and let him walk me home.

Abruptly, I grind to a halt. Right there, emerging onto the path, is a doe, her large, gentle eyes meeting mine with quiet curiosity. Behind her, two fawns with dappled coats glance my way, their delicate legs frozen in place. They stand there, serene and utterly unafraid. My breath catches at the sight, and a laugh escapes me as the tension washes away. It was just a deer and her fawns, not a bear or a pack of hungry wolves. It would seem that my imagination is as lively as my students'. They stand for a moment more and then dash into the woods.

I walk the rest of the way to the cabin. There's no need to hurry now. I open the door and step inside, a sense of calm washing over me. I head to the window and glance out, hoping to see my woodland friends, but all I see is the gentle sway of the trees. Above, the stars are just showing their light in the darkening sky. My reflection bounces back at me from the glass, and I let out a self-deprecating laugh. "So much for being an intrepid adventurer," I say. "Spooked by Bambi and friends. What's next? Confusing the wind for a wolf's howl?"

I laughed more today than I had the entire week. With the last of my giggle fading, I turn away from the window.

In the quiet of the night, I light a fire in the stove and enjoy the simple snap and pop of the flames as they catch. I think back to the first fire in this cabin and how Kane carefully placed the tinder and logs. It was so domestic and sexy. But tonight, I did it on my own and that's a major accomplishment.

I unpack my groceries and put water on to boil before changing into my flannel pajamas and slippers, ready to wind down.

Several minutes later, the kettle's whistle breaks the quiet, and soon, hot water meets cocoa—its scent is a warm hug. I think about another hug, where I impulsively wrapped my arms around Kane. What was I thinking? You weren't thinking, but that was perfect. I only wished I'd hugged him longer, so he had a chance to hug me back. If I hadn't stepped away so soon, would he have done that?

Settled in at the table with my notebook open, I jot down ideas for tomorrow's adventure. A trip to see Kane's fishing rig might intrigue the kids, but then again, fishing is life here—not quite the novelty I'm looking for. Instead, we'll explore the woods, and I'll definitely make sure we search for Devil's Club. I could weave in a lesson about the ecosystem and how everything connects from the forest floor to the sea.

A glance at my phone reminds me that I've got an early start tomorrow, so I quickly use the outhouse, brush my teeth, and toss another log on the fire, its heat is a cozy send-off to sleep.

As I crawl into bed, I imagine I'm the luckiest girl in the world. Eyes closing, my thoughts drift to Kane. How different he seems now from that first day on the dock, when he was tossing fish at me as if I were the target in a carnival game.

The tranquility of sleep is shattered by the sharp smell of smoke. Heart racing, I stagger out of bed and toward the stove, struggling through the haze. The flue must be clogged again. Mimicking Kane's actions, I grab a towel and shake the pipe, hoping to clear it. Instead, embers fall, setting the floor on fire. Panic grips me, my chest tightening, my hands trembling uncontrollably as I gasp out, "No, no, no."

I grab my phone, my mother's journal, the treasured photo, and Cubby the Bear from my bedside table and bolt out the door. The cold night air hits me like a slap in the face. The contrast to the heat of the cabin jolts me into full awareness. Horror courses through my veins as I fumble with my phone, fingers shaking as I dial Eliza's number hoping there's a connection. Relief floods me when there's a ring.

With each ring, the flames seem to grow larger in my mind's eye, licking greedily at the wood of the cabin. I can see them spreading, consuming everything in their path. There's no answer from Eliza, just the incessant ringing in my ears, a cruel reminder of my isolation in this remote wilderness.

Finally, after what seems like an eternity, she picks up, her voice groggy with sleep. I don't wait for a hello, I yell into the phone, "It's Timber, the cabin is on fire. I need help." I manage to get the words out before the line goes dead, leaving me stranded in a world of uncertainty.

I can't just stand by and watch. With a sense of determination, I set my items by the outhouse and run back into the inferno, my pulse racing with every step as I brace myself for what lies ahead.

Smoke bites at my eyes as I snatch the water bin, my

jacket, and boots, and flee once again. The damp cabin's wood does little to slow the fire's steady, hungry spread across the roof.

Frantically, I pump water from the outdoor well. Clutching the water bin tightly, I hurl water at the flames. It's a desperate attempt to bring things under control, but it's futile. It's like trying to hold back the tide with a spoon. I stand back, helpless, watching the fire devour what had become my Alaskan summer home.

Chapter Eight

KANE

My stomach tightens as I pull up to the chaos unfolding before me. Flames reach for the sky, hungrily consuming the cabin. Hailey stirs, the crackling inferno jolting her awake.

"Daddy." She points to the cabin. "Fire!"

"I know, Noodle, but stay put."

With a quick kill of the engine, the oppressive heat and choking smoke engulf us. Hailey covers her face with her blanket. Timber runs toward us. "I'm so sorry. I did the one thing you told me not to do. I burned down the cabin."

"Take the ATV to the edge of the property. Get yourself and Hailey a safe distance away." I unhook the firefighting trailer. "We'll unravel this mess later. For now, I have a fire to put out." As she drives toward the border of the forest, I unroll the hose and fire up the pump. The water blasts forth, a steady stream directed at the middle of the flames. All I can think about as I douse the roof is how grateful I am that Timber had the foresight to get out of the cabin and call for help. My next thought is this wouldn't have happened to a local. It also reminds me of how outsiders aren't suited for this life.

Within minutes, Rhys is there beside me. His twin, Reid, follows minutes later. As part of the volunteer fire department, they have the same setup: a trailer, water pump, and a hose, always ready to go.

"Is anyone else coming?" I ask.

Rhys and Reid unfold their hoses and put water to the flame.

"Eliza told us to call her if we needed backup, and she'd send others," Rhys says. "But for now, it's just us."

I look at my brothers and then at the fire and know that we've got this. We work in sync, the kind of teamwork only brothers can achieve.

The fire is stubborn, clinging to the cabin like a malignant growth, but we're relentless with the water, Rhys, Reid, and I dousing the flames with a fierce determination. Slowly, begrudgingly, the fire hisses its surrender as the water sizzles on contact.

As the billows of dissipating smoke start to reveal the charred remains, Rhys's voice cuts through the chaos. "Hey, look at this," he calls out, gesturing toward the roof.

Following his gaze, I spot the gaping hole where the cap on the flue should be. "Damn," I mutter under my breath, realizing the implications of its absence. My memory clicks. There was a clank when I'd shaken the pipe to dislodge what was stuck in the flue. A wave of realization washes over me. I'm the cause of this fire, not Timber.

I turn and spot her at the forest's edge, holding Hailey. Both of their eyes are wide and haunted.

"You got this?" I ask my brothers.

"Yep, go see to the girls," Rhys says.

I approach them, my boots squishing on the soaked ground.

Hailey scrambles from Timber's embrace and rushes toward me. I smell like smoke, but she doesn't care and jumps into my arms. "You okay, Daddy?"

"Right as rain, Noodle." I glance back at the fire and then turn to face Timber. "I know you're blaming yourself, but you didn't start the fire. This isn't your fault," I say before she can speak. "The cap on the flue was loose. That clank we heard the first day—it must've been the cap falling off. This is on me."

Her eyes, rimmed with red from smoke and, likely, emotion, search mine, as if seeking the truth of my words.

"I couldn't let you think you caused this," I say. "That wouldn't be fair."

"Are you certain I didn't?" Her voice falters, and I'm unsure if it's emotion or the smoke she'd inhaled earlier.

I nod. "Ninety-nine percent certain."

Relief gradually relaxes her features, intermingling with exhaustion. I notice a visible shiver run through her, a clear sign of the chill of the night. "Let's get you two someplace warm." I put Hailey down and return to my brothers.

"If you two can handle this, I'm going to take my girls home."

Rhys raises a brow. "Your girls, huh?"

"I meant Hailey and Timber. You know, the girls as in gender."

Reid laughs so loud I can hear him over the spray of the water. "Sure, that's what you meant."

Reid and Rhys continue to douse the last of the smoldering embers, the steady hiss of water on char making a calming backdrop to the mess.

"You should head back," Rhys says. "Get your girls warm and dry. We'll stay and make sure this doesn't flare up again."

One slip of the tongue and I'll be catching shit until Timber leaves, but I can't dwell on that now. The cold is biting.

Hailey's huddled under her blankets while Timber keeps a watchful eye over her. Reality sinks in. With the cabin gone, where will Timber sleep? Where is home for her now? She needs a roof over her head. Timber slides to the passenger side, and I take a seat behind the wheel. I'll manage the logistics of it all later. Right now, the priority is getting everyone back safely.

"I'm sorry this happened," I tell her.

Tears flow freely down her cheeks. "This cabin was important to you and your family's history. I'm so sad it's gone."

I shrug. "It's just a cabin. It can be replaced, but you

can't." I'm about to wrap my arms around her and offer comfort when Reid walks over.

Timber does a double take. "I thought the smoke was playing tricks on me for a second there," she says with a half-laugh. "There's two of you."

Reid chuckles. "I'm Reid, Rhys's twin. The better-looking one," he teases. "Wish it were under better circumstances, but it's good to meet you, Timber."

Her engagement in the conversation tells me she's going to be alright. She's strong, even when the world seems to be falling apart around her.

"Let's get you someplace warm and dry," I say.

She nods but looks at the cabin. "Where am I going to stay?"

That is the hundred-dollar question. "With me and Hailey. At least for now."

Timber places her things on the floor behind her seat. Hailey crawls from her back seat into the front and into Timber's lap. Normally, I'd tell her to go back and buckle in, but I can see that they need each other. Timber cradles my daughter with a tenderness that's as natural as it is heartwarming. I'm struck by the motherly way she envelops my daughter in her arms and Hailey lays her head on Timber's chest as if she's been doing that forever. It stirs something in me—a blend of admiration and a surprising jolt that tightens my chest.

I start the ATV, guiding it onto the path that leads to the ridge. On the way, I point out some landmarks still visible in the dusky distance: Misty Meadows, where my brother Nash lives; Crystal Creek, where Finn has a small lodge and a row of cabins he rents out. This time of year, night comes later, and daylight arrives earlier.

"Today, during class, the kids referred to a lot of places by name as they were navigating the island through our lesson. I learned that Eliza lives in Serenity Cove. Tommy's parents live at Bear Paw and Lucas says his home is called Long Neck Pass. What's your place called?"

My place remains unnamed. It reflects the terrain—unyielding and raw in a land where the elements carve out the days. Sentimental names seem unneeded. So, the townsfolk call it Kane's, but to me, it's just the ridge—nothing more than a speck in the vast, indifferent wilderness.

"It's never had a name," I reply over the engine's growl. "Just ... home, I guess. Sentimental names seem unnecessary."

The woods give way to the outline of my house, its size casting long shadows in the night. I cut the engine. We're immersed in an all-consuming silence. Gently, I take a sleeping Hailey from Timber and I nod for Timber to follow me. We climb the stairs, the wood creaking under our weight. As we reach the top, the size of the house seems to swallow us. I push open the door, stepping into the familiar coziness. This place, unnamed and lived-in, is about to become Timber's refuge, too.

"I'll be right back." I walk up the stairs and lay my daughter down in her bed, tucking her beneath the blankets with care. Her peaceful face, relaxed in sleep, eases some of the tension from my shoulders. I linger for a moment, watching her breathe, before turning back to the dim glow of the staircase.

I find Timber in the living room. She's standing still, a solitary figure bathed in the faint, flickering light from the last of the fireplace's embers. She's staring into the coals, lost in thought, the orange light casting shadows that play across her face.

As I step into the room, there's a sense of rightness seeing her there. It's as if the room has been waiting for her presence to complete it, for her to fill the space with a warmth that's been missing.

She turns at the sound of my approach, and in that glance, there's a mutual understanding. She's been through an ordeal, but here, in front of the dying fire, she seems to have found a moment of peace.

"I'm sorry for all this," she says, her voice a blend of exhaustion and regret. "And for pulling Hailey into it, waking her up."

"Hailey will be fine," I reassure her. "You made sure she was okay."

"It was the least I could do."

At the cabinet, I pull out a bottle of brandy and pour a modest amount into a glass. I hand it to her, and our fingers brush briefly. Her touch is as cold as ice, yet it ignites something that spreads through my entire being.

"Here, this will help with the chill."

She wraps her hands around the glass, the amber liquid catching the light. There's gratitude in her eyes before she takes a sip. Coming together under my roof for the night is a strange and unexpected comfort.

As Timber takes another sip, she glances around the room, her gaze lingering on the details of the house. "You have a beautiful place here."

I nod, looking around. "It serves us well."

She points to the lights in the kitchen. "Electricity?"

"Solar," I say. "We take advantage of the summer's lengthened daylight hours and charge our batteries for winter."

"Smart," she says, her gaze sweeping across the room. Timber sets down the emptied brandy glass with a gentle clink against the mantelpiece. I find myself watching her intently. She's dressed in Winnie the Pooh flannel pajamas and boots, an ensemble that makes her appear younger than I initially estimated, perhaps a few years my junior.

"Let me show you to the bathroom," I say, breaking the quiet. "You'll want to wash off the smoke."

She nods, following me down the hall to the large bathroom, where towels are stacked high, and everything is ready for use. "When you're ready, take your time," I tell her. Then I lead her to the guest room. "My sister left some clothes here the last time she helped with Hailey. If they fit, you're welcome to them. Eliza wouldn't mind."

For a moment, I hang back in the doorway, just taking her in. She's there, standing firm, a mix of toughness and tenderness that makes me want to wrap her in a hug. But then I pull back. This moment is significant, like a fork in the road, and I'm not sure which way to go.

Retreating to my room, the quiet takes on a different quality now, knowing she's just down the hallway.

I hear the shower running in her bathroom and decide to rinse off too in mine. With only a few hours left until dawn, I climb into bed, tugging up the blankets and staring at the ceiling. I send up a quiet prayer for this unexpected turn of events, hoping it brings something good—for both of us.

Chapter Nine
TIMBER

I'M jolted awake by the sound of something clanking nearby. I struggle to shake off the remnants of sleep. What time is it? I reach for my phone and see it's half past four. I'm relieved I didn't sleep through my shift at the community center.

For a moment, I lay still. Everything's foggy, and nothing looks right. Then, bam! It all hits me at once.

The fire. The chaos. The cabin reduced to ashes in the night. Kane's house.

I push back the covers and swing my legs over the side of the bed, shivering as the chill of the wooden floor seeps into my feet.

As I stumble to the bathroom, the noise from the kitchen grows louder, and the aroma of sizzling bacon drifts through the air. Relief floods through me at the realization that it must be Kane in the kitchen, making breakfast.

With each step, I ignore the heaviness in my bones and focus on the present moment and the day ahead. At home I might have called in sick, but here I can't. The parents need me to be there for their kids.

I gather my clothes but realize all I have is what's on my back. Those are worries for when I'm fully awake, and I won't be that until I wash my face and rinse my mouth, so I head to the bathroom where both water and electricity are at my fingertips. As the water washes away the remnants of sleep, the tension in my muscles eases. There's something soothing about the steady rhythm of the shower, the sound of water against the tile drowning out the noise of my racing thoughts—thoughts about the fire and Kane. But I don't linger. In a town where water is scarce, every minute in the shower is a minute less for someone else. Last night's shower was about removing the soot and ash from my skin. Today's is about a rebirth, a new beginning. I am like the phoenix who rose from the ashes to face another day. I step out and wrap a towel snugly around myself. I head out of the bathroom, intent on finding the clothes Kane mentioned his sister left behind.

Turning into the hallway, lost in thought, I bump into something solid. I stagger back, surprised. Kane's presence fills the narrow space, towering over me with an unexpected intensity.

I struggle to find my footing as I meet his gaze. There's a trace of something in his eyes, a spark of amusement that leaves me momentarily breathless.

"Sorry, didn't mean to startle you," he says, reaching out a hand to steady me.

Heat rises to my cheeks, embarrassed to be caught in nothing but a towel. "It's okay," I stammer, my voice high-pitched and breathy.

Kane's eyes linger on me for a moment longer than necessary, taking me in from head to toe. That look heats me to my core.

Clearing my throat, I attempt to regain my composure, but there's no chance of that when the man in front of me looks like he's starving and might gobble me up. "I'll get dressed," I say, gesturing down the hallway.

"Right," he says. "Eliza's stuff is in the closet. I'll leave you to it."

I stop at the door and turn to face him. "Is that bacon I smell?"

"Yes, breakfast is almost ready. Normally it's something simpler, like cereal, but I imagined that you would enjoy the comfort of a warm meal after last night."

"That's very kind of you."

As he turns to leave, a flutter of excitement flows through me. There's something about Kane, something magnetic and undeniable, that draws me to him. Is it the way he adores his daughter? The way he hides behind this gruff exterior, but at every turn does something kind, like pays for my meal, carries my bags, or makes me breakfast after a nightmare of a night. It could be all of those things, but I can't ignore how pleasing to the eyes he is as well. He's as big as a mountain, with eyes that seem to see everything. His hair is the color of tree bark, with bits of gray running through his beard. I've only seen a half smile on his face when he's looking at Hailey. Even the thought of that makes my pulse pound. I can't imagine what a full grin looks like.

I head to the closet to find something from Eliza's clothes. Among the assortment of tops and bottoms, I find a pair of stretchy yoga pants and a T-shirt emblazoned with the slogan: "I'm not lazy, I'm just in energy-saving mode." It seems fitting for today.

I make my way to the kitchen and take a seat at the table. The tantalizing aroma of sizzling bacon and eggs fills the air. Hailey is already digging into her breakfast with gusto. Kane joins us with two plates of food in his hands. He sets one in front of me, and we settle in, listening to Hailey talk about unicorns and how they eat fairy dust and rainbows at every meal.

When Kane finishes, he announces that he's heading out to feed the chickens, leaving Hailey and me alone. I take care of the dishes, eager to contribute in some small way to the household chores. As I scrub away, Hailey hops onto a stool next to me, ready to help. Her hair is a mess of knots and tangles. I don't want to overstep my boundaries, but I figure anything I can take off Kane's plate is good.

"How about braids today?" I set the last pot down and wipe my hands on a nearby towel.

Hailey shakes her head and frowns. "Daddy doesn't know how to braid."

"But I do. Would you like me to do your hair?"

"You can do braids?" She jumps off the chair and

opens a drawer that has a Minnie Mouse brush and some hair ties. "I like braids. May used to have a long braid that went down her back until she cut her hair."

I pause, thinking about my mom. I remember her long black braid too. It makes me a bit sad and nostalgic. I miss her, especially moments when she used to braid my hair and tell stories while doing it.

Even though I miss her, I'm remembering all the times we shared. Seeing Hailey so excited reminds me of the joy Mom brought into my life. Her love stays with me, even though she's gone.

"Shall we try?" I pat the stool Hailey just vacated, and she climbs up. After a few minutes of detangling and Hailey complaining about the tugs and pulls, I weave her hair into two French braids that hug her head and drop just past her shoulders.

As I finish up, Kane returns to the kitchen. "Nice job," he says. "Her hair hasn't been that tame in forever."

"It was my pleasure."

"Are you ready to go?" Kane asks.

I rush to my room to get my phone and jacket.

As we step outside, my eyes adjust to the morning light. I take it all in, from the towering trees to the shimmering pond in the distance. Birds chirp as if taking roll call to see who made it through the night. The natural beauty leaves me almost speechless.

"It's stunning here."

Kane smiles. "I agree."

As we climb onto the ATV and drive away, I turn to Kane and offer an apology for the cabin once more.

"It's not your fault," he reassures me.

We continue and Kane proposes swapping numbers for emergencies. I agree, seeing its wisdom. Yet, beneath the surface, I wish there was more to this exchange than just practicality. There's kindness in Kane's eyes when he hands me his phone. In that brief moment, I find myself longing for a deeper connection, a sense of companionship that goes beyond mere convenience.

But I quickly push aside those thoughts, reminding myself of my reasons for being here. I came here to find a man, but not this man. My inner voice whispers, *But you like this man.*

"I still feel responsible." I enter my number into his phone and put his in mine. "I did put wood in that stove."

"True, but that stove should have been safe, and I failed you." He takes one hand off the wheel and scrubs at his beard. "It could have been disastrous."

"It was. The cabin is gone."

"I know, but what if you didn't get out? If something happened to you, I'd never forgive myself."

I'd like to think it had something to do with me, but I imagine Kane would respond that way to anyone. No one wants to be responsible for hurting another.

"Let's not dwell on it. It's over. I'm here to teach another day, and you get to haul in more fish."

"That's true," he says. "I'll try to be on time today."

I nod, appreciating that he tries. "If we're not at the community center, we'll be at May's Café. I hope to find her that Devil's Club while we're out on our walk."

We stop at the building and Kane hands me a pair of gloves from the ATV. "For the thorns," he says. A surge of gratitude floods through me for his care and concern. The Devil's Club is notorious for its razor-sharp thorns, and Kane's foresight in providing me with protection fills me with gratitude. It speaks volumes about the kind of person he is: considerate, caring, and always looking out for others.

With a heartfelt "thank you," I slip the gloves into my jacket pocket. Hailey grabs her lunch bag, and Kane drives the ATV away. As I watch him go, I suddenly realize I never made a lunch for myself this morning. Typical. Not that I'd use Kane's supplies even if I was at his place. Well, I won't starve if I miss a meal. Shrugging it off, I turn back to my work, determined to power through the day.

Inside, I set about getting things ready, knowing that today's nature walk will be an exciting opportunity for the kids to learn about plants and wildlife. Hailey joins me and helps arrange the supplies like she's still taking on the job of my special helper. On the table is a jar of Nutella, and beside it, a note.

I found this in the back of the storage. An order placed but never picked up. It expires in a week. I placed another order, so you'd have a fresh one. - Rhys

I chuckle, setting the note back down. Well, it won't be the first time I've eaten a jar of Nutella for lunch.

Soon, footsteps approach. Lucas and Tommy rush in, excited. "Good morning, Ms. Moore!" they say in unison.

"Good morning, Lucas, Tommy. I'm glad you're both here. We're going to have a fantastic nature walk today."

Lucas's mother walks in with a paper bag and hands it to me. "I heard about the cabin. Not sure if you were able to save anything, so I brought you a few essentials. Things like clean underwear and a bra." She takes me in from head to toe. "I'm taller, but I think we're close in size, so this should hold you until you order more."

I peek inside the bag to find cotton underwear, a sports bra, and several rolled-up balls of socks. There's also toothpaste, a toothbrush, and deodorant. Her thoughtfulness overwhelms me, and a tear falls from my eye. This morning, I brushed my teeth with a washcloth.

"I'm so grateful for your kindness."

"It's not much."

"It's everything." I yank her in for a hug. She stands there stiffly until I let her go, and then she dashes out the door. It would seem that Port Promise isn't used to someone as overtly affectionate as me.

I walk to the front of the class. "Let's get ready to explore!"

Even early, excitement hums in the air for our outdoor adventure.

With supplies in hand, we head out of the community center and onto the trail that winds through the nearby woods. Along the way, I point out different plants and wildlife that I recognize. Many of the plants I see are only familiar because of my mother's journal, which makes me more convinced she spent time here. I point out the bushy bundles of leaves growing nearly everywhere on the path and tell the kids that they can eat the fireweed raw or cooked. When we come across stalks of wild rhubarb, I tell them to never eat the leaves.

"What happens if you eat the leaves?" Lucas asks.

"I imagine your stomach wouldn't like that, so never eat them and only eat the stalks when they are cooked."

We continue on the trail and walk past the cabin. Three of the four walls stand, but the roof is completely gone, and the inside is gutted. From the path, I can make out the stove and the skeleton of the metal bed frame. It hurts seeing it this way. When I first came, it wasn't much to look at, but in the two days I was there, I began to appreciate it for what it was—a piece of the town's history. Sadly, the chipped plate will no longer be witness to anything.

I turn to look at the kids, who are bent over, looking at something in the mud just off the wooden path.

"What did you find there?"

The kids shift and make room for me. What they're looking at shocks me. Right there in the yard of the cabin I was staying at is the biggest animal print I've ever seen. It's at least twice the size of my hand.

Lucas points to where a toe is missing from the print. I assumed its walk was off kilter.

"That's Old Grizzletoe. He got caught in a trap once and left behind a toe with some of his gold fur attached. No one has ever been able to catch him."

"Gold fur?" My research says that most of the bears

here are black bears, but I imagine they have variations in color.

"Cool, right?" Lucas says, and the little ones nod.

"We should head back." The last thing I need is to leave behind a legacy as the teacher who saw the signs and didn't heed them.

"He's not going to bother us. We are four people." Lucas looks at Hailey and Tommy. "What did we learn about bear attacks this year?"

Tommy stands tall. "They hardly happen."

Hailey raises her hand. "If you make lots of noise with our kind of bears, you'll scare them away."

I try to remember what I learned. Brown, lay down and pretend you're dead. Black, attack, meaning make yourself as big and noisy as possible. Grizzlies are another story altogether. If you run into one of them, you're most likely the next meal.

Since there are no brown bears or grizzlies on Prince of Wales Island, Old Grizzletoe must be a black bear who's gold. As I measure the logic in my brain against the risk, I realize that our group of four would probably be a deterrent, and I decide to move on with our day. Bears are a daily challenge for those who live here. They can't be a huge threat, or someone would have warned me.

"Who is up for looking for Devil's Club for May?"

All hands raise, and I explain how to spot it, but I warn them not to touch it. "Who will be the first to find it?"

Fifteen minutes later, Tommy hoots and hollers,

jumping up and down like he got six spots that matched on a lottery ticket. "Is that it?"

We rush over to check out the plant. "That's it, Tommy. It may look prickly, but it has some incredible medicinal properties," I explain. "It's been used for generations by the indigenous people of Alaska for everything from treating sore muscles to boosting the immune system."

I put on Kane's gloves and show the kids how to harvest the shoots, emphasizing the importance of being careful around the sharp spines. Everyone seems to hold their breath while I snap off a sizeable length and clear the thorns with the scissors I brought along. When it is safe to hold gloveless, the kids pass it around.

As the morning turns to noon, a sense of accomplishment washes over me. Not only are we contributing to Old Danny's health and wellness, but we're also learning.

Lunchtime hits, and I open the jar of Nutella. I realize I'm not being a great role model by eating sweets for a meal but everything I bought to make sandwiches was destroyed in the fire. I'm just grateful it was a few grocery items and some clothes that can be replaced. The biggest loss was the cabin and, of course, my Kindle. Some people lose everything when tragedy strikes. I grabbed what was irreplaceable. The rest can be ordered online or purchased at Rhys's store.

As I watch the kids unpack their lunches, a pang of envy washes over me. How I'd love to have even just a simple sandwich or a bag of chips right now. I'm considering plucking a handful of fireweeds when Hailey brings over food.

"Ms. Moore, Daddy packed lunch for us." Hailey shows me two sandwiches, chips, and juices. She hands me one of the sandwiches, pointing to the sticky note attached to it. "This one's yours because it has your name."

I glance at the note and melt at the simple yet heartfelt message. "Timber, I hope you have the best day ever."

This small act of kindness means so much to me. In this moment, a sense of belonging and gratitude envelops me, something I haven't experienced in a long time.

Kane might believe that the community doesn't help each other the way they used to, but he's wrong. I'm seeing it in everything they do. From the way his brothers rushed to put out the fire, to the bag of things Theresa brought me this morning. Then there's the little jar of chocolate happiness. Generosity is a muscle you have to flex. Port Promise just needed a little workout.

As the afternoon sun peaks and then begins its descent, Lucas and Tommy's parents arrive early to pick them up, giving quick waves and hurried thank-yous before whisking the boys away. Soon enough, it's just me and Hailey left in the community center.

I scribble a quick note on a piece of paper and tape it to the door, in case Kane forgot. "Gone to May's."

"How about we go to the café?" I ask, excitement bubbling at the thought of presenting her with the Devil's Club we gathered earlier.

Hailey jumps up and down. "Yes, let's go."

The weight of the Devil's Club in my hands fills me with a sense of purpose. It's a small thing, but knowing I can contribute something meaningful to May's herbal remedies brings joy to my heart.

We're greeted by the comforting aroma of freshly baked pie and coffee. May looks at my hands and claps. "Yay, you found some."

"It was a joint effort. In truth, Tommy saw it first, and I harvested it safely with the gloves Kane gave me. I hadn't thought about how I'd be able to get it for you without slicing my skin to pieces, but he did."

"That man is a keeper." She takes the Devil's Club and turns it over in her hands and grins. "Someday someone is going to steal his heart."

I tug on one of Hailey's braids. "I think someone already has."

"I'm not talking about his daughter." She points to a nearby booth. "Have a seat. For your trouble, let me treat you both to a piece of pie while you wait for your man."

"Oh, he's not..."

May waves the Devil's Club in the air. "But he could be. Now, how about that pie? I've got fresh wild blueberry or apple."

I lead Hailey to the table. "What do you say, kiddo? Apple or blueberry?"

"Blueberry," she says, and I hold up two fingers. May takes her Devil's Club into the kitchen and comes back minutes later with three plates.

She joins us and sits next to Hailey. "I hear the fire destroyed your cabin," she says before taking a bite.

A somber mood settles over me. "It did. I'm surprised the whole town didn't come to the rescue." I figured word of a fire would have everyone running, if not to help their fellow neighbor, then to make sure it didn't burn down their property. "Communities of this size need to be able to count on their neighbors."

"We used to." May's gaze is distant as she nods in agreement. "Things change," she murmurs. "People stick to themselves these days."

Her words strike a chord within me, a reminder that nothing stays the same. Change is the one thing we can count on, but maybe it can be a change for the good.

"When was the last time there was a community event?" I ask. "It seems like gathering everyone in one place could be a positive thing." It would also help me find what I'm looking for. On our trek today, I realized how far apart everyone lives. If I'm ever going to find my father, I can't go door to door. It would be so much easier if I could get everyone in the same place.

May's eyes show her excitement at the suggestion. "It's been years," she replies, a hint of wistfulness in her tone. "But I think you're right. It's time we brought back that sense of community."

I'm filled with renewed purpose. "Then let's make it happen. Kane says that when he was a kid, there used to be potlucks at the community center. Do you think we can do that?"

Her glasses sit at the end of her nose. She pushes them back and looks at me. "We'll have to make it appealing. Like free food. I can supply the dogs and burgers, and everyone can bring a side dish or a dessert to share."

"What can I bring?" Hailey asks. Her lips are dyed purple from the blueberries.

"You can help me make my mom's famous potato salad."

Satisfied that she's not left out, Hailey goes back to eating her pie.

"What makes it famous?" May asks.

"Capers and bacon."

May cocks her head and looks confused. "I thought I was the only one who did that." She rubs her chin. "Red potatoes or regular?"

I roll my eyes and make a *pfft* sound. "Red, of course, and the good mayonnaise, but not the sweet kind."

"That's the only way. Anything less would be disrespectful to the potatoes," May says.

I laugh because it sounds like something my mom would say.

As we continue to discuss plans, May's phone rings. She answers and steps away, her expression shifting to concern as she listens intently to the caller. When she returns, there's worry in her eyes as she quickly swipes up the pie dishes before everyone's finished.

"Have you ever delivered a baby?" she asks.

"No." Before she says another word, I know in my gut that Eliza is in labor.

"There's no time like the present."

"Is Eliza in labor?" Panic rises in my chest.

"Yes, and I need your help." May runs off.

I turn to Hailey. "Looks like you're going to be a cousin to baby Cody today."

Hailey doesn't complain about not finishing her pie. She puts on her coat and runs to the door. "I want to help too."

I take a deep breath, my mind racing. Delivering a baby? This is way out of my league. But there's no time to think, only act. I immediately take out my phone and message Kane. "Change of plans. Your sister is in labor. May asked for my help. Pick us up at her house."

Chapter Ten

KANE

My pulse quickens as I read Timber's message about Eliza being in labor.

I pull in my gear and steer the boat toward home. I'm sad my father won't be here for the birth of his second grandchild. And poor Matt won't be there to watch his first child come into this world. I was there when Hailey was born. There's nothing more amazing than watching your child take their first breath.

I push the throttle, and the engine roars to life, the boat slicing through the waves at a faster-than-safe speed. Suddenly, a jolt ripples through the rig, the helm shudders, and the engine sputters. Panic grips me as I wait for everything to stall. Today is not the day for mechanical failures. I pray for things to hold together a little longer. Miraculously, the engine steadies, its familiar hum returning with renewed strength.

The familiar sights come into view. I approach the dock, steer the boat into its berth, and secure the vessel to the metal cleats. Every second counts as I unload the day's catch, my mind solely focused on reaching Serenity Cove. With the last crate of fish on ice and safely stowed away, I sprint toward my ATV. The minutes stretch into eternity as I race toward my sister's house.

The scene at Serenity Cove is much like its name, deceptively tranquil, with shimmering water lapping at the shore and tall trees swaying in the breeze. Despite the calm exterior, I know that a different kind of energy courses through the air inside.

The sight of four parked ATVs lined up neatly in the driveway signals my brothers' presence and their readiness to help.

With Eliza's husband away on an oil rig, we are responsible for providing support and assistance. We'd do that anyway because she's our sister. We may not always agree, but family comes first. Together, we'll weather any storm that comes our way.

As I approach, the sound of an ax hitting wood comes from the back of the house. I step around and find Nash cutting wood. He sees me and stops mid-swing.

"I think she's got enough wood." I stare at the pile, already eight feet tall and ten feet wide. "Are you doing this for her or you?"

"Probably both. Every time she cries out in pain, I want to rush in and take that away, but I can't, so I'm better off out here where I can't hear. At least I'm doing something productive."

I walk over and pat my brother's shoulder. "Hang in there. She'll be okay. May knows what she's doing."

I walk back to the front door, and other than the sound of metal hitting wood, it's silent outside. It's as if the birds are waiting for Cody's arrival. With a mixture of anticipation and apprehension, I raise my hand to knock, but the door swings open before I can make contact, and Rhys stands there.

"Glad you're here so quickly," he says. "May says things are moving fast."

I'm grateful because Hailey's birth took what seemed like a lifetime. Though I felt helpless, like Nash does now, I stayed by Amanda's side.

Finn is in the kitchen washing dishes. Reid is in the living room, letting Hailey "do" his hair. He's got barrettes and bows everywhere.

Hailey looks up. "Daddy!" She runs around the couch and hugs me. "Cody is coming soon."

Her enthusiasm is infectious. "He sure is, sweetheart." Some might consider Hailey too young to experience all that comes with a home birth, but this is a way of life here.

As Timber emerges from the bedroom, I notice the way her hair is pulled back into a messy bun, strands escaping to frame her face. There's a subtle sheen of sweat on her brow, and yet she's absolutely beautiful. Despite the exhaustion evident in her features, her calm demeanor is a reassuring presence.

"Hey there." I can't suppress the surge of appreciation swelling within me at the sight of her. "How's it going in there?"

Timber laughs. "Oh, you know," she says, her tone

laced with a hint of exhaustion and a dose of humor. "It's just another day. Burn down a cabin one night and deliver a baby the next. There's no rest for the weary here."

"That's a pretty accurate statement."

She walks to the kitchen and fills a glass with ice. "I should get this to Eliza. May says the baby will be here within the hour." She disappears into the bedroom.

As someone who has lived a solitary life, wary of outsiders and protective of my family, I've often hesitated to let strangers in. But seeing Timber's genuine kindness and willingness to lend a hand, even to those she's just met, has challenged my notions about outsiders. While I may still approach new faces cautiously, Timber has opened my eyes to the possibility of finding friendship and support in the most unlikely places.

As I settle into the living room, my eyes are glued to the closed bedroom door. Heavy quiet hangs over the room, broken only by the muffled sound of Eliza's labored breaths and the background music to *Frozen*, Hailey's go-to for entertainment. The tension in the air is thick as fog. I look for something to do, but it appears everything from dishes to laundry has already been done.

"I bet it will be any minute now," Rhys says from beside me.

It seems like forever before we hear it—the cry of a newborn echoing through the house. A chorus of relieved sighs fills the room. Nash rushes inside, his forehead dripping sweat. "Sounds like we've got ourselves a new Hollister."

"You can't take his dad out of the mix," I say. "While Cody is half Hollister, he's also half Ryder, and that's good." Out of all the men Eliza could have chosen, she picked Matt Ryder, who is as steady as the mountain and patient as a saint. I can't wait for him to get here, so I can give him a pat on the back for being the kind of man we can all be proud of.

Several minutes later, Timber emerges from the bedroom as the newborn's cries echo through the house. She catches my eye and offers me a weary smile. "Hey, guys," she says, her voice soft, but her eyes filled with excitement. "Eliza would like you all to come in and meet Cody."

My brothers and I exchange glances, rise from our seats, and follow Timber back to the bedroom where May stands at Eliza's side.

I step inside, with Hailey next to me. Eliza is nestled in the bed with a tired but contented look on her face, cradling her newborn son. The room is warm and joyful, and time stands still. This is so different from when Hailey was born. Amanda looked at our beautiful baby girl and rolled to her side to sleep. I should have known then that she wouldn't stay, but I chalked it up to exhaustion. But right now, I push those thoughts aside to focus on Eliza and Cody.

"Hey, Sis," I whisper, approaching her bedside. "You did it. Mom would be so proud of you." Cody would be the first grandson and her only daughter's child. Poor Eliza had to go through all of this without a mother.

That makes me sad for Hailey because she's had to navigate her short life without her mother, too.

Eliza squeezes my hand. "Thanks, Kane," she says. "And thanks for being here."

"I wouldn't want to be anywhere else." I take in my nephew, this tiny bundle of new life. He's red, wrinkly, and nearly bald, but I can already tell he'll be a good-looking kid. How could he not—he's half Hollister.

Hailey tentatively approaches the bed, her eyes wide with curiosity. "Daddy, can I touch him?" she whispers.

I glance at Eliza, deferring to her.

Eliza nods. "Of course, sweetie," she says, her voice filled with kindness and affection. "You can touch him gently."

Hailey's eyes widen as she reaches out, her hand trembling slightly. With a gentle touch, she brushes her fingertips against the baby's fine hair.

Observing the tender exchange between my daughter and her new cousin fills my heart. For all the bad that came with Amanda, she gave me Hailey, and for that, I'll be forever grateful.

After a few moments, May shoos us out of the room, and I find myself lingering in the doorway. Timber takes the baby and cradles him in her arms with a tenderness that takes my breath away. I'm struck by how natural it seems. It's as if she was born to be a mother.

After seeing her with Cody, I allow myself to entertain the possibility of something more between us. It's not something I can rationalize or explain away. It's simply a knowing, deep-seated intuition that tells me

Timber is more important than I ever imagined. And at that moment, I know that I can't ignore this undeniable connection between us.

As Timber puts the baby in the bassinet, I realize how tired she must be. She walks out of the bedroom and closes the door behind her. She heads for the couch in the living room and sinks into the cushions, where she seems to find a moment's peace.

May steps out several minutes later. With a grin, she tells me to take Timber home. "I'll stay the night here, but she needs a hot meal and a comfy bed," she says. "Timber worked hard today. We should all be proud of her."

I give May a nod, appreciating her concern for Timber's well-being.

Turning to my brothers, May asks, "Who is staying and going? If you're staying, then you have to change diapers and cook breakfast." Before May can say another word, my brothers are on their feet, ready to hit the road. They quickly say their goodbyes and head out.

May's laughter echoes behind them as they exit the house.

"Let's say goodbye before we go," I say.

We enter Eliza's room, where Timber and Hailey exchange goodbyes with my sister. "Remember, Eliza, I'm just a call away," Timber says.

"Thank you so much for being here."

I kiss my nephew on the head and look at Eliza. "Did you call Dad, or do you want me to?" Eliza confirms that she has already phoned him, right after Matt, who should return home tomorrow.

When I lean down to kiss Eliza, she whispers, "Timber is a keeper, Kane. You should try to keep her."

I kiss her cheek. "Some things aren't up to me."

She shakes her head. "I think you could have a say in this."

"Go on now. We all need our rest." May waves us away like we're annoying insects.

Knowing Eliza is in good hands, I guide Timber and Hailey to my ATV, ensuring Hailey's buckled in the back seat. Timber finds a spot beside me. Somewhere along the journey, she leans against me, and I enjoy her gentle weight against my side.

The engine hums steadily beneath us as we navigate the winding trails back to the ridge. The rhythm of the ride lulls us into a comfortable silence punctuated only by the sounds of nature surrounding us.

It's not until we reach the familiar sight of my home on the ridge that I realize Timber has fallen asleep, her breathing slow and steady against my shoulder. Hailey stirs in the back, unbuckling herself and climbing out of the parked vehicle. I signal her to be quiet as I lift a sleeping Timber out of the ATV. She stirs for a minute, lays her head against my shoulder, and she's out again.

With Timber in my arms and Hailey beside me, I remember that even in tough times, there's beauty. Putting Timber on the couch, I'm hopeful about what comes next.

Chapter Eleven

TIMBER

I SNAP AWAKE. The last thing I remember is sitting next to Kane, driving to his home, and now I'm lying on his couch with him looking down at me. I scramble to sit up.

"How did I get here?"

"Daddy carried you." Hailey peeks from behind her father.

"Did you hurt yourself?" I pull down my T-shirt, which had ridden up over the waist of my pants. "May was right when she called me sturdy. I'm no lightweight."

Kane laughs. "I catch fish that weigh more than you."

I scrub the sleep from my eyes and laugh. "Isn't whaling illegal?"

"Stop, you're perfect, exactly the way you are."

Charmed and embarrassed, I realize there's nothing I can say but, "Thank you."

"Are you hungry?" he asks.

I nod. "I'm so hungry. Even Beaver Bolognese sounds

good. Who knew helping May could be so exhausting." I rise from the couch. "Let me know what you want and where I can find the ingredients, and I'll cook. It's the least I can do since you're providing me a place to sleep for now." That only reminds me that this is a temporary solution. Given my increasing attraction to Kane, staying for long wouldn't be wise. It's risky to get too attached to him, considering the heartache it could cause. Plus, there's Hailey to consider—strong attachments could make things complicated for her too.

Kane shakes his head. "It was part of the deal. We provide room and board and a small salary for your services."

"I know, but this is your house, and I don't want to intrude."

He brushes off my concerns with a gruff, "It's no problem." Though reassuring, his words somehow suggest my presence could be an issue. Perhaps I'm reading into them because his proximity will challenge me. All I want to do is fall into his arms, and that's a dangerous place for me.

"I'll make dinner," he says. "You were up most of the night, worked all day, and helped deliver a baby."

He walks into the kitchen and pulls out a package of ground meat, a jar of spaghetti sauce, and a pasta pack.

I follow him and take a seat at the center island. My eyes focus on the ground meat. "I was kidding about the beaver."

He chuckles as he washes his hands and gets a pan from under the kitchen sink. "It's beef, but you'll have to give the other a try sometime. It's not as bad as you imagine."

While I generally play it safe when it comes to food, I'm tempted to live on the wild side and try it someday. "My mom used to tell me to try everything legal twice. She said you can't have a genuine experience on one try because you often go into it with preconceived notions which skew your experience."

"It sounds like your mother was wise." He crumbles the meat and puts it into a frying pan, then glances at Hailey, who's dumping a box of dolls on the living room floor. "Hailey, go wash up before dinner."

"Can I play first?"

Kane looks at her sternly. "No, you need to wash up." He turns to me and says, "This is a daily event. She argues with me about everything."

Hailey stomps away, and I laugh. "Wait until she grows up. Girls are tough, but that independent streak will come in handy one day."

"I expected it at some point, but not at five."

"Kids can be challenging, but you're lucky to have her. There are so many people who can't have children." Suddenly, I choke up but immediately swallow my emotions like always. I'm tired and emotional. Holding a baby brought out all those feelings I try to avoid, like emptiness and brokenness. "I wanted children, but it wasn't meant to be." I don't know why I'm telling him personal things, but probably because his sister just gave birth, and watching her dream come true makes me sad that mine never will. "I always wanted them. I dreamed of having three when David and I got married."

"You're married?"

"No, not anymore. He wanted children more than he wanted me."

"I'm so sorry." Kane stops stirring the beef and looks at me. "That must have been hell helping Eliza." He walks over and hugs me. It's not a one-handed hug you'd give an acquaintance, but a full-on bear hug with both arms swallowing me. I thank the universe for a wish granted. It's good to be in his arms, and I bury my face in his shirt and inhale. He smells like pine, sunshine, and an ocean breeze. "I'm sorry you had to go through that."

I reluctantly break away. "No, that was a magical moment. I've never seen a baby born except on TV. Honestly, it was a beautiful experience. I'm blessed that I was allowed to be present."

Kane laughs. "I was here when Amanda gave birth to Hailey, and I wouldn't call it magical. That woman called me every name under the sun." He looks around as if to make sure Hailey can't hear. "She wouldn't even hold her or feed her or anything."

I couldn't fathom the idea of not wanting to hold my child. I mean, if I carried it in my body for nine months, nurturing it, experiencing every kick and flutter, how could I not embrace her when she finally arrived?

"That had to have been hard. What did you do?"

"I called in reinforcements. My mother was alive then. She came in and took over."

"What happened to Hailey's mom? Were you married?"

He returns to the pan, stirring the meat, browning it thoroughly before adding the sauce. All I wish is that he'd hug me again.

"We weren't married. Amanda is a do-gooder, but her focus has never been on people. She left us at six weeks to save the seals in Namibia. She pops in on occasion, but there's never any warning."

A lump the size of a fist lodges in my throat. "Did you have any help?"

He nods. "Yes, my family stepped in. During the first year, my brothers ran their businesses and mine to ensure I had the money and resources to care for us. After that, my mom and Eliza watched Hailey while I fished. Then my mom got cancer, and it was just Eliza." He puts water in a big pan, sets it on the burner with the flame high, and then calls out to Hailey. "What are you doing up there?"

There's a giggle before she races down the stairs in a Cinderella dress. "I dressed for dinner."

I look at my borrowed yoga pants and T-shirt. "I may be underdressed."

"You look great," Kane says.

My stomach flips and then flops at the compliment. "If you keep being so nice to me, I may never want to leave."

Hailey twirls in her blue dress. "I've got a Snow White dress you can borrow."

"I appreciate the offer." It tickles me that she thinks it would fit.

Kane places three plates on the table and then stares into my eyes. "I don't see that as a bad thing. Besides, finding another place will be near impossible. This is where you'll stay."

Every cell in my body surges with a fiery intensity, sending electric currents straight to my core. But I remind myself that I'm not here forever. This is temporary.

"I've got a new boss in Phoenix that might have a problem if I decide not to return."

"New job?" Kane's shoulders tense, and a shadow passes over his eyes, making me wonder if my leaving will affect him.

"Yes, I took a promotion to be a testing coordinator. It pays better than teaching, and honestly, I'm tired of people's games." I'm mostly tired of the favoritism and being overlooked and ignored when positions open in my school.

"I like games," Hailey says.

Kane ruffles her hair, which was nicely braided this morning, and now looks like a nest for birds. "You also like spaghetti, so let's eat."

Dinner passes in a blur, Hailey recounting every step we took on our trek. "We found the Devil's Club." She frowns. "Tommy found it, and Lucas found Old Grizzle-toe's paw print. We even stopped by the burned cabin. Will Grandpa be sad?"

I'm immediately brought back to the panic and then

the guilt. My stomach tightens, and the acid rises to my throat. Although Kane repeatedly reminds me that the fire isn't my fault, I still hold myself responsible.

"Grandpa will understand," Kane says. "The thing about living in a place like this is nothing is forever." He looks at Hailey. "If you're finished, you can go play for a while."

Hailey skips off to the living room to play with her dolls.

Waiting until Hailey is out of earshot, I say, "The cabin has been around for a long time. Surely, your dad will be sad to lose all the memories it held."

"My father left the island after my mother passed." Kane sighs. "He's been traveling for months. I'm sure he's afraid to come home to the emptiness. He won't be bothered. Everything he loved is already gone."

I ache for Kane. "Not everything. You guys are still here. He'll come home, eventually. Probably sooner than you think. He's got a new grandson."

He shrugs, the movement a subtle shift in his posture. "We'll see," he replies, his tone carrying a hint of resignation.

Later, while Kane fights Hailey to bathe and get ready for bed, I borrow his computer to order some clothes from Amazon. There isn't Prime Delivery here, but I'll make do with what I have for the time being. I have a closet with some of Eliza's clothes, my flannel PJs, and the gift Theresa brought to school today.

"Did you order what you need?" Kane asks when he returns, looking exhausted. He pulls two wine glasses from an upper cupboard and takes a bottle of cabernet from a nearby rack. "You should let me pay for those since I technically burned down your home."

"While I appreciate the offer, you have a boat to pay for, and I can afford to get my clothes." It warms me that he is willing to pay for what I lost in the fire. While I don't want to admit it out loud, I am grateful that I didn't create the situation that burned down the cabin. How does one recover from that? The guilt would be immeasurable.

He hands me a glass and takes a seat on the couch. "Join me?"

"Sure." I'm happy to join him for a glass of wine. It will give me time to get to know him better, to get accustomed to this town. "So, tell me, why didn't the cabin have solar power or indoor plumbing?" It appears that many places have modern amenities, and some don't. I'm curious as to why some buildings have moved into the twenty-first century and some remain in the dark ages.

"There are too many trees, so the sun can't get past the canopy to charge the panels, and the cabin was built long before indoor plumbing was a thing. This house sits atop the ridge, so I get plenty of sun. As for the water here, I get much of what's in the house from the lake, which gets replenished yearly with snowfall. For waste, I have a septic system. My house is a modern marvel compared to most."

"That makes sense." He shifts on the leather sofa so he's facing me, and I immediately want to run to the bathroom to fix my hair or put on lip gloss. Though we've been together all evening, this seems more intimate. There was dinner and now there's wine. With Hailey in bed, it's just the two of us, and it almost seems like a date. I let go of that thought and remind myself that this isn't that.

"I bet it was all a shock when you arrived at the cabin Eliza didn't describe it accurately."

I take a sip and savor the smoothness. "She left out a few details, but she said it had everything I needed, and that wasn't a lie. At first, I imagined I'd hate it, but I was game to try."

"And?"

"I actually liked the rustic vibe of the place. It's life-affirming to know you don't need all the bells and whistles to survive."

His eyes widen, and he looks at me, as if searching for deception in my words. "Most women spend a week here and then bolt as fast as they can in the other direction."

"Hailey's mom stayed longer, didn't she?" His shoulders slump forward, and guilt washes over me for bringing it up, but I'm curious about them. What was she like? What did he see in her? Why would she leave a man like Kane? I wave my hand in the air. "It's none of my business."

"No, it's okay. Amanda came here as part of a Save the Whales campaign. We hooked up a few times, and then she was gone. I had no illusion that she'd stay, but then she showed up a few months later, pregnant. I wanted to do right by her and Hailey, and I proposed." He shakes his head and looks into the distance as if replaying a scene. "She said no. She didn't want to be married to anyone." He looks at me and shrugs. "I thought that since we had a child together, she'd stay, but she wasn't interested in any of that 'domestic stuff,' as she called it. She wanted the wind in her hair and the sand between her toes. She wanted Alaska today and Galapagos the next month." His tone is nonchalant, but there's a hint of sadness underlying his words. And I wonder if he's sad for himself or Hailey?

"What did your family think?"

"Honestly?"

"If you're willing to share."

He chuckles. "They thought I should have kept my dick in my pants, but they all love Hailey, so they're glad I didn't. At least my mom got to spend time with a grandchild before she died."

"Did your mom like her?"

Kane sips his wine. "Amanda is a likable person. I think she means well, but life threw her a turn that she wasn't ready to navigate."

I'm familiar with what it's like to have an absentee parent. I knew from a very young age that my father didn't want me, and that does something to a child's self-worth. I suppose not being wanted at any age hurts. When David cast me aside, he destroyed me. "I feel bad for Hailey," I say, my voice cracking slightly.

Even now, thinking about it brings a familiar ache to my chest. Am I healing? Maybe. But there are still moments that trigger those old wounds, making them fresh all over again. Seeing Hailey struggle with the same emotions stirs up a whirlwind inside me. I want to protect her from the pain I know all too well.

"I do, too, but all I can do is be the best father I can be. It was easier when my mom was here because she had raised a girl, and I could ask her questions. I miss her." As Kane speaks, I notice a shift in his demeanor. His usually stoic expression relaxes, revealing a vulnerability that tugs at my heartstrings. His words carry a weight of sorrow and longing, and I can see the pain etched in the lines of his face. That's a pain I'm all too familiar with.

"I miss my mother, too. I'd do anything to have another day with her." I reach out and gently squeeze his hand, offering comfort in the face of both of our losses.

"Me too. There are so many things I wish I had said to my mom before she passed. Even telling her I loved her once more would have been so good." He shifts his shoulders, as if trying to shake off the weight of his emotions, and then he smiles. "I should have gotten a few more hair tips for Hailey. I'm a total failure as a stylist."

Remembering Hailey's pigtails on the first day of school, I laugh. "You are, but I can show you some easy ways to tame it."

"I'd appreciate that," Kane responds, his gratitude evident in his voice.

"Hailey's hair is a lot like mine. While it's fine, it has a lot of waves to it. I can definitely help," I assure him.

"It's times like these when I realize Hailey is missing out on a mother's love."

"I think you're doing a great job." I chew my lip for a second before asking what's on the tip of my tongue.

"What if Amanda comes back and wants a second chance? Would you take her back?"

He frowns and shakes his head. "Not for me. I'm a once burned, twice shy guy. But if she came back for Hailey and genuinely wanted to make things right for our daughter, I'd be open to having her around. Everyone deserves a second chance, but she'll never return to stay. She bounces in and out when it's convenient for her."

I want to ask if that bouncing in and out includes his bed. I can't imagine not wanting that as I stare at this man before me. I've only known him for a few days, and he's got me hugging him on a whim and staring at his lips like they were the only thing in focus in a blurry world. It's ridiculous how quickly he's woven himself into the fabric of my thoughts, each thread tingling with anticipation whenever he's nearby. And yet, here I am, toeing the line between curiosity and restraint, wondering if the same magnetic pull is tugging on him.

"My turn."

My heart beats double time as I wonder what he'll ask. Will they be questions I'll want to answer? As I think about it, there isn't anything I'm hiding. Just things I'm working out in my head, like the possibility of my father being here.

"What do you want to know?"

"Same thing. What about your husband? If he came back, would you give him a second chance?"

As I hesitate, considering his question, I catch a subtle shift in his expression. There's a look of something in his eyes—perhaps curiosity, or a hint of something more. It's a momentary glimpse into his thoughts, leaving me wondering if his interest in my answer extends beyond mere curiosity.

I think about that for about five seconds. "No, he was all wrong for me. I'm a forever person, and he was a for-now kind of man. Besides, he's remarried and has twin boys. He's got everything he wants and needs."

Saying it out loud is like ripping off a bandage. It still stings, but there's a strange sense of relief too. Maybe it's acceptance, or maybe it's just realizing that I'm better off without someone who couldn't see my worth. I deserve more than someone who's only in it for the moment.

Thinking about his new life, a pang of something—regret, maybe?—surfaces. But it's not for losing him. It's for the time I wasted trying to fit into a life that was never meant for me.

"He was an idiot," Kane states bluntly.

"Why would you say that?"

"Because he left you." Kane's gaze is unwavering as he meets my eyes.

Insecurity creeps in, and I say, "I'm no great catch."

"As an expert on great catches, I'd say you're wrong," he insists, sending a flutter through my chest.

"Who am I to correct an expert?" I say with a nervous chuckle, taking another sip of wine to mask the rush of emotions coursing through me.

"Exactly," he agrees, his expression unreadable as he turns away, leaving me to ponder the significance of his words. He rolls his glass in his palms, the movement so effortless it mesmerizes me. And then I notice how big his hands are, how they dwarf the delicate wine glass, making it seem almost fragile in his grasp. That's how I felt when he hugged me—delicate, fragile, and cherished.

"Before I head to bed," Kane continues, interrupting my thoughts, "I want to thank you for all you've done since your arrival."

"It's been my pleasure. It's nice to be needed."

"We definitely need you." His gaze lingers on me in a way that seems like he's peering straight into my soul. "What did you think when you arrived? Was it less than what you expected?"

"Less? Oh, heavens, no. It was more than I could have hoped for." From the moment I arrived, I had a purpose, and each day brings new moments of connection and understanding. In Kane's company, I find myself more at ease than I've been in a long time, as if I've finally found a place where I belong.

"We are a bit much here. I think the term is extra."

"Speaking of extra, should I be concerned about Old Grizzletoe?"

"No more than you should be concerned about other wild beasts. I bet the fire drew his attention, and he came to check things out. If you run into him, make a lot of noise, and try to make yourself look as big as possible." He waves his arms through the air. "Does having him around scare you?"

"Scare?" I imagine myself jumping up and down, waving my hands in the air.

Kane nods, his eyes never leaving mine, as if he already knows the answer but wants to hear it from me.

I take a deep breath, gathering my courage before admitting, "Yes, I'm scared, especially when the kids are with me. But I learned early on that fear is temporary, but regret lives with you forever. And I don't want to regret anything, so I'll continue to walk through the woods, gather herbs, look for rocks, and explore, but I'll be more aware while I'm doing it."

"I'd rather not have any regrets either." Kane's gaze seems to linger on my lips. He leans in, and for a moment, I'm certain he's about to kiss me.

Do I want that? My brain screams yes! But just as I'm about to meet him halfway, he pulls back, stands, and stretches his arms out with a groan. I chastise myself. First for daring to want it, and second for entertaining the thought that someone like Kane could ever be interested in someone like me. He's made it clear he's been burned before, and I can't shake the feeling that he's guarding himself against getting hurt again. After all, why would a man like Kane risk anything when he could easily stay unencumbered to avoid the pain?

"I should get to sleep. Four in the morning comes early." He walks to the kitchen to place his glass in the sink. "Help yourself to anything you need or want." He stares at me again, and I can see some kind of debate in his eyes, and somewhere deep inside, I hope that he'll come back and kiss me, but as soon as he looks away, he says, "Good night, Timber. Sweet dreams."

After Kane leaves, I sit in his living room and finish my wine. I'm usually good at reading the signs, but I was way off tonight. He wasn't staring at my lips because they looked plump and appetizing. I probably had wine dripping down my chin because I drool over this man whenever I find myself alone with him. That lean forward wasn't the prelude to a kiss. It was merely forward momentum to get him to his feet so he could go to bed.

Silly me. I take my glass to the kitchen and wash up, so we aren't faced with a mess in the morning. But as I rinse off the soap suds, a wave of relief floods through me. That almost kiss? Phew. Dodged a bullet there. Sure, it might have been nice in the moment, but let's face it— it would've turned my life into a mess of complications. After all, he's not just any guy. He's the father of one of my students. And here I am, staying in his house. Yeah, it's definitely not a good idea.

With a sigh, I mentally brace myself for bedtime rituals. Theresa's toothpaste and toothbrush await—a reminder of her kindness. Pulling on another one of Eliza's quirky T-shirts, I smirk at the slogan emblazoned across it: "solvem probler." Well, ain't that the truth? Could it be I'm conjuring problems where there are none, letting my imagination run wild? Tomorrow's a fresh start, a chance to shake off the nonsense and tackle whatever comes my way. Bring it on.

Chapter Twelve

KANE

I PACE THE BEDROOM, thinking about the colossal mistake I nearly made.

"Unbelievable," I grumble to the empty room. I was so close to kissing Timber I almost tasted the wine on her lips. Truth is, I wasn't that close, but I imagined it. I stared at those lips for seconds—long enough to know she has a freckle above the upper, and when she purses them, they are shaped like a heart.

Discussing regrets got me pondering—would kissing her have been one more for the list? Pulling back made sense. "What was I thinking?" She's Hailey's teacher, for crying out loud, and a guest in my house. "All I need is another one-night stand and, three months later, an unexpected visit telling me she's pregnant."

I freeze when I realize what I said. There would be no knock on the door because Timber can't have kids. Watching her with Hailey, I know she'd make an excellent mother. She's completely in tune with those around her and does sweet things Amanda would never consider, like holding back when the conversation isn't for Hailey's ears or ensuring Hailey is included by asking her questions. She knows when to listen and when to steer a kid right.

Her ex is blind to so many things. The way I see it, you don't need to father a kid to leave your mark. It's like tracking a path in the woods. It's the staying, the walking through it day by day, that matters. When I called him an idiot, I'm not just spitting words against the wind. If she was mine, I'd stick it out. Fertility be damned.

Those vows state things like sickness and health and richer or poorer. I've never seen or heard vows that say, I'll stay until you can't give me kids. Marriage is a partnership where sacrifice is a given, but unconditional love is as well. They could have adopted. Hell, they could have raised mini goats and called them family. My house is big enough for many children, but I'm content to have Hailey. I don't need a half-dozen children to make me a man. The love of a good woman does that on its own.

My dad's leaving makes sense. It's sad, yeah, but I get it. The place he calls home reminds him of her every single day. And without her, it just isn't home anymore. I imagine leaving is his way of looking for some peace. I can't say I wouldn't do the same.

I had a long talk with my mother before she passed. She worried I'd never know the kind of love she and my father shared. I told her not to worry because I have Dad, Hailey, and my siblings. "It's not the same thing," she said. She explained that Hailey would grow up and build her own life. My brothers would eventually marry. Eliza had a family with Matt. Two days before she died, she held my hand and made me vow to let my guard down and let someone in.

"You can't give up on love because of Amanda. Open up to people and let them in if you want them to stay," she said. It's only been a few months. I'm not there yet, but I'm trying. Changes of that magnitude don't happen fast.

I consider Timber. Would I want her to stay? Yes. She's not what I'm used to, but she may be exactly what I need. She's the type of woman I could fall hard for, but I'd rather not start something I can't continue, and I don't want to get to the end of summer and force her to decide between me and that new job that pays more. But boy, do I want to kiss her.

Thinking about Dad, I wonder about love, the kind that knots two lives so tight it's near impossible to tell where one starts and the other ends. Is it wise to lean on someone like that, to need them so much? But then again, isn't that the point of it all? To risk the fall for the chance to fly? Dad did, and even if he lost his balance when she was gone, for a while, he soared higher than anyone I've known.

Questions swirl as I shed the day's clothes and climb into bed. Would she have come closer if I hadn't stepped back? And that look she gave me. Was it just a trick of the light, or did she want that kiss as much as I did?

I'm not usually one to dwell on what could have been. It's not like when Sarah Blakely said yes to being my date at that dance and then left with someone else because he had a better ATV. That's kids' stuff.

I wonder if that near-kiss was a narrow escape or a missed opportunity. Mom's advice seems more real than ever, but a trickle of fear seeps into my heart. It's like waiting for a bite on a still morning. You've got the line out, the bait set, but there's no telling when the fish will strike or if they will at all. You just need to be patient and keep your line in the water. And when you get that nibble, will the fish be there, or will they steal the bait and move on to another line?

Chapter Thirteen
TIMBER

My alarm tears me from my dreams at four in the morning. I am kissing Kane, and it is glorious. But as I shake off the fog of sleep, a thought arises—the real thing would be even better. Dreams set the stage, but it's real life where it all counts.

I shake off all the tingles rushing through my body. With a Herculean effort, I fling myself out of bed, a feat akin to a fish flopping around on dry land.

Rushing to the bathroom, I squint at my reflection, half expecting to see swollen lips and a blush staring back at me. Yet, to my surprise, I'm normal morning me with pillow creases and a wild mane. I splash water on my face to wake up. Once my teeth are brushed and my hair is in order, I face the day.

Back in my room, I tackle the wardrobe battle. With a grunt of determination, I wrestle my way into a pair of Eliza's jeans, which are one size too small. The struggle is like trying to zip up a tent while wrestling with a bear. But finally, after much huffing and puffing, victory is mine.

Feeling slightly ridiculous, I leave the bedroom, ready to tackle whatever challenges the day throws at me. After all, I can conquer anything after a morning battle with a pair of jeans.

I tiptoe into the kitchen. It's tranquil. The only sound is the gentle hum of the refrigerator. With a sense of purpose, I set about whipping up a delicious breakfast for Kane and Hailey.

I rummage around the cupboards until I find the necessary ingredients for pancakes. Flour, check. Eggs, check. Milk, check. As I gather the supplies, I reflect on last night, how Kane and I opened up to each other. Does that count for something more? We shared laughs and stories, not just thoughts in my head. Sure, it wasn't a date, but it was real. And real conversations have to count for something, don't they? What if what we're building isn't just in dreams? It could be the start of something.

With practiced ease, I mix the batter, the rhythmic whisking soothing my nerves. The aroma of vanilla fills the air as I pour the batter onto the hot griddle.

As the pancakes sizzle, my mind replays the dream, the vivid memory of Kane's lips pressed against mine. There is a rightness to it, a sense of belonging, and in that dream, everything else fades away. It is only us, and it is perfect. The shock of reality, the sound of the alarm—it was like cold water dousing a flame. Now, standing here, flipping pancakes, that dream is like a cruel tease, a reminder of what isn't.

Sure, Kane may be intriguing, but what future could there possibly be when I'm set to leave in August? The job back home in Phoenix is the role I thought I wanted and it's more money. I need the money to fix up my mom's house because that's where I have my memories of her. But now, there's Kane. His presence has cast a new light on everything, making me question what I really want. Phoenix is familiar, safe, but it's also a return to the old me. Kane represents something new, a change I hadn't planned for. The thought of leaving makes me feel both excited and pained. It's a tug-of-war between the comfort of the past and the pull of a new possibility.

I sigh, leaning against the countertop and closing my eyes. It's tempting to get lost in the moment's allure, ignore the practicalities, and surrender to the pull of attraction. But deep down, I know better. If we get involved, it will turn into heartache when my time here ends, and I've had enough heartache.

Yet, despite my rationalizations, a small part of me still holds hope. Hope that there's more to this attraction than meets the eye.

For me, that sliver of hope looks like a question mark drawn in the sand, likely to be washed away by the tide of reality. What would it mean to give this a chance? Could I entertain a fleeting romance, knowing the expiration date is as searing as the desert sun back in Phoenix? Could we try to stretch this connection across the miles, a long-distance bid to keep the flame alive? I can almost envision the late-night calls, the flights to see each other, the constant texts.

Could that work? The practical part of me lists the cons. The emotional side counters with "what if." The list is long on both sides, but "what if" weighs more heavily. It's a dance of possibilities in my head, each step choreographed by a heart that's learned to be cautious yet yearns to tango.

But for now, I push those thoughts aside, focusing instead on flipping the pancakes, determined to savor this moment of domestic bliss before the realities of the day come crashing back in.

Moments later, Kane and Hailey come downstairs together. Hailey beams as she takes in the spread before her—pancakes, orange juice, and me. Kane's gaze flickers with an intensity that leaves me slightly unsettled. A whisper of doubt tiptoes through my mind. Did I overstep my boundaries? Was surprising them with breakfast too much, too soon?

"Wow, you made us breakfast?" The look on his face is pure joy.

I lift my shoulders in response, trying to play it cool. "I was up first." But deep down, a spark of happiness ignites within me. With a grin, I join them at the table, handing two pancakes to Hailey before serving up a hearty stack of four for Kane and keeping the final two for myself. As I settle into my seat, their gratitude washes away any lingering doubts, and I bask in the simple pleasure of sharing this moment with them.

"How did you sleep?" His voice is gentle, but there's

a turbulent undertone that matches the stormy look in his eyes. His tapping fingers betray a hint of nervousness, mirroring my own. Are we both experiencing this tension, or am I alone in this?

Caught in the moment, I struggle to find the right words. I'm not about to tell him that I had a hot, steamy dream about him kissing me and how his hands roamed over my body.

"Good, what about you?"

He stares at my lips for a moment, as if he, too, had a dream about them, and is looking for evidence. Heat climbs up my cheeks, a sign of the havoc he stirs within me. Every glance he offers is a riddle, his eyes holding back unsaid words. It's in these quiet exchanges, these fractions of seconds where our worlds collide and retreat, that I find myself lost in the what-ifs.

"Slept like a baby," he says, his voice steady. But his brief glance leaves a hint of hope, or maybe it's just my wishful thinking.

"That's excellent." I turn to Hailey, who is halfway through a pancake. It makes me happy to see her enjoying what I made. If I had been able to have a child when I was trying, he or she would be about Hailey's age. For a minute, I let myself pretend everything around me is mine. I never asked for riches, jewels, or fancy cars. All I ever wanted was a place to call home and a family to call mine.

"Big day of fishing today?" I raise an eyebrow, hoping he'll share his plans with me.

"Same old, same old, but I'll try a new location

farther out. I don't normally push the boundaries, but knowing you'll be here for Hailey, I might do that." His voice is a blend of casual conversation and subtle sincerity. The subtext isn't lost on me. This isn't about changing his routine, it's about trust. There's a delicate thread extending between us, tethering him to me in ways that surpass our day-to-day interactions. "It means I'll be late, but I'll leave the Polaris for you, and you can come home when you like."

The way he says "home"—a word so simple yet weighted with unrealized dreams—feeds into my fantasy. Being trusted with Hailey is a sacred responsibility that I cherish. As he discusses his plans, my mind wanders to the evening ahead. The house will be quieter, filled with the lingering essence of his presence. Hailey will be there, a sweet girl with his eyes, and in caring for her, I'm caring for him. It's a responsibility I take on willingly and happily.

"How will you get home?"

"I'll ask Rhys to drive me, but don't think you have to keep Hailey. I can get one of my brothers to step up. I don't want to take advantage of your kindness. It's just that I'm trying to get this new boat as soon as possible."

His words tumble out in a quick succession, an abrupt detour from the ease of our earlier conversation. The mention of his brothers stepping in implies a retreat, a polite but clear boundary being drawn. The change is stark, leaving me to grapple with a whirlwind of questions. Does he regret extending the offer, or is he trying to shield me from an imposition?

But seeing how badly he needs the new boat, I'm happy to help. I know what it's like to want things that are out of reach, and if I can help him get to his goal faster, that would be a good thing.

"Sure, I can do that." It's good to help, to be part of his journey toward a dream.

His eyes meet mine. "Thank you," he says. That simple exchange, the smiles we share, says everything about the trust and friendship growing between us. "I don't think Aurora has that many trips left in her."

"Aurora? How did your boat get that name?"

"She used to be my grandfather's, and he named her after the Borealis."

"And you kept the name?"

"It's bad luck to rename a boat. Mine is bad enough already that I don't need to borrow any more trouble," he says with a hint of a smirk, yet his tone is playful and edged with a touch of mock seriousness.

I let out a small laugh, understanding the jest behind his words. "So, superstitions are the sea captain's gospel now?" I tease back, playing along. It's clear he's not wholly serious, using humor as a way to lighten the conversation about what seems to be a run of tough luck.

I think about the vessels lined up at the docks, each with a woman's name proudly displayed on their sterns. It's a longstanding nautical tradition, but I wonder about the emotional toll of such a choice. What happens when the person for whom the boat is named departs or passes away? To me, it seems such a name might transform the boat into a floating memorial, a constant echo of someone absent, more a shadow than a tribute.

"What will you name the new boat. As its first captain, you get that honor, correct?"

"I do and it will be Seas the Day"

"I like that," I say, and it's the truth. It speaks of living in the present, of adventure and capturing opportunities. Perhaps, in this small act of naming, he's also setting a course for the future, one that isn't overshadowed by what or who is no longer with us. I appreciate the name, not for its playfulness but for the freedom it signifies.

"Me too. It embodies everything I feel when I climb aboard my troller."

"Then seize the day so you can get your new boat. Don't worry about being late. I'll feed Hailey and give her a bath."

Hailey's head pops up, eyes filled with hopeful anticipation. "Can we have a bubble bath?" she asks, her voice pitching high with excitement.

I nod, "Of course, bubbles it is."

Kane observes the exchange. He knows Hailey's in good hands, and there's a mutual understanding between us. I'd care for Hailey like she is mine.

"That would be wonderful, but I don't want to take advantage."

"Neither do I, so it would bring me great pleasure to help. I know having me staying in your home wasn't part of the deal."

"True, but if I'm being honest, I like having you here."

That smile of his, it's more than polite. It's as if he's happy not for the help, but for the company—my company. And that thought alone fills me with joy.

"You do?"

"Yes, it's a big house, and while I love being with Noodle," he reaches over and bops Hailey's nose, drawing a giggle of delight from her, "sharing conversation and enjoying a good glass of wine with another grown-up? That's the thing that hits the spot after a day out at sea."

His words resonate with me, and the cold uncertainty of being an unwelcome guest is replaced by a sense of belonging. I realize now that my presence is not merely tolerated but appreciated—perhaps even needed.

Kane drizzles the warm syrup over his pancakes. "This was very nice of you. I thought it would be a cereal kind of day, but this is so much better." Kane takes a bite of the pancakes and closes his eyes. A moment of quiet fills the room, and I hold my breath, waiting. When he speaks, his voice has a soft edge to it. "They taste like my mom's. Did you use the mix in the cupboard?"

The question takes me by surprise, and it takes a moment for me to respond. His compliment, filled with nostalgic kindness, washes over me, and a swell of unexpected happiness rises within me.

"No." I shake my head. "My mother would have reached out from wherever she was and given me a good pop on the head if I did. She was a true believer in making things from scratch. She always told me that boxed food lacks the love it takes to make it good."

He takes a bite. "It definitely tastes good."

We sit in silence and eat. Every time I glance at Kane, he's looking at me. Caught in his gaze, I feel like a mystery he's intent on figuring out. It's a little unsettling, but also thrilling to be seen so closely.

He finishes his last bite and says, "Hailey, sweetheart, when you're finished, get your brush so I can comb your hair. We still need to clean up and feed the chickens before we leave."

"Why don't you feed the chickens while Hailey and I clean up and get ready, unless the chickens are one of her chores."

"No, this will actually save time. Hailey's more likely to pick each one up and say good morning, which takes a lot of time. If you're willing to do the dishes, and her hair, it will be like killing two birds with one stone."

I laugh. "No need to kill the birds. I'm happy to divide the chores."

He rises and places his plate in the sink. When he returns, he kisses me on the cheek. The soft press of his lips throws me completely off guard. For a heartbeat, everything stands still.

When he steps back, his eyes widen, and his mouth falls open. "I'm so sorry. I just … it's a habit." His apology is rushed.

"It's okay," I say, the corners of my mouth lifting in a genuine smile. Despite the surprise, the kiss leaves a lingering sweetness, not only on my skin but somewhere deeper. It's a small, intimate connection that seems as natural as it is unexpected, and I can't shake the feeling it stirs inside me.

"Are you in the habit of kissing all girls on the cheek?"

He shakes his head so hard I fear he'll scramble his brain. "No, I never kiss anyone." His denial is so serious it only stokes my fearlessness.

Despite knowing it isn't wise, I tease him anyway. "Too bad. I bet you're a great kisser." There's a thrill in this light-hearted banter, a flirtation with what-ifs that I know I should probably avoid—but don't want to.

He's caught off guard, words faltering for a fraction of a second, his eyes locking with mine. There's a question there, but any further response is cut short by Hailey's voice piercing our little bubble.

"I kissed Tommy once on the lips, and he said he didn't like it."

Hailey's innocent interjection changes the dynamic. His previous look of curiosity at my teasing comment about being a great kisser shifts abruptly. When Hailey mentions her own experience with kissing, it's a jolt back to reality for Kane. His brows furrow, signaling a shift from the playful tension between the two adults to his protective parental mode. "No kissing boys until you're thirty-five."

I bite back a laugh. Thirty-five, he says. By that benchmark, I'd have missed out on a lot—the sweet taste of a first kiss, the bitter end of a marriage, and the rich lessons each heartbreak brought. Sure, I could have dodged the pain, but then, I wouldn't have grown. The kiss on the cheek, light as it is, is another piece of the universe's puzzle laid before me. I don't have the full picture yet—why that kiss, why now—but I trust that it's all part of a larger design. Every experience, every connection, has its moment, even if its purpose isn't immediately clear. This kiss, casual as it is, might just be the universe's way of telling me there's more in store for me.

Once Hailey is finished, we clean up. I wash while she rinses, and when we're done, I pull her hair into a ponytail.

"There you go, princess. Grab your jacket. It looks like it might rain later." Hailey bustles around, looking for her things, while I open the refrigerator to make lunches. I gather sliced turkey, cheese, and bread. I'm not sure how much food Kane needs, but I imagine with his hard work, he'll need a few sandwiches. If he plans on staying out late, he'll need more. I whip up several meals and fill his cooler with water bottles I find in the kitchen corner, bagged chips in the pantry, and cookies he has hidden on a top shelf—probably to keep out of Hailey's reach. On the counter is a notepad and a pen. It's likely the one Kane used to write my note. It was such a sweet thing to do. It reminded me of the notes my mom used to tuck into my lunch bag. Each little message was like a hug, a reminder in the middle of a school day that I was loved. I want Kane and Hailey to feel as wanted and appreciated as I did as a child.

So, I scribble a quick note for each of them. Nothing too heavy, just a nudge to make them smile. For Hailey, it's a smiley face to brighten her day, and for Kane... Well, it's a whisper of something more, something that says I'm here, thinking of you even when you're miles out at sea.

When Kane comes in, he sees everything ready to go. "You made our lunches too?"

"It isn't a big deal. It's best when people work together as a team."

"I agree, but I'm not used to that. If you keep being this nice to us, we may never let you go." His words hang in the air for a heartbeat, and I can tell they've caught him off guard just as much as they have me. There's a brief look of surprise in his eyes—the kind that says he hadn't planned on being so candid. Then, a half-smile tugs at the corner of his mouth, and he holds my gaze, steady and unwavering.

"I'm sure you'll welcome it when it's time for me to go," I say, my voice light, but inside, my stomach does a slow somersault. The idea of being wanted, of someone hoping I'd stay, sends a ripple of something sweet and terrifying through me. I catch a glint in his eye that makes me wonder—does he sense it too? This pull, this back-and-forth we're doing around each other's lives. He's so different from my ex-husband, who never seemed to grasp the concept of us, of teamwork. And here is Kane, valuing my presence, almost as if he's reluctant to think about a time when I'm not here. "Shall we?"

We walk outside to the ATV. Kane buckles Hailey into her seat, and I take the passenger side. As we drive along the path, I'm awestruck again by his land's beauty. I can't understand why more people don't stay in this place, and then I remember the plans May and I made yesterday.

"Did I mention that we're going to do a community potluck a week from Sunday?"

Kane's brows furrow slightly. "It's a great idea, but I'm not sure how many will come."

"I don't know either, but it might be fun," I say optimistically. "Isn't being a part of a community what this town was founded on?"

His expression shifts as he considers my words. "That was then, but things changed."

"They're going to change again," I say, meeting his gaze with determination. "And who knows, maybe this potluck will be the start of something new."

"Maybe."

We drive for another twenty minutes. Each time the ATV hits a bump, he instinctively reaches out to steady me. His hand is quick to ensure I'm safe, an action that makes my pulse quicken. I'm so aware of his closeness, and it seems like more than just a reflex. When we arrive, his hand falls away, leaving a ghost of his touch. I step down, my skin still tingling from the contact.

He helps Hailey out and then walks us to the door, where he kisses her on the cheek. As he steps away, a swirl of anticipation stirs within me. There's a fleeting moment where our eyes meet, and in that instant, I'm filled again with boldness that only comes from not wanting to let a moment slip away. Before I can second-guess the impulse, I close the distance, reach up, and plant a kiss on his cheek.

"Have a great day," I say.

I watch him walk away, and there's a sudden drop in my stomach, a mix of gladness for the connection we just shared and the disappointment of him leaving. I'm left standing there, slightly breathless, wondering what the rest of the day will bring and how long it will be until he comes back.

Chapter Fourteen

KANE

THE SEA'S CHURNING up something fierce today, matching the storm brewing inside me. Aurora is battling the waves, her old metal frame groaning against the swell. She's been a good boat, but every trip out is a gamble these days.

When Timber kissed me on the cheek, it was like a jolt through my system. I didn't expect it, yet I hoped for something, some sign. It wasn't the kiss I wanted—no, I wanted something deeper, but I'm treading carefully, unsure of crossing lines that might change everything.

In that moment, I wanted to pull her in for a real kiss, to show her just how much her being here meant to me, but I held back. It's a precarious balance between this growing need for her and the protective walls I've built around Hailey and myself.

I attempt to shake her from my thoughts and focus on the day's goal of catching lots of salmon. Beyond the usual boundaries I set for myself, there's a stretch of water where the current runs just right, and the depth drops off, giving way to the rich feeding grounds that salmon can't resist. Though it's far out there, Dad used to say it was like a dinner bell for the fish—the way the river runoff hits the saltwater, mixing up a perfect cocktail of fresh and brackish that the salmon love. It's where he and Grandpa would bring in hauls that were the stuff of local legend. While I would have liked to experience it with Dad, I have no idea when he'll return, and my needs can't wait. I steer Aurora toward it, thoughts of a new boat fueling me.

As the familiar shoreline fades into the distance, and the only sounds are the slap of waves against the hull and the call of seabirds overhead, there's a sense of calm. My grip on the wheel is steady until I reach my destination hours later. I carefully drop the nets, watching as they disappear into the blue depths.

Time slips by, marked by the rocking of the boat and the sea. My arms work in time with the waves, pulling in the nets heavy with thrashing, silver-bodied salmon. Each one that hits the deck is a whisper of a new start, a sturdier boat beneath my feet, and a safer future for Hailey and me.

I allow myself a rare moment of pride as I survey the swelling hold. It's a good day's work, the kind that could mean a real change in luck. The thought of that new boat, sleek and reliable, edges closer to reality with each fish I ice down.

Hunger hits, and I go for the cooler. Timber's packed lunch is nothing fancy, but you can sense the care put into it. I tear into a sandwich, and it's good, really good. Then I spot her note under the chips. Unfolding it, her handwriting greets me, neat and sure.

Kane,

This is just a little something to keep your strength up out there. Don't worry—I've got you covered. Good luck today and come back safely.

Warm food and warmer smiles are waiting for you back home.

T

Just a few words on a scrap of paper, but it's like sunshine breaking through the clouds. She's here with me, in a way, out on the water. It's funny how something so small can lift you. I read it again, and I can almost hear her voice. I'm chasing the day's catch, but it's Timber's thoughtfulness that catches me off guard, making me grateful in ways I don't expect.

I stare out at the horizon as I remember her face—her smile. It's a strange sensation, unsettling but not unwelcome. For a moment, I let it wash over me, that sense of wanting something more. This thing building between us—it's like a current, strong and silent. I'm not sure where it's headed, but it's clear now. Ignoring it isn't an option anymore.

A distant murmur of the storm has been a low growl on the horizon for hours, but as the first drops of rain pelt the ocean's surface, they're like cold little warnings against my skin. I should head back and steer Aurora to the safety of the harbor. But the nets are full, bowing deeply in the water. The haul is too good to abandon.

With Timber watching over Hailey, it seems safe to take some risks out here. I push Aurora harder, thinking of the future I'm trying to build. There's a saying that rings in my head— no risk, no reward—and today, that seems truer than ever. It's a shot at a better tomorrow. Comfort seeps in. The idea of this being my new normal —it's a tempting thought. But as the storm picks up, so do my doubts. It's a gamble, out here on the rough waters, and so is letting someone in. But maybe, the risk is worth the chance of a reward, like having Timber as part of my forever.

Heaving the nets aboard, my muscles scream while rain slicks my face, mingling with the salt spray kicked up by an increasingly angry sea. I've got the rhythm down, a routine I've done a thousand times before, but today, my thoughts betray me. All day, I've shoved these thoughts aside, telling myself there's no room for distraction. But now, as I'm surrounded by the ocean's roar, I let myself think of her—the softness of her lips and that damn near-kiss.

A sudden squall hits, Aurora lurches, and for a split second, I'm a rookie again, fumbling.

The net catches my foot and coils around it. For a terrifying moment, as the boat tips precariously, I'm nearly dragged overboard into the icy water. I fight it, kick hard, my chest pounding louder than the storm.

I manage to free myself. A harsh laugh is caught in my throat, more from relief than amusement. It's a mistake that shouldn't happen, not with my experience. But then, I hadn't counted on being so damn distracted.

As I haul the last of the catch in, the wind howls at my back. I know it's time to go home. The storm won't wait for the likes of me, and there's too much to lose now.

The tempest's fury intensifies as I steer Aurora from within the confines of the weather-beaten cabin. With every giant swell, she groans, a sound that echoes the fear tightening in my chest. The sturdy metal around me is the only barrier between me and the chaos outside. Yet, as the waves crash against us, the cabin offers little comfort. The glass windows, streaked with salt and rain, are my only eyes to the outside world, now covered by the storm's rainy wrath.

Despite the cabin's protection, the cold seeps into my bones. My clothes cling to my skin, damp remnants of the struggle on deck. I'm shivering, partly from the chill and partly from the onset of a realization I've been trying to ignore. Aurora isn't invincible.

I'm fighting the wheel as Aurora pitches and rolls. This is bad, worse than I expect. I need to get out of this mess, not just for me, but for Hailey. She needs her dad. And Timber—she's stepped in without asking for anything in return. I can't leave her to explain to my little girl why I didn't come back. My brothers, they're tough, but I'm the one they count on to hold things together.

I'm praying for a miracle. Then something happens

—the engine gives one final shudder before silence falls. It's not the miracle I want, just more complications. My hands fly to the ignition, turning it over repeatedly, but there's nothing. Just the dull clunk of a dead heart. I bang my fist on the helm.

I scan the instrument panel, desperate for some sign of life, but it's as dark and lifeless as the depths below us. There is no radio, no transponder—all the modern lifelines rendered useless. The only thing left, my last hope, is the emergency beacon. I snatch its sturdy case and, with a press, release its cry into the storm.

The boat lurches, a cruel reminder that I am at the mercy of the sea. I brace myself, wedging my feet against the edges of the seat to stay upright. Once a sanctuary, the cabin walls now seem like a trap as Aurora is flung mercilessly by the surging waves.

In this moment of dire isolation, my thoughts turn to Timber's note. I grip it in my pocket like a lifeline, the paper saturated with seawater. The words now gone, are imprinted in my mind and offer comfort. It's like holding onto a piece of calm in the midst of this tempest. In my head, I see her handwriting, the loops and lines of a quick message that's now a light in the darkness.

I imagine making it back, seeing Hailey's relief, experiencing Timber's embrace. They push me to fight through this.

I picture sitting Hailey down, telling her the story of the worst storm I ever saw. Timber is by my side, a subtle smile telling me she's proud I made it. They're why this isn't just a fight for survival—it's a fight to return to the life that suddenly holds so much promise.

I'm not one to pray, but I whisper words, half to the ocean, half to whatever fate may be listening. "Let me see them again. Let me embrace my child, who looks at me like I'm her world, and don't let me die before I can taste Timber's lips."

Chapter Fifteen
TIMBER

THE STORM PELTS the community center. Tommy's and Lucas's parents pick them up, leaving the building emptier than it was just moments ago.

"Should we go to May's for a visit and hope the rain stops?" I ask Hailey.

She races to get her coat while I gather the flyers the kids made that morning. I like all of them, especially Hailey's. It's full of smeared blue and green paints, like the ocean where her dad sails. There's a sun in one corner made with yellow handprints. She proudly told me the gray spot was supposed to be her dad's boat, and the sun was happy about the potluck. We make our way out the door and into the storm. The wind fights with our coats as we hurry through the heavy rain. I keep the flyers safe in a folder close to my chest

Reaching May's diner, the warm air slices the chill. Inside, the storm seems distant. Dusted with flour from her baking, May smiles and waves toward an empty booth. "You two look like wet cats." She reaches behind the counter, pulls out two towels, and tosses them to us. "Dry off, and I'll get you some drinks to warm your bones."

While May fixes us hot drinks, I admire the proud handiwork of the children. May serves us cocoa for Hailey and coffee for me, with the scents weaving through the cinnamon-infused air.

"Well, look at these masterpieces!" May says.

"We plan to post them everywhere, like you suggested, but the weather needs to cooperate."

May carefully selects one for the window and pins it up. I can't see it from where we're sitting, but Hailey's face lights up, and I know it's her art on display for the whole town to see. The other flyers lay on our table, a splash of vibrant creativity among the white ceramic mugs and the dark wood. There's a picture of the community center, stick figures holding hands around it, and on another, a garden with flowers bigger than the people tending them.

Peering out the window, I can't shake thoughts of Kane out at sea. The diner's cozy chatter fades as I imagine the storm's fury he must be facing. Hailey's here with her cocoa, happily drawing, and I hide my worry behind a steady smile, trying to keep the storm in my heart from showing. But inside, I'm on that boat with him, experiencing every wave and gust, hoping he's okay. I hold on to the hope that he'll come back to us. I'm trying to stay strong, for Hailey's sake.

Leaning on the table, May says, "Where's that man of yours?"

"You know he's not mine." In my mind, the words form a different truth. The thought is a wishful what-if or maybe that I tuck away into a corner of my heart. I look to the window where the rain pelts the pane. "He's still out there."

Unfazed, May smiles and brushes flour from her hands onto her apron. "Well, wherever he is, he's a seasoned fisherman and can weather anything thrown at him. You don't have to worry about that one."

And just like that, she shifts my worry to confidence regarding Kane's ability. "You're right," I agree, watching Hailey from the corner of my eye. I'm looking at things from a position of inexperience. I remind myself this is familiar territory for him.

The noise of the storm fades, leaving silence behind. We should head out. I gather our belongings and tell Hailey, "It's time to go." She springs from the booth, clutching her napkin artwork.

"It's time for us to leave," I tell May, catching her attention as she cleans the counter.

"Drive safe, Timber," May says.

"Will do. Thanks for the cocoa and coffee. What do I owe you?" I reach for my wallet.

May shakes her head. "Nothing, it was my pleasure." She looks at Hailey. "Thank you for the art. It made my day."

I nod, appreciative, and Hailey echoes a "thank you" as we leave.

Outside, a fresh canvas unfolds where the storm has passed. The ATV seats glisten with raindrops, and I sweep the moisture away. Hailey climbs into her damp seat, undeterred by anything. After buckling her in, I start the engine and we begin the journey home. I'm looking forward to a peaceful evening. I think about Kane returning, his clothes damp and his eyes tired, but he's safe. I can almost hear the clatter of dishes as we clean up from dinner. The low hum of our voices fills the kitchen. In my mind, we're laughing while Hailey tells him about her day, and everything seems complete. I imagine us sharing stories and the comfort of being together, the storm nothing but a memory.

Once we arrive, I park the ATV. "Let's go in and think about dinner."

"Let's have ice cream and cookies," she says.

I chuckle and lead the way to the house. "Let's start with something warm—grilled cheese and tomato soup —and then we'll talk about ice cream."

Her face falls but recovers fast. "Okay, and a movie night?"

Stepping into the kitchen, I'm hit with a sense of gratitude. The warm glow of the lights, the hum of the refrigerator, and the certainty of the gas flame are all luxuries that are comforting tonight. "That's a deal."

As I cook, there's a cozy normalcy to it all, a stark contrast to the cabin's solitude. I think about Kane coming home, how he'll step through the door with stories etched by the sea—tales of close calls with the waves or the thrill of the catch.

The soup bubbles away and the sandwiches crisp up nicely, but there's a knot forming in my stomach with each passing minute. Hailey's voice is a bright thread through the growing dusk, yet my eyes keep looking at the clock. It's later than I expected.

At first, I tell myself when he said he'd be home "late," the definition of "late" was loose, especially for a fisherman. But as the evening wears on, "late" starts to seem more and more like "too late." A chill seeps in, not from the evening air, but from the worry that's pooling inside me. Then again, I volunteered to feed Hailey and bathe her. Somehow, I must have expected he'd miss dinner and bedtime.

I consider calling Eliza, but I dismiss the thought. What would I say? That I'm worried because he's not back at the time I arbitrarily decided was "late?" I'd sound foolish, paranoid.

We sit down to eat, and the savory scent of melted cheese mingles with my rising concern. Hailey is blissfully unaware, her spirits as high as her laughter, but with each chime of the clock, I glance toward the window, half-expecting to see Kane's silhouette.

Post-meal, we set the plates and used soup bowls in the sink. "Next up is movie time."

Hailey nods enthusiastically, and for a moment, I let her excitement push away the cold knot of worry in my stomach. We settle on the couch, the opening credits casting a soft light in the dim room, and for the length of the film, I immerse myself in the adventure, sharing laughs and glances with Hailey.

Yet, even as we watch *Willy Wonka*, a part of my mind ticks away with the clock on the wall. I hoped Kane would join us, laughing at the silly parts. But the space beside me remains empty.

Movie time shifts to bath time. I run the water, making sure it's just the right temperature, and Hailey splashes among the bubbles. Her carefree joy is a stark contrast to my growing unease. The sound of wind against the house prompts me to check the window, and the dark outside offers no comfort.

I tuck Hailey in, her room bathed in the pale blue night light she can't sleep without. "Dream of ice cream castles," I say.

"And chocolate rivers," she adds, already half in dreamland.

Downstairs, the silence presses in. I curl into the couch, drawing the blanket tighter around me, trying to recall May's words. "He's a seasoned fisherman."

But Aurora and her troublesome engine are haunting me. Kane has been late before, but never this late. I have never been on the troller myself, but from Kane's frustrated updates, I know it has seen better days. He's skilled, no doubt, but even the most experienced sailor can't always predict the sea's whims.

Another gust of wind lashes the house, more ferocious than the last. Instinctively, I rise and peer through the window, searching for any sign in the pitch-black night. The clock ticks on, a relentless reminder that time—and perhaps the sea—waits for no one.

It's ten o'clock now. The void of Kane's absence fills

the room like a tangible presence, and I can't sit idle any longer.

With a trembling hand, I reach for the phone, and dial Eliza's number, hating that I might disturb her rest, especially now, with a newborn in the house. The line clicks, and after a couple of rings, a groggy voice answers.

"Hello?" The man's voice is thick with sleep.

"Who's this?" I ask.

"I'm Matt, who's this?"

"It's Timber, the teacher covering Eliza's summer program," I begin, my voice betraying my worry. "I'm sorry to call so late, but it's about Kane—he hasn't come back, and the storm..."

Matt's sleepiness vanishes, replaced by a sharpened tone. "Kane's still out? That's not like him. He knows better than to risk the storm. That damn boat."

His words confirm my fears, sending a shiver through me that has nothing to do with the night's chill. The room spins slightly, and I brace against the kitchen counter, my concern for him growing into a knot that threatens to choke me.

"I'll alert the Hollisters. We'll start looking for Kane now. Don't worry, Timber, we'll find him," Matt assures me, but the edge in his voice is unmistakable. This is serious.

I hang up the phone. The taste of metal fills my mouth, the early signs of panic that I try to swallow down. Despite the complexity of our attraction, the idea of Kane's absence becoming permanent is unbearable.

With Matt's assurance that they will search, there's nothing I can do but wait.

Throughout the night, I am stationed on the living room couch. Every creak and whisper of the house calls me to the window, searching for signs of his arrival. But as the first light of dawn washes the room in a pale glow, the reality that Kane is still out there, somewhere, hardens like ice in my stomach.

The thought of Hailey, possibly without her dad, sends a shiver down my spine. Her mom's distant, Eliza's got her hands full, and her uncles ... they're great, but they're not Kane. It would upend everything. Could I step in? Should I? These questions churn in my mind.

I've got responsibilities, too—my job, this town, other kids who count on me. But as the minutes tick by, the temptation to hunker down next to the phone, to call someone, anyone, grows. Yet I force myself to stick to the routine, for Hailey's sake, for normalcy.

With a heavy heart, I wake Hailey. She blinks up at me, her first words are a sleepy question. "Where's Daddy?"

The truth hangs heavy on my tongue, but she deserves more than a well-meaning fib. I kneel beside her bed, brushing a strand of hair from her eyes. "Daddy's been delayed, sweetheart. There was a big storm, and sometimes that can happen. People are looking for him, and we hope to see him soon."

Seeing Hailey's worried frown, my stomach clenches. I wrap my arms around her, holding her close, vowing to protect and comfort her. The fear that Kane might not return sends a surge of determination through me—to be a steadfast presence for her, no matter what. Inside, I'm a storm of worry, but for Hailey, I'll be a shelter until he's home.

I maintain a calm exterior as I help Hailey get ready, but inside, my thoughts are a whirlpool of concern. Each time she looks up at me, I wonder if she's searching for the same reassurance I'm aching to give. "Will Daddy be home soon?" she asks again, and I can only nod, offering a hopeful, "Very soon," even as my stomach knots tighter.

After breakfast, we step out into a world that seems unchanged, under a sky too blue for my inner turmoil. "Let's go feed the chickens," I suggest, trying to usher in some normalcy. I've never done it before, but I say, "Hailey, can you show me how?" Her face lights up, eager to be the guide. As she leads the way, I follow, grateful for this moment of leadership that makes her feel big and important.

After the chickens are fed, Hailey scampers to gather her things for the day. I stand in the kitchen with bread and bologna. Should I make sandwiches for Kane? The act is like stitching normalcy and hope into the fabric of an uncertain day.

I decide yes, because hope is something you do, not only something you feel. Making his sandwich, placing it alongside Hailey's in the lunchbox, is my quiet act of faith. It's a declaration to the universe. I expect him back. I'm waiting, we're waiting. It's normal, it's hopeful, it's necessary.

Hailey and I walk in silence to the ATV. I secure her into the passenger seat and climb in beside her. The engine rumbles to life. The path to the community center unfolds with familiarity, each turn a route I've navigated with Kane. What once seemed so vibrant and full of life is dull and lifeless.

As we ride, Hailey sits quietly, her usual chatter absent. She stares ahead, and I wonder if her young mind is trying to make sense of the uncertainty or if she's conjuring images like me. Images of her father, safe and sound, coming home.

We pull in front of the community center, and the ATV grinds to a halt. I help Hailey off, and her hand finds mine, a small act that speaks volumes.

At the door stands May. Seeing her there, out of place against the backdrop of the building instead of her usual spot in the diner, sends a jolt of fear through me. She's a fixture behind her counter, not here. This isn't right. My stomach drops, and I tighten my grip on Hailey's hand, readying myself for the kind of news that can tilt your world off its axis.

We approach, and I tell Hailey, "Why don't you start getting the art supplies out today? I'll be right in."

Hailey walks inside and I turn to May. "What do you know that I don't?"

"They've received a signal on the beacon. Kane's vessel—it's way off course, further out than it should be."

I feel a jolt of panic. The beacon? Off course? My mind races with what this means and what comes next. The uncertainty is suffocating, but I'm comforted by the fact that he turned on the beacon. That has to mean something good.

"Is he okay?"

"Hard to know until they find him."

Hearing the hesitation in May's voice, I search her face for any glimmer of hope, any sign that this is just a precaution, that Kane is okay. I force calm into my voice, steady and sure, despite the tremor of fear that's breaking through. "They'll find him," I say quietly, almost in a whisper. "Kane knows that boat, knows the sea. He'll hold on. He has to." And I cling to that belief because the alternative is too scary to entertain.

"He'll come home, Timber," May says, but her voice lacks the conviction I need right now.

"Okay," I say. "We'll wait, and hope."

Taking a moment, I prepare myself for the day ahead, drawing on every ounce of strength to be the pillar Hailey and the other children need.

As I step inside, the silence of the center is a stark contrast to the tumultuous rush of my thoughts. I find Hailey in the art room, her small hands diligently setting out paints and brushes, her brow furrowed in concentration.

"Good job, Hailey," I say, my voice steady. Hailey's smile is a small comfort, a reminder of innocence and trust. But then Tommy and Lucas arrive with their parents, and their parents' masked concern adds weight to the facade I'm trying to maintain. The question in their eyes is as clear as the words they whisper to me. "Any news about Kane?"

I shake my head slightly, forcing out the facts. "No news yet, but they've picked up the beacon signal and are looking for him." Repeating it, I'm clinging to the hope those words carry, trying to keep the worry from my voice for the sake of everyone listening. "They'll find him."

They nod, grateful for the reassurance, however fragile. They turn to their children, bending down to plant kisses and whisper encouragement before leaving for the day.

I'm left with the kids, their presence a balm to the helplessness that gnaws at me. They gravitate toward the art supplies Hailey has laid out.

"Let's make something special today," I suggest, hoping to channel their energy into creativity and maybe, just maybe, keep my mind off the waiting, off the beacon, off the relentless sea, off Kane.

Chapter Sixteen

KANE

SLEEP IS a luxury that the sea doesn't afford me, not when each drop of rain pounds against the Aurora, not when every wave threatens to be the one that swallows me whole. My hands are numb from gripping the bucket, my shoulders aching from heaving water over the side, hour after relentless hour. The storm's gone now, but it's left me in a bad way.

Dawn's first light brings no comfort, only showing the mess of my boat. She's handled this better than I expected, but we're not clear yet. I am aware of every bruise, every strain of muscle, as if my body is keeping track of the costs of survival. My arms throb in a steady rhythm, in sync with the relentless headache that's been pounding since last night. The only thing that keeps me moving is the thought of Hailey. Her laughter is the sweetest memory. I have to make it. My family can't survive another loss so soon. Then there's Timber, who has entered my life and become more important than I ever imagined.

I need to eat, to stay strong. The cooler, secured by bungee cords, hasn't budged. Timber's thoughtfulness is inside—one of the turkey and cheese sandwiches she made before I left. The bread's a little soggy, the lettuce wilted, but I've never been picky. The water bottles are a lifeline. I ration them in my head, planning for days, even though the thought of being out here that long is like a punch to the gut. I have no idea where I am or how far I drifted. I only hope that someone picks up the signal from the beacon and finds me.

My stiff fingers grasp a water bottle, its plastic crinkling in the quiet. I swig it slowly, letting the coolness settle in my chest, a small relief against the gnawing hunger and fatigue.

The sky clears, the heavy gray yielding to blue. The sea's rough beauty remains the same, but now it seems like a prison. I count each minute, hoping someone's searching for me.

I make one more attempt at the engine, praying with everything I have left. The motor coughs, sputters—a teasing whisper of life. For a fleeting moment, hope flares. But then, silence. Dead silence. Defeated, my hands fall to my sides, and that's when I hear it—not the sea, not the wind, but my mother's voice, as clear as if she were standing beside me. "The ocean's no place for quitters, Kane." Her words cutting through the noise like a lighthouse beam through fog.

She's been gone for months, but she's pulling me

back from the brink of surrender. I can't see her, can't touch her, but she's here with me, in the middle of the sea. Her strength, her resolve—it's a legacy that's my lifeline, even as my body protests every movement and my skin prickles with cold.

With a deep breath that does little to fill the sails of my spirit, I retrieve the binoculars from the cabin, their lenses foggy from the damp. I wipe them against my jacket, as much as it's worth, and bring them to my eyes. The initial scan of the horizon reveals nothing but the merciless stretch of ocean.

Her voice comes to me again, a whisper in my mind. *Try again, Kane. Always persevere.* It's something she'd tell us kids when we were about to give up on anything, from fixing a bike chain to solving a hard math problem.

The binoculars almost slip from my wet hands, but I tighten my grip, steady them, and look again. That's when I see it—a speck, far off, a blemish on the endless sea. I track it. Are they coming for me?

I can't afford hesitation. I scramble for the flare gun. My last chance. I fired two flares into the storm last night. Both went unanswered. This last one—it has to count.

The sea spray stings my face as I take aim. The flare bursts into the morning sky, a bright red cry for help. I watch, binoculars pressed to my eyes, as the speck alters course, growing steadily. Someone's seen it. Relief is a wave that almost knocks me to my knees.

They're close enough for their horn to carry over the water, but far enough that it'll be some time before they reach me. Anticipation surges through me. Fifteen, twenty minutes, I calculate, squinting through the binoculars, the vessel growing larger with each tick of my watch. Each second feels like an hour, each minute a day, but they're coming.

In my mind, I list all the things I'll do if I get another shot. There's Hailey, my little girl with her wild imagination and infectious laughter. I'll spend more time with her, do whatever she wants. Yes, even if it means sitting with my knees crunched under a tiny table, sipping air from a plastic teacup, letting her paint my nails any color she likes, and my hair... Well, she can tie it in as many ribbons as she wants. I'll listen to her stories, her dreams, and I'll share a few of my own.

Next is Timber, steadfast, her subdued smiles and perceptive eyes that seem to cut through the surface straight to my core. I've circled the emotions I have for her, constantly telling myself she isn't the one for me, that she'll just be another to walk away. But even if she does, is that the greatest loss I could suffer? No. The true loss would be in never taking that chance, in living with the question of whether she might share the same feelings. Hailey's in the mix, and it doesn't make things impossible, but it complicates things. Yesterday's trials brought it home—life doesn't guarantee us any tomorrows. Time is a currency in short supply. Out here, where each breath is a victory over the void, I grasp a simple truth. It's not about finding the right time. It's about deciding to leap.

Then there's the new boat I've been eyeing, sturdy

and reliable, not like the battered Aurora, that's barely keeping me afloat.

My regrets are stacked like unused nets at the dock, especially the almost-kiss with Timber. She leaned in, I pulled back, and it's haunted me ever since. When I get back, I'm going to find her, pull her close, and not waste another second.

A shiver racks my body that has nothing to do with the cold. It's fear and relief, balancing like a tightrope walker across my heart.

The horn blasts again, closer now, each sound quicker than the last, like it's counting down. And I know, with clarity, that this is my turning point. This is where the promises I made to the unforgiving sea become the actions of a man who's been given another shot at life.

The approaching boat grows bigger against the lightening sky, more detailed by the minute. It's familiar, owned by Old Danny. The one I've seen cutting through the waters since I was a boy. Its presence has never been more beautiful.

A wave of relief washes over me as my pulse races. My brothers are the first I see as they pull alongside the Aurora, their faces a mix of anger and relief that's as familiar as the lines of my own hands. Tears blur my vision as I fall to my knees, overwhelmed by the sight of them. I whisper a shaky thank you to my mother, knowing her presence guided me through the darkest hours.

They waste no time securing a tow line to my

battered vessel, efficient despite the choppy waves that make the task treacherous. Sobs of gratitude escape my lips, and I shout, "Thank God!" My brothers' stern faces morph into joy. They understand the depth of my emotions. This moment, this rescue, seems like a rebirth.

"You idiot, Kane!" Rhys yells over the sound of the engines. "What were you thinking?"

I don't have the words, just a weary shake of my head. But before I can attempt an explanation, I'm pulled into a crushing embrace. His anger extinguishes like a snuffed candle, swiftly replaced by a wave of relief.

"You're lucky we found you," grunts Nash, as he too wraps me in a hug that speaks volumes more than words could. Finn and Reid are next. At first, they threaten to throttle me, but hug me instead, and then help me onto the other boat.

The sense of family and belonging seeps into me, holding back the cold that's settled deep in my marrow. They hand me a thermos, and I wrap my peeling, raw hands around it. It's soup, still warm, tomato by the smell, made by Eliza. The first sip is cautious, but then I gulp it down, its heat a salve to the chill that's claimed every corner of my body.

Matt turns the helm over to Nash and approaches with a slap on my back that's got the force of normalcy behind it. "I've been back on land for a day, man. Barely had time to hold Cody before Timber called us to find your sorry hide."

Relief floods through me. I knew I didn't have to worry. Timber cares for Hailey like she's her own. Gratitude swells within me for this woman who has embraced both me and my daughter, giving us a sense of family and belonging we didn't even know we needed. My brothers wrap me in blankets, but my body shakes uncontrollably, a mixture of cold and overwhelming emotion.

"Welcome home man, and congrats on Cody."

Matt's grin is a flash in the dim light, pride mixed with relief. "He's got lungs on him, that's for sure. Eliza is an amazing woman. I wish I'd been there for the birth." He looks at all of us. "Thanks for stepping in."

I nod, and my eyes catch sight of my boat latched to Old Danny's vessel. The question of how they got it burns through my weariness. "How'd you get Old Danny to release the boat?" I ask, knowing the man's reputation for being as stubborn as the tides.

Matt laughs. "Turns out Timber's got a knack for finding Devil's Claw right when May needed it for his salve. How could he say no after that?"

A new wave of gratitude hits me, stronger than before. I don't know what I did to deserve her, but I'm determined not to let her slip away.

As we move, the Aurora follows, tethered to the back. Her hold is still crammed with the fish I almost lost to the depths. I think of the irony that in saving me, my brothers have also saved the catch—the very livelihood that I risked everything for.

The journey back is a blur. The rocking of the boat tempts me with the sleep I've long been denied. But I resist, holding on to the clarity of this second chance, to the faces of my family members who risked the angry sea to bring me back.

Hours later, the dock comes into view, and a swell of gratitude rises in me. Timber, who's barely set foot in this place, has already staked a claim in our lives. In just a few short days, she's become part of the rhythm of my world. She didn't just watch over Hailey. She went beyond, becoming someone we rely on, someone who belongs.

It's remarkable how quickly things change—a stranger one day, a lifeline the next. I'd never have pegged Timber as someone who'd dig in deep and fast, but here we are. She's stepped into the chaos of my life, into the heart of my little girl, and without meaning to, into a corner of my mind that's always been wary of newcomers.

The boat touches the dock, and as I step off, shaky but on solid ground, I'm hit with a need to find her. Not just to say thanks for raising the alarm, which I'm more grateful for than words can say, but to let her know that she's made a difference. To make her aware she's needed.

Everything blurs around me until she comes into focus. Standing there, she meets my gaze with a quiet strength, understanding shining in her eyes. I never thought I'd need anyone new in my life. But as I walk toward her, every step more certain than the last, I realize she's become as necessary to me as the salty air I breathe. It's a new sensation, raw and daunting, but it's there, as real as the deck beneath my feet.

Chapter Seventeen
TIMBER

Kane steps into view, and for a moment, the world falls away. It's just him and me. The noise of the dock, the cries of the seagulls, even the wind, seem to hush. He's alive. He's safe. Relief washes over me like an overwhelming wave.

Suddenly, Hailey's hand slips from mine. "Daddy!" she screams, her voice piercing the thick salt air, filled with joy. She dashes forward, a bright streak against the wooden planks, her small legs carrying her as fast as they can toward her father.

Kane catches her effortlessly, holding her tightly against him, his face buried in her hair. The long embrace speaks volumes of the ordeal and the relief. It's a poignant sight that grips at my heart, stirring a blend of emotions inside me.

Together, they walk toward me. Kane's eyes find mine across the remaining distance. His gaze is intense.

May, standing beside me, leans in and whispers with a soft chuckle, "Your man is back."

For once, I don't correct her. "Yes, he is," I say, my voice stronger than I expect, ringing with a new truth.

As they approach, well-wishers pat Kane's back with hearty slaps, tossing comments like, "Glad you made it!" and "Rough night, huh?" Despite the friendly greetings, Kane doesn't engage. His eyes remain laser-focused on me, his stride purposeful.

Goosebumps prickle across my skin, a mixture of anticipation and something else—an awakening of feelings I've tried to ignore. The closer he gets, the more pronounced the sensation becomes, stirring a heat that seeps through my veins.

He stands before me and sets Hailey on her feet. "Hang tight, Noodle." He looks at me and his eyes convey a message clear and raw—he's going to kiss me.

He leans forward. His lips brush my ear, and his voice is low and gravelly, husky from the sea wind. "All I thought about last night was that kiss I wanted but didn't take," he confesses, sending shivers down my spine. "I'm going to kiss you. If you don't want it, step back."

I don't move back. Instead, I close the space between us, pressing my body against his. The world fades into a blur, the noise of the dock slips away, and all that remains is the heat of his body warming mine.

I reach up, wrapping my arms around his neck, pulling him down to meet my lips. Our kiss is deep and sensuous, a mingling of relief and desire. His lips are firm yet tender, moving with an intensity that tells me he's been holding back, waiting for this moment as much as I have.

As our kiss deepens, the rest of the world hits pause, respecting the gravity of our reunion. This kiss—it's not just a kiss. It's a declaration, a fierce acknowledgment of the night apart and the moment we are now seizing.

When we finally pull apart, the intense connection doesn't need words to define it. I don't know what the future holds, and right now, it doesn't matter. We're here, together in this moment, and now is all anyone ever has.

May clears her throat, drawing our attention to her. Her expression is a mix of amusement and concern as she turns her focus to Kane.

"I hate to interrupt this reunion," she says, as she points toward his hands. "But those hands of yours need tending to, Kane." His skin, raw and peeling, catches the light, reminding me of the night's harshness.

"May I borrow him for a bit?" May asks, her tone gentle, yet insistent, understanding the importance of the moment but prioritizing Kane's well-being.

Kane leans in once more and his lips graze mine in a quick, tender kiss.

He bends down and kisses Hailey's cheek. "Be right back, Noodle," he says. "May is gonna patch me up."

Hailey's smile stretches wide. "Okay, Daddy!" She bounces on her toes and claps her hands. "Hurry back. I want to show you my drawing!"

"Sure thing, kiddo."

I watch Kane walk away. For a moment, a pang of reluctance washes over me. It seems like I've only just claimed him, and already I'm hesitant to let him out of my sight. But I set the emotion aside, reminding myself that he'll be back soon.

With a deep breath, I redirect my focus to Lucas and Tommy, who have been engaged in their own nearby play, unaware of the emotional storm brewing nearby.

"Alright, you two," I point to the building. "Let's head back to the community center."

They begin singing in unison, "Kane and Timber sitting in a tree, K-I-S-S-I-N-G."

"There was no tree," I say, shaking my head. How do kids always know that song? It's like it's embedded in their DNA.

As we step into the center, Hailey makes a beeline for the art corner, ready to dive back into her project. She doesn't know how dire the situation was for her father, and I'm glad I could insulate her from that. All she knows is that everything is right in her world.

Glancing at the clock, a combination of restlessness and anticipation washes over me. Kane said he'd return soon, and every passing minute seems like an eternity.

Hailey picks up a marker and works her magic on the paper in front of her. She draws three stick people and when I ask who they are, she proudly tells me it's her family. Pointing at the tallest, she exclaims, "Daddy." Then, pointing at the smallest, she says, "Me." Her finger moves across the one with the big smile. "This is you."

I experience a combination of emotions. Warmth fills

me at the sight, but there's a pang of longing too. I've always wanted a family. Hailey's art makes me wonder if a long-term relationship with Kane is possible. Does he want that too? It's a question that lingers in my mind, stirring uncertainty. But for now, I focus on the joy of this moment, cherishing the time we share and remaining open to whatever the future may hold.

Lucas and Tommy's parents arrive unexpectedly early. They explain they heard on their radios that Kane was found and thought it would be good to come in early so me and Hailey could be free to go home and care for him. With the boys gone, a quiet descends upon the room, broken only by the occasional giggle from Hailey as she draws all the things she wants, like a dog, a horse, and a unicorn.

I steal glances at the clock, willing time to speed up, eager for Kane's return. But amidst the anticipation, I remind myself to savor this moment—the quiet before the chaos of emotions that will surely come when Kane walks back through that door. So, I lose myself in the simple pleasure of creating art with Hailey.

As Hailey proudly holds up her masterpiece, a shadow falls across the doorway, drawing our attention. My breath catches as I turn to see Kane filling the space. His hands are bandaged, and there's salve on his face, but he's as handsome as ever.

As Kane's gaze sweeps the room, his eyes lock onto mine. Excitement flutters in my chest. "Hey there," he whispers. His voice is weary but filled with affection. "Are my girls ready to head home?"

My girls... His words send a rush of giddiness through me, a sensation I can't quite contain.

"We're ready whenever you are," I say.

Together, the three of us make our way out of the community center. And as we walk, a sense of hope stirs within me, a belief that this could be the start of something beautiful for all of us.

Chapter Eighteen

KANE

The familiar creak of the front door announces our return. Stepping inside, the scent of home wraps around me—wood, sea salt, and a hint of vanilla from Hailey's favorite lotion. Relief washes over me, soothing the raw edges of exhaustion. I made it. I'm safe.

Hailey skips ahead, her laughter filling the space as she recounts her day, oblivious to the fear that gripped us all. Her resilience is a marvel, and her joy lifts my weary soul. I smile, despite the weight of fatigue pulling at me.

"Daddy, look!" She waves a drawing above her head, her stick figures dancing on the paper. "This is us!" She points out each figure with pride, her eyes shining with innocence and love.

"That's beautiful, Noodle." My voice is thick with emotion. I reach out, ruffling her hair. "You're quite the artist."

She runs off to her room, her energy boundless. I exchange a weary yet grateful glance with Timber, the woman who's become my anchor. Her eyes meet mine, and the air between us crackles. The kiss we shared still lingers in my mind.

"Come here," I murmur, my voice barely above a whisper. "Please."

She steps closer, her eyes searching mine. I pull her into my arms. "Thank you for everything." The world narrows to this—her body against me, the steady beat of her heart, reassuring and grounding.

"Are you okay?" she asks, her voice laced with concern.

"Better now," I reply. "Better because you're here. Better because I finally kissed you."

"About that," she says.

I'm afraid she's going to say something that might ruin the moment, like the kiss didn't mean anything when it meant everything to me.

"It was amazing."

A smile spreads across my face. "It was that good? No room for improvement?"

"Well," she continues, a playful glint in her eye, "you could kiss me again, and then I can compare the two."

I don't need any more encouragement. I lean in, capturing her lips with mine. This kiss is different—still full of the relief and desire from before, but now there's a layer of playfulness, an exploration. Our lips move together, and I can feel the heat of her breath, and the soft sighs that escape her mouth.

Just as the kiss deepens, promising more, a small voice interrupts. "Daddy? Can I have a bubble bath?"

We break apart, breathless and flushed.

"Of course, Noodle. Let's have a bite to eat and then I'll run your bath." I turn back to Timber, seeing the same mixture of amusement and longing in her eyes. "To be continued," I whisper, earning a soft laugh.

In the kitchen, Timber quickly whips up some sandwiches and heats up a jar of Eliza's chicken noodle soup. It's quick and easy, but perfect for the moment.

After dinner, we settle on the couch to watch a short show with Hailey. Timber sits close, her shoulder brushing against mine. I can't focus on the show. My mind replays the kiss, craving more. The anticipation is almost unbearable.

Finally, I can't wait any longer. I get up and say, "Hailey, let's get that bath started."

Together, we head upstairs. Hailey beats us to the bathroom, turning on the water and dumping in far too many bubbles, but I don't care tonight.

"Alright, Noodle, let's wash your hair," I say, rolling up my sleeves, but Timber looks at my bandaged hands. They are probably in far better shape than I would imagine they'd be, but May's medicine is always a miracle worker.

"I'll get the hair, you just relax," Timber says.

Watching the routine is comforting. Timber washes her hair, rinses off the suds, and wraps her in a fluffy towel. The simple scene seems like a small victory—a return to the life I was so afraid I'd lost.

Once Hailey has brushed her teeth and is in pajamas, she picks out a book for her bedtime story. Timber leans against the door and watches while I sit on the edge of her bed and read. Hailey's eyes are heavy with sleep, but she fights it.

"And then the princess said..." I read, my voice soft and steady. Hailey's eyelids droop, and she snuggles deeper into her blankets.

By the time I finish the story, she's fast asleep. I lean down, pressing a kiss to her forehead. "Goodnight, Noodle," I whisper.

Timber and I quietly step out of Hailey's room, closing the door behind us.

We head downstairs, the weight of the day finally catching up with me.

"I'll clean up the dinner dishes," Timber offers. "You go take a shower."

Reluctantly, I agree, needing to wash away the day's grime and clear my head. I have to keep my hands out of the water because of the bandages, but the sensation of hot water flowing over my body feels amazing. It's a small respite from the day's troubles.

By the time I come back down, Timber has tidied up, and the house is calm and cozy. We head to the couch. As my body sinks into the cushions, she settles beside me. Her presence is comforting, and thoughts of wanting this to last fill my mind.

"Snuggle with me?" I ask, my voice vulnerable. "I don't want to be alone."

"I'm here." She curls into me, her body fitting against mine as if we were made for this. Holding her close, my fingers trace lazy patterns on her back, letting all remaining tension drain away.

Her breath evens out, matching mine, and the world outside these walls ceases to matter. In this quiet, in this moment, I find peace. Tomorrow will bring its own challenges, its own uncertainties, but tonight, I rest in the comfort of Timber's presence, holding onto the hope that this, whatever it is, can be the start of something beautiful.

I wake with a start, the sound of footsteps thudding upstairs. Timber, nestled against me, stirs, eyes snapping open. Without a word, she hops off the couch and races to the kitchen, starting breakfast.

I heave myself up, my body protesting with every move. My arms tremble and my legs wobble, sending sharp pangs through my muscles. A low, involuntary sound escapes my lips as I finally stand upright.

"Morning," I mumble, making my way to the kitchen. Timber pulls out the eggs and cracks them into a bowl. I lean in, pressing a quick kiss to her cheek. "Thanks for that."

"I liked being next to you."

I look over my shoulder, hearing Hailey's footsteps approaching. "Me too. More than you can imagine, but we need to be careful to not confuse Hailey."

She nods. "I completely agree."

Hailey bursts into the kitchen, her face lighting up

when she sees us. "Good morning, Daddy! Good morning, Timber!"

"Morning, Noodle," I say, scooping her up into a hug. "Ready for breakfast?"

"Yes!" she giggles, her arms wrapping around my neck.

As Timber continues cooking, I set Hailey down and start setting the table, our movements in sync as we prepare for another day. In my head, I'm plotting the next moment I can pull Timber aside and kiss her.

That moment doesn't happen for a while. That evening, right after we get home from Timber's day at the community center, Eliza shows up unannounced with a batch of homemade cookies. Another day, it's Rhys dropping by to help with some house repairs. Finn insists on taking me for a drink, claiming I need a break after everything that's happened. Then, Reid stops by with a new book he thinks I'd enjoy. And finally, Nash shows up unexpectedly, wanting to drink a beer and stare at the pond.

In between these visits, it's Hailey's uncanny knack for bad timing that keeps interrupting any chance Timber and I have for a moment alone. It's as if she can sense our longing and chooses those exact moments to need my attention or ask for one more story before bed. It's frustrating, maddening even, how my whole family seems to be a collective cockblocker.

Despite the constant interruptions, every moment with Timber is cherished. Driving her to the community center in the mornings and picking her up in the afternoons becomes a routine. We cook together, clean up, and enjoy games and shows with Hailey until her bedtime. By then, exhaustion takes over, and we retreat to our rooms. Yes, there are kisses, but they aren't the passionate ones that lead to breathless nights lying naked beside each other. The desire for more is strong. Hope remains that soon, time will be carved out to be together, uninterrupted and without distractions.

Gravel crunches under my boots as I step from the ATV and head toward the community center. Inside, there's a flurry of activity. Hailey, Lucas, and Tommy are busy drawing, while Timber hangs up their art. She nods to the corner where two of my brothers stand with an older man. When the man turns, I freeze. It's Dad. Shock mixes with relief, and a bit of hurt.

He's been gone three months—since Mom passed. Each day without him seemed to stretch out endlessly.

"Dad?" The word is half-choked, revealing more than I intend. He looks rested and not so sad. His once-tired eyes now seem brighter, and the lines on his face less pronounced, as if the time away has eased his burdens. He's quick to embrace me, a rarity in him that speaks volumes. As we stand there, holding on, the familiar scent of pine and motor oil fills my senses.

His hair is grayer, but his posture is straighter, less burdened by grief. The dark circles under his eyes have faded, and he's even wearing a faint smile—a stark contrast to the man who left shattered and withdrawn.

"When did you get here?" I ask, pulling back slightly. I'm torn—glad he's back, frustrated he left. We all missed her, but we stayed and faced our pain together. He went away, needing space, perhaps to find his own way to cope. Now, seeing him here, I realize how much I needed him, how much we all did. Guess we handle grief differently. He's back, and that's all that counts.

"Just a few minutes ago," he replies, his voice steady but soft. "I wanted to see everyone, to be here with you all."

I turn to Nash and Finn. "Why didn't you tell me Dad was coming home?"

Nash exchanges a glance with Finn before speaking up. "We didn't know. We just got here a few minutes ago for a delivery," he says. "Hank dumped him off on the dock along with our packages. We saw an Amazon order for Timber and delivered it personally."

I look back at my father. "I'm happy you're here, Dad."

"I'm glad I'm back too. Old Danny called." He rubs his beard. "Now what's this about you burning down my cabin and getting lost at sea?"

At that moment, Timber drops something, causing a clatter.

"Whoops!" Her voice cuts through the chatter as she lunges for a fallen stapler. She rights herself and meets my father's eyes. "About being stranded on the open water—

that was all Kane. But the cabin, we ... kind of teamed up on that one."

"Not true." I'm not willing to let her take the blame. "I shook the cap free."

"I built the fire, and without fire, there would still be a cabin. So, if we use that logic, then I burned down the cabin." She looks at my father. "I'm very sorry."

I glance at Timber, seeing the guilt still etched on her face. The memory of the fire flashes in my mind—panic, the crackling flames, and the acrid smell of smoke. It was a reckless mistake, but it was mine. Seeing Timber shoulder some of the blame twists something inside me.

Dad studies us both for a moment, then sighs. "It sounds like an adventure gone wrong," he says finally. "But I'm just glad you're both safe. We can rebuild a cabin. Lives are harder to replace." Dad's smile returns, and everything seems normal.

Hailey rushes over with another stick figure drawing. This one shows all the Hollisters, Matt, and baby Cody. Timber stands next to me, and in the sky is a stick figure with wings representing Mom.

Seeing the drawing, my throat tightens. Mom with her angel wings, watching over us—it's a comforting yet bittersweet image. The constant sadness turns into something more bearable—it's replaced by a warm, nostalgic ache.

I glance at Timber, who catches my eye and gives me a reassuring smile. She has been our rock. I squeeze her hand, the familiar firmness a reminder of all we've endured together.

I expect to see sadness in Dad's eyes, but instead, I see joy.

"You know exactly where your grandma is. She's up there watching over us all," Dad says warmly as he takes the picture. He looks at Timber. "Can I hang this one?"

Timber nods, smiling as she hands him the stapler. Dad carefully hangs the drawing high on the wall, a visible reminder of the love and memories that bind us together. When he's done, he turns to us. "What else needs to be done?"

Timber takes charge, directing the men on where to move the tables for Sunday's event. Her natural leadership shines through, and I am proud of her. As we finish setting up, I wrap my arms around her shoulders, pull her close, and press a kiss to her temple.

"Great job," I whisper. Timber smiles up at me, her eyes shining with shared understanding and gratitude. Together, we've faced so much, and together, we'll keep moving forward.

"Who set this up?" Dad asks.

All eyes turn to Timber. "I thought it might be nice to remind everyone of the town's promise," she says. "Sure, life gets busy, but it's important to take moments to belong and enjoy each other's company."

My father's eyes widen at the display of affection, and he clears his throat awkwardly.

"I see I've missed quite a bit," he says.

"I'd say," Eliza's voice comes from the entrance. Next to her is Matt, who holds Cody.

Dad's steps quicken, eyes lighting up as he scoops

Cody into his arms. He coos, his rough voice surprisingly gentle.

Just then, Rhys and Reid burst inside, their faces lit up.

"Hey, what's going on here?" Rhys calls out, his eyes locking onto Dad. Reid is quick on his heels, his expression one of disbelief.

"Dad. You're back."

Dad turns to them with a broad smile, stepping forward to pull them into tight hugs. "It's great to see you guys."

As Reid hugs Dad, dad pats him on the shoulder. "We had no idea you were coming. You could have called."

Dad looks at all of us—his gaze lingering on each face, his breath catching slightly. "It was time I came home," he admits. His voice is thick with regret and relief. "I missed too much. There's no place else for me but here."

Rhys, always the one to probe deeper, folds his arms and studies Dad closely. "So, you're back for good?"

Dad nods. His eyes meet each of ours. "I'm here to stay, help with the grandkids, and make up for the time I lost."

Relief washes over me. As the oldest, I've carried the weight of trying to fill Dad's shoes. Knowing he's here to stay means I can finally relax, confident that he can resume his role as the head of the family.

"How about we talk over dinner?" Dad asks. "I could really go for some of May's famous pie."

After Lucas and Tommy are picked up, we leave the community center and head to May's Café. It's a place full of our memories, and it's time to make a few more. May's pie, with its perfect crust and sweetness, is just what we need to finish off this day right.

Timber walks next to my dad. "What should I call you?"

Dad chuckles. "Peter is fine," he says, then looks at our intertwined hands and adds, "Actually, call me Pops."

The word hangs in the air. Dad not only approves of Timber, but he sees her as part of the family. That speaks volumes. Even Dad, with his reserved ways, can see Timber's here to stay.

Chapter Nineteen

TIMBER

I'M IN THE KITCHEN, prepping for the potluck and making a batch of my special potato salad with capers and bacon. Hailey is upstairs gathering her toys, giving us a rare moment together alone. The kitchen is a whirlwind of activity, but in our little corner, time seems to slow down. Kane expertly chops the cooked potatoes while I cook the bacon, our movements synchronized in a comfortable rhythm.

"So, capers in potato salad, huh?" he asks, leaning in a little closer, his voice low and sexy.

Who thought cooking could be so damn hot, but that voice and his nearness is absolute foreplay.

"It's a game-changer," I say. The truth is, he's the game-changer. I never thought I'd have these feelings about anyone again. Hell, I don't even think I felt this strongly about my ex. What's harder is knowing he's feeling the same way and not being able to act on anything because we are almost never alone except for late in the night when we're too exhausted to do anything about it.

We continue working, the air between us thick and simmering with sexual tension. Every brush of our hands, every shared glance, builds a quiet, growing need to be together—alone. When Kane laughs, it's a sound that cuts through the noise, making my pulse race.

"Alright, taste test," I say, holding out a spoonful, my fingers grazing his.

He takes a bite, his eyes widening. "Okay, you were right. This is amazing."

"I told you."

Hailey bounds down the stairs, her arms full of toys. "I'm ready!" she announces. It's been so long since their community gathered, and they have so much to celebrate. Kane's dad and his brother-in-law Matt are home, and little Cody is the newest resident to welcome.

We race around the kitchen gathering everything we need and head out. The drive is short, but the anticipation makes it seem so much longer.

As we arrive, I see Kane's father and brothers have taken charge of the makeshift barbecue—a rustic contraption fashioned from a halved metal barrel and a grate. The air is thick with the aroma of sizzling hot dogs and burgers, a scent that speaks to a feast.

Inside, the residents have outdone themselves, the tables groaning under the weight of heaping bowls of potato salad, baked beans, and plates piled high with fresh berry tarts and other sweets. Why they haven't gathered in years baffles me. It's obvious they enjoy each other's company. It just shows me that people can make time for anything they want if it's important enough, and community is important. But now, as I observe the day unfolding before me, I experience a sense of accomplishment. All this took was an idea, a few handmade flyers, and May's enticement of free hotdogs and hamburgers. This event brings everyone together, which not only helps strengthen the community, but also helps me.

I weave through the crowd, scanning each face for a hint of familiarity. Today, I'm more than just a potluck participant. I'm searching for a connection to my past. Looking for features like mine. Blonde hair, blue eyes—anything that might lead me to my father.

I move closer to a group of elderly townspeople standing in a circle, their faces etched with deep lines and wise eyes, each wrinkle carrying the town's history. Gathering a surge of courage, I clear my throat and step into their collective gaze. "Excuse me," I say, then introduce myself. "I'm Timber." My voice carries a certainty I lack inside. "I'm looking for someone who might have passed through here. Has anyone ever come across a woman named Aspen Moore?

Just then, Kane walks over, his presence momentarily drawing my attention. Our eyes meet, and a spark ignites between us. He leans in, his lips brushing against my cheek in a familiar, comforting way. "I'm going to join my father and brothers outside," he says.

As he pulls away, the sensation of his touch lingers, and I wish he was kissing my lips instead of my cheek. Turning back to the group, one of the elderly men steps forward, his eyes narrowing slightly as he looks at me. "Aspen Moore, you say? That name doesn't sound like it belongs to anyone from around here," he says with a shake of his head. "What's your relationship to her?"

"She was my mother." A stir of emotions wells in me as I speak her name out loud. "She passed away, and I realized I know very little about where she came from."

The man's expression changes, his earlier curiosity shifting to sympathy. "I'm sorry to hear that, young lady. Everyone should know their family history. It's tough not knowing, isn't it?" He looks around at his companions, hoping perhaps for a spark of recognition, but there's none. He points to a lady across the room. "Ask Rose Whitaker over yonder."

With a nod, I thank the group for their time and continue on my journey. My path takes me through a maze of festively adorned tables toward a woman meticulously placing the final touches on a spread of desserts arrayed on a side table. On the way, I almost bump into Theresa, Tommy's mom.

"Oh, Timber!" Theresa exclaims with a warm smile. "I was just about to look for you. I wanted to let you know that Tommy won't be here all next week. We're visiting family in Oregon."

"That sounds like a lot of fun. Thanks for letting me know," I reply, trying to keep my disappointment at not having him in class for a whole week hidden. "I hope you have a great trip." She waves down a friend from across the room and I continue on my quest.

"Mrs. Whitaker?" I interrupt, and she turns, her face lighting up.

"You must be Timber."

"I am. It's nice meeting you."

"This is a good thing you did."

I look around and see everyone enjoying themselves. "It's wonderful so many people showed up."

She looks around. "Practically the entire town."

I hesitate, then plunge forward. "I was wondering if you've ever heard of someone named Aspen Moore. She was my mother and recently passed. I'm trying to learn more about her past and think she may have spent some time here."

Mrs. Whitaker pauses, her eyes narrowing as she searches her memory. "Aspen Moore ... The name doesn't ring a bell, I'm afraid. Did she grow up here?"

"I don't think so, but I can't be sure," I admit. "There's so much I don't know." That was the truth. My mother didn't share much, and she didn't dwell on things. I remember once getting an F on a test. She told me that the F didn't have to move forward with me. It was yesterday's F, and it wouldn't matter to tomorrow's A. I could leave it behind and never mention it again.

Mrs. Whitaker gives my hand a comforting squeeze. "Have a chat with May," she suggests. "She's the one who greets everyone at the café. If anyone knows anything, it'll be her."

I depart from her, experiencing a tightness that constricts my chest. The memory of May's previous words comes back to me. Despite her intricate knowledge of everyone's comings and goings, she too had no recollection of my mother. I've once again hit a dead end.

Drawn almost magnetically, my steps guide me toward Kane, seeking comfort in his familiar presence.

As I approach, he's flipping burgers and laughing with his father. It's wonderful to see. Just watching him, the steady calm of his movements, lifts the heaviness inside me. It's strange how his presence can do that. How he can give me a sense of stability when everything else seems to slip away.

Maybe Mom was onto something with her live-in-the-present philosophy. As much as I crave answers about her past, perhaps it's time to focus on the here and now. For a moment, I let go of the questions and uncertainties, allowing myself to be present, just as she would have wanted.

I rest against the trunk of a nearby tree. A quiet realization dawns on me, sparking a thought—perhaps my journey here wasn't for the reasons I imagined. Could it be the universe guided me to this place not to find my father, but to cross paths with Kane? This thought, both surprising and sweet, makes me smile.

Kane looks up, his eyes finding mine. "Hey," he says, as he reaches out to draw me closer. "Did you talk to Lucas's parents?"

"No, what's up?"

"He won't be in class next week. They're taking him on the boat."

"Weird, because Tommy is gone too."

"Really?" He smiles. "That means it's just you, me, and Hailey."

"Yes, that's awesome."

He winks. "A week without early mornings. You know that means we might have more energy at night."

I know exactly what he's thinking and a sliver of anticipation threads through me and lands heavy and aching in my core.

Seconds later, Hailey runs past me and says, "You're it." Kane and I get caught up in a game of tag that takes us down the path and into the woods. Hailey's joyful giggles blend with the rustling leaves and distant bird calls, creating a moment of pure, carefree joy.

After three "you're its," the game winds down. Hailey clings to my leg, her small face flushed with the exertion. "You're fast, Timber!" she says, a grin spreading across her face.

"Not as fast as you," I say, ruffling her hair. She beams up at me before dashing off toward the community center.

Alone, Kane pulls me into the trees and kisses me. It's not the type of kiss you share in public. This is a bedroom kiss. The kind that happens before clothes fall to the floor. It's nothing like the brief, chaste pecks we've shared this week in between impromptu family visits that lasted way into the night. It's deep and consuming, a searing connection that sends a shockwave of heat through my entire body. His lips move against mine with a passion that whips up a storm of emotions inside me.

His taste is intoxicating—a sweet trace of soda

lingering from his last drink, mingled with the essence of barbecue smoke—distinctly Kane, hauntingly familiar, and utterly appealing.

My skin tingles where his fingertips brush against it, tracing small, electric paths down the side of my arm and back up to cradle my face. I lean into his touch, my own hands finding the solid muscle of his shoulders, gripping them for support as my knees weaken with the intensity of our embrace.

The world narrows down to the space where our bodies meet. The soft rustle of leaves above us and the distant sounds of the community center fade away, leaving only the sound of our synchronized breathing. Time seems to stretch and condense all at once, every second elongated and filled with the awareness of his presence.

As our lips part, I gasp for air, my chest knocking against my ribs as if it's fighting for escape. Kane presses his forehead against mine, his breathing ragged, his voice husky. "I've been waiting to do that all day," he says.

The grin that spreads across my face seems as wide as the sky above. "Me too," I whisper back, my voice steady despite the thundering of my pulse.

In that secluded spot behind the trees, with Hailey's joyful shouts just a whisper on the wind, I realize that no matter what I came here searching for, what I found is something far more profound. As we step back into the sunlight, our fingers intertwined, ready to face the world again, I know that this moment, this kiss, is just the beginning of something new and utterly exhilarating.

After another hour of talking and visiting and ogling over Cody, Kane and I gather the leftover food and pack up the unused supplies. The community center slowly empties, the atmosphere shifting to a quieter, more reflective mood.

Kane glances at me. "Did you have fun? Was it everything you expected?"

How was I supposed to explain that in many ways it was more than I could have imagined, and in some ways, it fell short of what I hoped. Kane is so suspicious of outsiders and their motives. While I didn't come here to fall for him, I did. How will he feel when I tell him the truth? That it wasn't just the job that brought me here. I stare at him for a moment and realize the easiest way to come clean is to tell him everything.

"You should know I didn't come here just for the teaching job," I say. "When I was going through my mom's things, I found a postcard. It wasn't just any postcard—it was one from Port Promise. The exact one in your brother's store, the one of the dock. There was a heartfelt inscription on it, written with such tenderness that I could only imagine it was from someone who loved her deeply." I pause, but Kane stays quiet, so I continue. "I hoped, maybe even believed, that it was from my father, whom I've never met. I would've come for the job anyway, but I was hoping to find some family too. After my mom passed, I had no one left. Imagine being the last of your family."

His jaw tightens, and his shoulders tense. "I can't imagine," he whispers.

"When researching the town, the job listing appeared, almost like a sign, as if a higher power was guiding me here." A small sigh escapes. "Asking everyone about Aspen Moore led to no answers. The hope was that someone who knew my mom might know my father. Not finding him is disappointing, but spending the day here with you and Hailey offered some much-needed perspective."

"And what's that?"

"That the universe put me exactly where I need to be, even if I never find my father."

Kane's brows furrow, a shadow of hurt crossing his face. "All those nights we talked, and you never said a word."

I swallow hard, a pang of guilt catching in my throat. "Those nights were about us, Kane. I refused to taint them with my unresolved past. Besides, I was caught up in your stories, and the way you painted this place with your words. I didn't want to interrupt that."

He shifts slightly. "I was just filling in the blanks, telling you about the town. You could have told me anything."

"I wanted to," I admit, my voice trembling. "But every time I tried, I felt this ... hesitation. Like if I started looking for answers, I'd lose the magic of what we were building. I didn't want to risk that."

Kane steps closer, his eyes searching mine. "Do you think finding your father will change anything between us?"

"I don't think so," I whisper. "I just know that after

my mom passed, I felt lost. When I found that postcard, it gave me hope. Coming here, meeting you, it's been more than I could have dreamed. But I also felt this void, this need to know where I come from."

"We all have our voids to fill," he says. "But you don't have to do it alone. You should've trusted me."

"I do trust you, Kane. More than anyone. That's why I'm telling you now. I'm sorry I kept it from you."

Kane reaches out, taking my hand in his. "Whatever reasons brought you here, I'm glad you came."

His words, simple and sincere, give me a squeeze of emotion. I'm glad he knows because now there's nothing coming between us. As we finish tidying up, certainty settles in my chest. Here, with new friends, potential family, and a community that's slowly becoming my own, I'm learning that sometimes, the universe doesn't just send us on a journey. It brings us to a place that could very well be home.

The hum of the ATV lulls Hailey into a deep sleep in the back seat. I glance at her before my eyes shift to Kane. "She's out cold," I say.

He nods, his grip tightening on the steering wheel. "Yeah, she's had a long day."

Silence settles between us.

As we pull into the driveway, he cuts the engine, and the sudden stillness makes his next words seem even more significant. "Timber, we both know where this is leading if we ever catch a moment alone."

My breath hitches, and I turn to face him, my eyes searching his. "Is this the right time to talk about it?"

He sighs, running a hand through his hair. "It needs to be said. If we continue to go forward, I'll need to plan. All I've got is an old box of condoms and a huge amount of desire."

A blush creeps up my cheeks, but I meet his gaze steadily. "Kane, I can't get pregnant. And it's been a long time for me too."

He looks at me. "I don't want to mess this up because we didn't think things through."

Before I can respond, a small noise comes from the back seat. Hailey stirs, mumbling something in her sleep. The moment is lost, and we both turn to look at her.

Kane sighs, his shoulders relaxing. "Guess that's our cue."

We share a look, that says there are more conversations and moments to come. For now, we unbuckle Hailey and carry her inside.

Chapter Twenty
KANE

THE FIRST LIGHT of morning filters through the kitchen window as I crack eggs into the hot skillet. Today, I have plans that'll take us away from the usual routine. Having no boat until the new one arrives next week gives me plenty of time to fulfill the vow I made when I was stranded. Quality time for Hailey. With Lucas and Tommy not showing up at the community center this week, Timber is free too. After yesterday's potluck, where she didn't get the answers she hoped for about her dad, I want to give her a day to remember, something to lift her spirits.

I'm busy at the stove but also prepping for our outing. There's a picnic basket on the counter, already packed with smoked salmon, sharp cheddar, fresh apples, and a loaf of French bread. We're heading out to my favorite spot, a secluded cove perfect for a quiet day of clamming and unwinding.

"Good morning, Daddy." Hailey's voice cuts through the silence.

"Good morning, Noodle," I greet Hailey as she scurries into the kitchen, her hair a tousled mess from sleep. "Can you go wake Timber? Tell her breakfast is ready and we've got an adventure planned."

Hailey's eyes widen, and she grins before she takes off running down the hallway.

About ten minutes later, Timber walks in, dressed in one of the new outfits she recently ordered—a simple yet flattering pair of jeans and a soft flannel shirt that accentuates the blue in her eyes. It's a casual look but suits her, and I realize I haven't yet commented on her new wardrobe.

"You look really nice," I say as I place the plates on the table. "I mean, you always look nice, but I didn't get a chance yesterday to say how great those new clothes look on you."

"Thanks, Kane." A smile brightens her face. "What's this about an adventure?" she asks.

"You'll see." I love stirring up a good mystery. "It's a surprise. But I think you'll love it."

Breakfast passes quickly. Having Timber and Hailey here, sharing these moments, it's like I'm building the life I've always envisioned. I see how Timber looks at the mountains, her eyes full of wonder, and I know she's starting to get why this place is so special. I'm determined to make sure she falls in love with Alaska, just like I've fallen for her.

We're soon out the door, heading to Eliza's place to

pick up the skiff. The road there cuts through thick groves of spruce and hemlock.

As we drive, a pair of rabbits scurry across the path, their white tails flashing briefly as they vanish into the underbrush. I gently touch Timber's shoulder, guiding her gaze. "See those?"

"Yes, what kind of rabbits are those?" she asks.

"Snowshoe hares," I explain, a warm satisfaction spreading through me as I see her interest piqued. "They're all over here. They get white in the winter to blend in with the snow."

She nods, her gaze lingering on the spot where the rabbits disappeared. "It's so lush here," she says, looking back at the forest. "So different from the desert where I come from."

"Yep, all the rain we get keeps it that way." I focus on the winding road, hoping these moments are planting the seeds for her to fall in love with this place.

We're descending when I spot a bald eagle perched majestically in a tree, surveying the cove. I slow down, stealing a quick glance at Timber. "Check that out," I say, pointing toward the eagle.

Timber follows my gaze, her mouth falling open. "It's huge." Her voice is filled with awe.

"Yep, they're all over Alaska. Part of the scenery." I lean in closer, taking advantage of her distraction to press a quick kiss to her cheek. She turns to me, looking happy.

As we pull up to Serenity Cove, Eliza and Matt are outside, getting a stroller ready for a walk with Cody.

I park the ATV. "Morning, Eliza, Matt!" Hailey

unbuckles and runs ahead, eager to peek at her baby cousin.

"It's a perfect day for an outing," Eliza says.

With a nod, I face Timber. "We're taking my skiff out for the day."

"The forecast says it will be clear. It's perfect for an adventure," Eliza says.

"Ever been clamming?" I ask Timber, hoping she's interested. If not, we'll simply picnic and enjoy the scenery.

"No, never, but I'm looking forward to learning something new."

"That's the spirit." I love how she's always open to anything, from staying in a dry cabin to finding Devil's Claw for May.

Eliza pushes the stroller up the hill but calls over her shoulder, "I want some clams too."

We load up the skiff with our gear and the picnic basket, ready to head to the cove.

"Alright, let's get this day started."

Chapter Twenty-One

TIMBER

WE DON our life vests and push off from the shore. The probability of a peaceful day on the water lays before us. The gentle hum of the skiff's motor blends with the lap of the waves against the hull. The open water stretches around us, a vast expanse under the clear blue sky. I watch Hailey, sitting comfortably toward the front—no, the bow, I correct myself, remembering the seafaring term.

Suddenly, Hailey's excited voice cuts through the tranquility. "Daddy, look!" She points toward a spray of water in the distance.

"Whales," Kane says, spotting the telltale signs of a pod just ahead. My eyes follow his gaze, a mix of awe and surprise bubbling up inside me.

He slows the skiff, careful to maintain a respectful distance as we approach the pod. The gentle giants glide through the water, their powerful bodies barely causing a ripple on the surface.

"What kind of whales are they?" I ask. "Are they dangerous?"

Kane shakes his head, a reassuring smile on his face. "They're humpbacks. And no, they're not dangerous to us as long as we keep our distance. They're gentle giants."

"There." Kane points to one particularly enormous whale, her dorsal fin marked with a distinctive notch. "See that one? She's been around as long as I can remember. Humpbacks can live up to fifty years or more."

I lean over the side, watching in fascination. "She's beautiful."

Hailey claps her hands in delight as the whale arches and sends another spray into the air.

Kane maneuvers the skiff carefully, ensuring we're parallel to the pod's path. "They're magnificent, aren't they?" he says, keeping his voice low, almost whispering, as if speaking too loudly might break the spell.

I nod, my eyes not leaving the whales. "It's incredible to see them like this, so close." I watch as the mother whale guides her calf, teaching it to breach. Now and then, a massive tail slaps the water, sending up a shower that catches the sunlight.

"It's moments like these," Kane says, his gaze shifting between Hailey and the whales, "that really make you appreciate how amazing this place is."

We spend a good while just drifting, the magnificent creatures occasionally surfacing close enough that we can hear their breaths—loud, whooshing exhales that seem to echo across the water.

Kane restarts the motor as the pod moves away. "Let's head to the cove."

A lump forms in my throat. The beauty and serenity of the moment leave me both awed and at peace. Hailey keeps glancing back to where the whales had been, as if hoping they might reappear.

I turn to Kane, my voice soft. "That was ... amazing. Thank you for this."

Kane smiles. "I'm glad you enjoyed it."

We finally arrive at Kane's favorite clamming spot, a secluded cove with a strip of sandy beach flanked by rugged, tree-lined cliffs. The tide is low, exposing the wet sand. Kane anchors the skiff and helps Hailey and me onto the shore.

As my feet sink into the cool, wet sand, I take in the serene beauty. The cliffs rise majestically around us, their rugged faces softened by the green of the trees. The cove is like a hidden sanctuary, untouched and pristine. The sea air fills my lungs, invigorating and calming all at once.

I glance at Kane, seeing the pride and contentment in his eyes as he surveys the cove. It's clear this place holds a special significance for him, a private retreat where he can connect with nature and find peace. The fact that he's chosen to share it with me fills me with gratitude and something deeper, something more intimate.

Hailey's laughter rings out as she skips ahead. Her joy is infectious. I watch her with a smile. The sense of belonging washes over me. It's as if the cove has wrapped us in its embrace, inviting us to share in its secrets and treasures.

Kane's hand rests gently on my shoulder, and I turn to him, meeting his gaze. The kindness and openness in his eyes speak volumes. This isn't just about showing me a beautiful spot to dig for clams. It's about sharing a piece of himself, inviting me into a part of his world that he holds dear.

As we begin our search for clams, I find myself more attuned to the rhythms of the cove—the gentle lapping of the waves, the calls of distant seabirds, the sand between my fingers. Each moment is precious and magical.

"Are you ready for this?" Kane asks.

"I can't wait. What do I do?"

"Alright, let's look for air holes—that's where the clams are," Kane explains, pointing out the small, round openings scattered across the sandy flat.

I nod, eager to learn but a bit unsure of myself. Kane steps closer. "Here," he says, moving behind me. He wraps his arms around me, his hands covering mine on the shovel handle. The intimacy quickens my pulse.

"You want to skim the top layer of sand gently," he says, his breath warm against my ear. "Just clear enough sand so you don't smash them when you dig deeper."

We move together, our bodies in sync as he guides my hands. His chest presses against my back, and I'm acutely aware of the heat radiating from him, the steady rhythm of his breathing. The physical closeness is electric, heightening my senses and adding a layer of tension to the moment.

We work the shovel into the sand, lifting the top layer with care. Kane's voice is a soothing counterpoint to the rush of emotions swirling inside me. "That's it," he encourages, his hands steadying mine. "Now go a little deeper, but gently."

His words, while meant for the act of clamming, somehow are charged with sexual innuendo. Deeper. Gently.

I follow his lead, and the resistance of the sand gives way to something more solid.

"Do you feel something hard?" he asks, his tone sending my thoughts racing. A rush of excitement hits me, and I instinctively push back against him. Yes, I do. "Just a little deeper," he says, digging the shovel in another inch.

We uncover a clam. "Got one!" I say, holding it up proudly, trying to shake off the heat climbing up my neck.

His eyes crinkle at the corners. "See? You're a natural. That's a butter clam. You can tell by the smooth, oval shape and the distinct, concentric rings on the shell."

Hailey, watching us, squeals in delight and rushes over to join the fun. She mimics our actions, her small hands eager and determined. "Look, another one!" she shouts, triumphantly holding up her find.

The game of finding and digging up clams turns playful, with Hailey splashing us with handfuls of seawater. Eventually, our bucket fills with the fruits of our labor, and we're ready to relax.

We flop down on the picnic blanket spread out earlier. Hailey jumps up to chase a bird, and I lean over and kiss Kane. It's spontaneous—a celebration of the great day we're having. Hailey notices the kiss and pauses in her play. She looks at us.

"Are you going to get married? People who kiss get married," she says innocently.

The question leaves me blindsided, and a rush of emotions sweeps through me—surprise, a pinch of panic, and a hint of something deeper. Kane and I exchange a quick glance. Is this where she thinks we're headed? My heart races, caught between the innocence of Hailey's logic and the complexity of adult relationships.

Marriage? This was supposed to be a summer job—a brief escape into the wild beauty of Alaska. I never expected Kane, but that doesn't mean I don't want him. But knowing this might end when the first leaves start to turn might crush me. I glance at Kane again. Maybe having some of Kane, even if only for a season, will be better than having none of him.

He clears his throat, as if searching for the right words. "Well, kissing is a way some adults show they care about each other," he says, "but it doesn't always mean they get married. It's important that they really like spending time together, just like we do."

I add, "Yeah, we're having a lot of fun together, aren't we? And today was all about enjoying this beautiful place and learning how to clam."

Hailey nods, satisfied with our explanation, then her

attention shifts back to more immediate concerns. "Can we eat now?" she asks.

"Absolutely." I'm relieved by her quick acceptance but still haunted by my thoughts. "Let's open up that picnic basket and see what we've got."

As Kane and I open the basket for lunch, Hailey busies herself chasing a bird. Our laughter, the sound of the waves, and the occasional call of a distant gull create a perfect backdrop for our meal.

After lunch, we pack up. Kane hoists the last of our gear onto the small boat, shaking the sand from his jeans as he does. Today's field trip is enjoyed by everyone, and the conversation on the boat is light-hearted. The skiff cuts smoothly through the water. The familiar coastline stretches out before us. As we get to Eliza's, we tie up at the pier and start unloading.

Eliza comes out to meet us as we place the full bucket of clams on the dock, her excitement showing through a delighted squeal. She quickly composes herself and turns to Hailey. "Hey, sweetie, would you like to stay with Uncle Matt and me for a few days? Uncle Matt won't be here long, and he'd love to spend some time with his favorite niece."

Hailey looks at Kane for approval.

Kane nods, and I step forward. "Does Hailey need anything? Should we bring her clothes, toys, or something else?"

Eliza shakes her head with a warm smile. "This is like her second home. We have everything she needs."

Then Eliza's gaze shifts to Kane. "Do you think you

can find something or someone to keep you busy while she's gone?" Her eyes shift to me, then back to him as she winks.

Kane shakes his head at his sister's obvious scheming. She's not just coordinating aunt and uncle time. She's pushing him closer to me. And honestly, I'm grateful for it.

Chapter Twenty-Two

TIMBER

As we return to Kane's house, I try to play it cool, like I'm not a bundle of nerves and excitement every time the ATV bumps and our shoulders brush. I'm a woman who started the day sifting sand for clams and now I'm sifting through unexpected emotions.

My mind races, considering the possibilities. What if this attraction is just a fleeting moment, another dead-end like the last relationship that left me shattered? But then I glance at Kane, at the easy confidence in his smile, and the affection in his eyes, and my doubts dissolve.

The way he gently nudges me when our shoulders touch, the way he looks at me like I'm the only person in the world—it's all so new and exhilarating. I think about what I want, and it only takes one second to decide. I want him.

"We're here," Kane announces as he kills the engine, his voice breaking through my swirling thoughts.

"That was fast," I manage, attempting a casualness I

can't quite muster. I hop off the ATV with what I hope is the grace of a gazelle but is probably more akin to a newborn calf.

He rounds the ATV and offers his outstretched palm. It's both sweet and completely nerve-wracking. I grip and squeeze so tightly that he flinches. *Touch his hand, Timber, don't clutch it like a lifeline.*

He leads me inside. The house is normally cozy and familiar, but tonight it's charged with a new, crackling energy. He drops my hand and heads into the kitchen, flipping on a light. "Do you want something to drink?" he asks, as if this were just any normal evening and not the prelude to my deep internal debate about whether I'm ready to take our relationship to the next level.

"Water's fine," I say, reminding myself to hydrate. Hydration is key when your emotions are doing the hundred-yard dash.

As he hands me the glass, our fingers brush, sending a shiver up my arm. I laugh, a nervous sound. "Look at me, a jittery mess. You'd think I'd never been alone with a man before."

Kane's steps closer, his nearness sending another wave of shivers through me. "Hey, there's no pressure for us to do anything. Whatever happens is because we want it for ourselves, but it's okay if we just hang out and watch TV, too."

He's giving me an out or perhaps taking one for himself.

I meet his gaze. The weight of my decision anchors

me in place. "I know," I reply. "But I want ... this. With you."

Kane's eyes search mine, looking for any hint of uncertainty. Finding none, he sets our glasses on the counter and gently cups my face in his hands. "Then that's what we'll do. We'll take this moment, this night, and make it ours."

The straightforwardness of his words, the sincerity in his voice, makes it so easy to lean in, closing the distance between us. Our lips meet in a kiss that starts slowly but grows more urgent, more insistent.

As we pull apart, breathless, Kane looks pleased. "So much for taking things slow, huh?"

I laugh, the sound bubbling up freely, mixed with newfound excitement and relief. "Well, we have endless daylight—why waste it?"

"Exactly my thoughts." His hand finds mine, and he leads me down the hallway. Together, we walk into a night that seems boundless, ready to explore our connection without doubt or expectation.

Tonight, we simply are, and that is more than enough.

As we head to the bedroom, a mix of excitement and anxiety surges through me.

This is it. The moment when everything changes. My mind is a whirlwind of thoughts—what if I'm not enough? What if this ruins everything? But his hand in mine is a steadying force, an assurance that we're in this together.

In the bedroom, we stand hesitantly, the reality of

where we are and what we're about to share sinking in. Then, with a shared breath, we move closer. Each step heightens my awareness of what's about to happen. My pulse is in my throat, the anticipation mingling with fear. The idea of being naked in front of him, of seeing him, is both thrilling and terrifying.

"Shower first?" he asks.

"Yes."

"Together?"

I hesitate, my mind flashing to every insecurity I've ever had about my body. But then I see the look in his eyes—earnest, caring, filled with nothing but admiration. I nod. "It saves water."

We walk to the bathroom, where he turns on the shower and then returns to me. His fingers brush the hem of my shirt, a silent question. I nod again, my chest pounding.

As he gently unbuttons my shirt, a fleeting moment of vulnerability tightens in my chest. This is really happening. I'm about to be completely exposed to him.

He eases the shirt from my body and discards it. The way he looks at me tells me he sees me—all of me—and he's nowhere near disappointed. He traces the lace of my bra. It's a moment where I silently congratulate myself for not choosing a practical one.

"You're perfect," he whispers, not just with his lips but with his eyes, and it bolsters my courage.

Emboldened by his acceptance, my hands find their way to his shirt, fingers trembling slightly as I undo each button. With every inch of skin revealed, I take him in, the sight of him both familiar and thrillingly new. The contours of his muscles, the softness of his skin, the smattering of hair that I touch with eager fingers. His chest rises and falls more sharply with each piece of clothing that falls to the floor.

Kane's hands shift from tracing the delicate lace to my jeans. The button gives way easily, and as he slides the zipper, his fingers graze my skin, sparking tiny fires wherever they touch.

For a brief instant, I experience a wave of shyness, almost consumed by the intense intimacy of the moment. But then I catch the look in his eyes—open, honest, admiring—and any insecurity melts away.

This is it. I'm really going through with this. It's going to change everything, and that's okay. With a shared understanding, my hands now move to his belt, unfastening it with quiet clicks that sound loud in the hushed air of the room. His jeans are next, and as I pull them down, there's a change in the atmosphere, a profound sense of anticipation mixed with trust.

We face each other, only our underwear separating us. Slowly, with deliberate movements, we shed these final barriers. The fabric slides down our legs, pooling at our feet, leaving us bare and exposed in the most intimate way.

Kane reaches for me, his hands framing my face, pulling me into a kiss. His lips move against mine with a passion that's controlled yet desperate, a contradiction that perfectly captures the complexity of our emotions.

"Are you sure?" he whispers, his breath mingling

with mine, his body radiating heat that draws me in even more.

In response, I press closer, wrapping my arms around his neck. "Never been more certain," I say. The warmth of his presence caresses my skin before his lips meet mine once more.

Together, we step into the shower, letting the warm water sluice over us. It seems to wash away any remaining hesitations. The steam rises around us, a misty veil that blurs the edges of reality, giving the moment a timeless quality.

Kane's hands explore the lines and contours of my body. His fingers trace the path of the water, down my shoulders, over my collarbones, pausing with a soft reverence at the curve of my waist. Every touch sends shivers through me, creating an intense heat that moves through my body.

My own hands are not idle. They roam across the broad expanse of his back, tracing the muscle and sinew beneath his skin. The slick surface offers no resistance, allowing my hands to glide easily, exploring him for the first time. Our movements are slow, almost meditative, as we discover each other beneath the warm cascade.

Each caress, each touch, builds the heat between us. His fingers slide lower, tracing the curve of my hips, sending jolts of electricity through my body. The intensity in his touch mirrors my own desire.

My breaths come quicker, the air thick with the steam and the heady mix of our anticipation.

His lips find the sensitive spot on my neck, and I

gasp, my hands clutching at him, pulling him closer. The water streams down, but all I can feel is the fire he's igniting within me. It's a fire that consumes every part of me, leaving no room for doubt or fear, only the overwhelming sensation of him.

Kane's hands cup my face, his thumbs brushing my cheeks as he kisses me deeply. It's a kiss that speaks of passion, of the connection we've always shared but are only now fully realizing. His touch is everywhere, grounding me and setting me ablaze at the same time.

My hands move to his chest. The steady rhythm of his heartbeat under my palms anchors me. As our bodies press together, skin to skin, the reality of this moment hits me again with full force. This is real. This is happening. And it's everything I've ever wanted.

Together, we move under the warm spray, our hands and lips exploring, discovering, claiming. Every touch, every kiss, is a new revelation, a new spark that adds to the inferno between us. We are lost in each other, in the sensations, in the undeniable attraction that binds us.

Kane pulls me closer. The sound of our breathing is heavy and mingles with the rush of water.

"Timber." His voice is barely audible above the shower's spray, yet every syllable vibrates through me. "This is everything."

I nod, unable to form words, my chest swelling with a mixture of joy and an overwhelming sense of belonging. In the water, we are not just washing away the sand and salt of the day, but also any barriers that might have once stood between us.

As we continue to explore, kiss, and hold one another, the world outside fades to nothing. Here, there is only us, and in this moment, we are infinite.

Suddenly, the water shifts from hot to shockingly cold. I let out a startled laugh, stepping back from the spray. "I don't think we saved any water," I joke, shivering slightly as Kane reaches out to shut the taps.

He pulls me against him, his touch igniting a fire that makes the cold seem irrelevant. "To hell with it," he says, his voice low and husky.

We leave the shower, our laughter trailing behind us as we grab towels. Wrapped in the plush fabric—and each other's heat—we pad over to the bedroom. Despite the cool air, all that registers is the fire racing through my veins, a blaze stoked by every touch from Kane.

Kane drops his towel, and I take in his magnificence. Everything about him is chiseled and hard. My knees go weak just looking at him. With a gentle tug, my towel falls to the floor.

He steps closer, the intensity in his eyes mirroring the rapid pulse thrumming through my veins. His hands find my waist, and he lifts me effortlessly. The world tilts for a breathless moment, and then I'm on the bed beneath him, the softness of the duvet a stark contrast to the firmness of him.

His eyes search mine, seeking confirmation, finding the answer in my eager response as I pull him closer. "I can't believe we're finally here," I whisper.

"Yes," he breathes out, the word more a vow than a simple affirmation as his lips meet mine.

Chapter Twenty-Three

KANE

Timber has somehow broken through my emotional barriers with ease. Now, the thought of not spending every moment by her side feels impossible. This isn't about jumping into anything too quickly. It's about acknowledging the profound impact she has. This is more than a casual fling after a night out—it's something special, and she needs to understand how much it means. Her physical strength, witty sense of humor, and the kindness she shows everyone make her flawless. Even her belief in destiny bringing us together is endearing. The details of how we ended up here don't matter. What matters is that we are here now, naked in this bed, and this moment will be unforgettable.

She spreads her legs, inviting me to join her in the intimate space between them. But I resist the urge to plunge into the depths immediately. Instead, I want to savor every moment, to take my time exploring every inch of her. The anticipation builds, and a surge of desire races through my body. I want to prolong this moment, drawing out the tension until it's almost unbearable.

With a soft kiss, I begin at her mouth, my lips capturing hers in a slow, lingering dance. Her hands find purchase in my hair, pulling me closer. I kiss my way down her neck, pausing to suck gently at the pulse point. The rapid pace of her heart beats against my lips. Her skin tastes sweet, a heady mix of soap and her own unique scent.

I move lower, my kisses trailing down her collarbone, across her chest, and over the swell of her breasts. She gasps as I take a nipple into my mouth, flicking my tongue over the sensitive bud, her body arching into me. My hand finds its way to her other breast, kneading gently, reveling in the soft moans that escape her lips. Her reactions fuel my desire.

With deliberate slowness, I kiss my way down her abdomen, feeling the tremors that ripple through her body. I pause at her navel, dipping my tongue into the hollow before continuing my descent. When I finally reach her feet, I start anew, tracing every curve and contour of her toes, savoring the delicate arch of her foot.

Slowly, I make my way back up her legs, my hands following the path of my lips, kneading the muscles, skimming the heat of her skin. Her breaths come quicker, shallower, each exhale a soft plea for more. I pause at her knees, savoring the anticipation that builds between us before resuming my exploration. Every inch of her body is a map to be discovered, and I am eager to chart its paths.

My mouth leaves a trail of fire along her inner thigh, but just as I approach her most intimate area, I veer away, teasing the sensitive skin along her hips. She responds by threading her fingers through my hair, urging me closer with a gentle pressure. But I resist, determined to savor every second, to revel in every sigh that comes from her lips.

I navigate her body like I'm on a quest to find hidden treasures. The air is heavy with the intoxicating scent of her, and it ignites a primal fire within me.

Finally, our eyes lock in an exchange full of desire. Her lips part in anticipation, an invitation to continue this teasing game of near touches and whispered breaths. With an expression that's both gentle and playful, I accept, shifting my focus to where she wants me most, ready to dive deep.

As her eyes lock onto mine, I start with a gentle kiss. The softness of her touch against my lips sends a rush of heat through me. With a playful and teasing flick of my tongue, I trace every inch of her most sensitive areas, savoring the sweet sound of her gasps and moans as they escape her lips. The taste of her skin lingers on my tongue, like a delicious and addictive treat. Her body trembles beneath me. As I continue to explore with deliberate kisses and tantalizing strokes, her breathing quickens, and her hands find their way to my hair, urging me on. I relish in her response, knowing that I'm bringing her pleasure and that she's completely in the moment with me.

As she reaches the peak of ecstasy, her body tenses

with pleasure, and a soft gasp escapes in the most delicious way. In that moment of pure bliss, she surrenders to the sensations, her grip on the sheets becoming white-knuckled as she rides the powerful waves of her climax. She unravels beneath me while I maintain the connection. My grip remains firm on her thighs, while I hold my mouth tightly against her until her shudders subside.

Basking in the glow of having brought her such pleasure, I take a moment to drink in the sight—her flushed cheeks, her heaving chest, the way her eyes flutter open to meet mine, filled with a mix of satisfaction and anticipation. I move back up her body, trailing kisses along her skin, savoring each inch as if it were the first time I tasted her.

The intensity of the moment hits me with full force. My arousal is almost unbearable, a hunger that borders on desperation. I press myself closer to her, feeling the rapid rise and fall of her chest against mine. She looks at me with trust and desire, and I know this is where I'm meant to be.

With a final kiss, slow and deep, I press against her entrance. I take a moment to relish the sensation, the way she fits against me, the way her breath hitches in anticipation. And then, with a gentle push, I enter her, and a surge of ecstasy pulses through my entire being. We move together, a slow, deliberate rhythm that builds in intensity.

The room fills with the sounds of desire, our breaths coming in ragged gasps and our bodies slick with sweat.

Her nails dig into my back, and I pause, savoring the sensation of her wrapped around me.

I push and pull, building up the tension until she is writhing beneath me, pleading for release. Every touch, every movement is electric, sending jolts of pleasure through my body.

Her eyes meet mine, and the intensity of her gaze sends a shiver down my spine. It's not just about the physical connection. It's the emotional connection, the understanding between us that makes this moment so powerful.

As I move inside her, the world around us blurs. All that exists is the two of us, lost in the rhythm we've created together. Her fingers dig into my back, pulling me closer, as if she can't get enough.

The tension builds to an almost unbearable peak. She is on the edge, teetering on the brink. Her pleas become more urgent. Her body trembles beneath mine.

With a final thrust, she shatters, her cries of pleasure filling the room. The moment she pulses around me, I let go, a wave of release crashing over me. It's overwhelming, all consuming, and perfect.

As we come down from the high, I hold her close, our breaths mingling. What we've just shared is more than physical. It's proof of the depth of our bond.

Timber's eyes meet mine, tender and soft. She takes my hand, lacing our fingers together.

I lean in and kiss her. It's gentle and says everything I feel without words.

This kiss speaks to a future together. When our lips

part, I rest my forehead against hers, our breaths mixing. I am complete and at peace.

"I'm falling for you." The words slipping out before I can stop them. But I don't want to take them back. They are the truth, and I want her to know it.

"I'm falling for you too," she says, her voice filled with the same raw honesty that grips me.

In the aftermath of our shared passion, we lie together, wrapped in each other's arms, the world outside forgotten. It's just us, here in this moment, and it's more than I ever dared to hope for.

As I hold her close, I know that this is where I'm meant to be. With her, in this bed, sharing this moment and whatever comes next. It's a beginning, and I am ready to embrace it with all that I am.

Chapter Twenty-Four

TIMBER

As the day unfolds, Kane and I lie in bed, sated and spent from our lovemaking. He dozes off, his body warm beside mine, his breaths quiet and even. I think about what transpired. It wasn't just sex. It was something more that goes beyond physical pleasure. It's two hearts finding each other.

In that moment, lying beside Kane, I realize I could fall in love. Deep down, I know he feels the same. You can't fake what happened between us. I slip away, careful not to disturb his peace. Standing beside the bed, I watch him sleep. A rare smile curves his lips, one I've seldom seen in everyday life.

I quietly exit, closing the door behind me as I head toward the smaller shower near my room. Stepping into the cascade of warm water, the space seems unexpectedly cavernous, a big difference to the closeness we just shared. As the water washes over me, thoughts of him swirl in my mind, mingling with considerations of what to wear when I get out.

Lost in these reflections, I rifle through my wardrobe, realizing I have nothing fancy or particularly feminine. Yet, a grin tugs at my lips as I imagine his reaction—how he wouldn't care about my outfit choice, how his eyes will light up just seeing me.

With a newfound sense of confidence, I exit the shower, dry off, and choose comfortable jeans and a simple cotton shirt. I know he'll appreciate the person in the clothes far more than the outfit itself, and that thought alone is enough to quicken my heartbeat.

In the kitchen, I discover a package of thawed ground meat in the refrigerator and a can of pasta sauce on the counter. I realize I'm going to have to broaden his culinary experiences from spaghetti with meat sauce or pancakes for supper. I cook the pasta, brown the meat, and add the sauce. As it simmers, I set the table.

I hear footsteps and turn to see Kane entering, just a towel around his waist. His gaze holds a hunger that I'm not sure pasta will satisfy.

"I missed you." He closes the gap and gently cups my face. His eyes search mine. Is he looking for something in particular? Something like regret? Well, he won't find it here. Whether that was one moment in time, or we get to repeat it with abandon, I will never regret it. He brought me back from being broken and unloved to cherished and desired.

"I missed you too," I reply. "I figured with all the exertion ... you might be hungry."

"I'm starving." He leans in and presses a tender kiss to my lips. "But not for spaghetti."

That's how the next round starts. It begins in the kitchen and ends on the bearskin rug in front of the fire.

The next couple of days pass in a blur of passion. Kane delivers coffee in bed each morning after we make love, and I introduce him to other culinary delights like meatloaf, which I make from a mix of deer and beaver. It isn't my favorite, but it seems to be Kane's. At night, we eat dinner by the lake, laying out a blanket on the grass to keep us warm and comfortable. We make love under the stars, the warmth of our bodies and the blanket shielding us from the cool evening air. On day three, it's time to get Hailey.

We take the ATV down the mountain. The farther we get from the house, the thicker the tension seems to grow. Our three days alone have been filled with discovering each other, our new love blossoming in the isolation. Daily calls with Hailey have been comforting, but we both really miss her. Had she missed us as much as we did her? Every mile away from our sanctuary makes the questions between Kane and me louder. What will Hailey's return mean for our intimacy? We haven't discussed how to handle things moving forward, and that uncertainty gnaws at me. Is he as uncomfortable as I am about it?

Finally, I blurt what neither of us is saying. "I'll miss sleeping with you."

It's true. My relationship with Kane goes beyond physical intimacy. It gives me a sense of belonging, which is exactly what I came here for. He also makes me seem delicate and vulnerable. I have never been described as slim—even May refers to me as sturdy. But standing next to Kane, I am small in comparison.

He reaches out and takes my hand, giving it a reassuring squeeze. "We'll figure it out."

I want to believe him, but deep down, I know it won't be the same.

We arrive at Eliza's and Kane parks the ATV by the door. It doesn't take long before it flies open, and Hailey rushes out. I expect her to run straight to her dad, but she doesn't. She squeals, "Timber," and throws herself into my arms. "I missed you so much."

"I missed you too," I say, picking her up and turning her around before setting her in front of her father.

Kane is smiling. "I rate higher than Olaf, but you rank higher than me."

I probably should feel bad, but I don't. I like that Hailey misses me.

Kane squats down. "Come here, Noodle." He lifts her with ease and sets her on his hip. "Where's your Aunt Eliza?"

"Feeding Cody. She said to come in."

"Where's Uncle Matt?" Kane asks.

"He's in the shower."

We enter the house just as Eliza exits the bedroom. "Hey, you two. How are things?"

"We had a wonderful time, Eliza. Thank you for everything." I turn away, my cheeks burning. Eliza knows exactly what we were up to, and part of me is thankful for her intervention, even if it makes facing her a bit awkward.

Eliza throws a victorious fist in the air. "Mission accomplished."

Moments later, Matt comes from the room, hair wet but fully dressed.

"Thanks for taking her," Kane says.

Matt nods. "It was our pleasure. She's a good little helper." He looks at me and Kane and says, "She'd make an excellent big sister."

Matt's words leave me speechless. Hailey beams up at us, her eyes shining with excitement. "I want a little brother or sister."

My smile falters for a fraction of a second, the weight of Hailey's innocent wish pressing heavily on my heart. That's something I can never give her.

Kane, noticing my discomfort, quickly changes the subject. "By the way, my boat's ready. They called yesterday. I'll pick it up on Monday."

"Need any help getting it?" Matt asks.

Kane shakes his head. "No, this is where you're needed," he says, glancing at Eliza. "Besides, I need to make sure I can handle her on my own." He tousles Hailey's hair. "Are you ready, Noodle?"

As soon as we're on the ATV, Kane says, "I'm sorry. They didn't know."

Most of me is okay with it, but a part of me is sad that I'll never experience carrying a child of my own. I close my eyes and imagine that baby, and what I see is Kane's brown hair and those stormy blue eyes.

"You know what sounds great right now?" I don't wait for anyone to answer. "May's fresh pie."

Kane looks at me and nods. "Pie it is."

Shortly after, we arrive at May's Café.

"Look what the cat brought in," May says as we enter.

"We're here for pie." Hailey is so excited she literally bounces to a nearby booth.

"Today is apple blueberry," May says. "Three slices with ice cream?"

"Yes," Hailey says. "And whipped cream too."

I give Hailey a high five. "I like how you roll."

A few minutes later, May arrives with three plates of pie. She sets them down and takes a seat next to Hailey.

I've learned that's the way with May. She doesn't ask. She just does.

"I've been thinking about your mom since the potluck. It is possible that we knew her by something different, as her name doesn't ring a bell. You know, a nickname. Karen Burrows goes by Sunflower now that it's unpopular to be a Karen. Do you have a photo of your mom?"

I don't know why I didn't bring one to the potluck. Maybe it's because the only printed photo I have is a recent one, taken just this year. I imagined no one would recognize the girl she was from a picture of the woman she became. Instead, I pull up an old photo on my phone, one from when I was a baby, where Mom looks happy, holding me in her arms.

I turn the phone to May, and she grabs it, her eyes widening. "Sarah," she whispers, the name barely escaping her lips. The tears come first, followed by deep, wrenching sobs.

I stare at her. The room falls into a heavy silence that seems to stretch on for a lifetime. May clutches the phone to her chest as if it's a lifeline, her body shaking with each sob.

"Oh, my God. You know my mom." My eyes well up with the weight of the moment pressing down on me. May reaches for the napkin dispenser and pulls out a few to wipe her eyes.

May nods. She swallows several times before speaking. "Your mom was my Sarah."

I remember when May ran out to the dock that first day, thinking I was someone else. Despite our differences, she saw something in me that reminded her of my mother. The pieces of the puzzle that have been my life suddenly appear different, and a single thought crystallizes with shocking clarity: "That means ... you're my grandmother."

I stare at her, my mind racing to make sense of this bombshell. A mix of emotions floods through me—shock, confusion, and an intense need to understand how it all came to pass.

"Why didn't I know about you?" I ask, my voice barely above a whisper. The question hangs heavy between us, filled with years of lost time and unshared memories.

May looks pained, her hands trembling as she reaches for another napkin. "It's a long story, one that's difficult to tell."

"I need to know," I say. "I've been in the dark for far too long."

"When your mother left here, there were problems. I told her everyone would forgive her and to let it pass, but she refused. The last time I heard from her was after I sent a postcard asking her to come back." She wipes a tear from her eye. "She called me and told me she loved me but that she had to let me go."

Kane, sitting across from me, leans forward, his voice filled with awe. "Wow, you came here because of that postcard, looking for your father, or a tie to your mother, and you ended up with a grandmother."

Hailey, sitting beside me, reaches out to touch my arm. "You're so lucky. My grandma is in heaven, and I can't see her anymore."

I turn to Hailey, her words tugging at my heart. "I am lucky." I turn back to May. "Why did she let you go?"

My heart aches for May, for the mother I thought I knew, and for myself—caught in the aftermath of choices made long before I could even speak. The realization that my mother lived carrying such a heavy burden makes my throat tighten. Why hadn't she come back? What had been so terrible to sever ties so completely?

A tear slips down my cheek, unbidden but not unwelcome, as it carves a warm path on my skin. "I can't imagine how hard that must have been for both of you." My voice trembles with the effort to stay composed.

May nods, her eyes glossy with unshed tears. "It was devastating. I always hoped she would come back, that she would see how much we all missed her and that ... that whatever mistakes were made could be forgiven."

The table is like an ocean between us, and impulsively, I reach over and take her hand in mine. "I'm here now," I say, needing her to know that despite everything, I'm present, and I'm real, and maybe, just maybe, I can be a part of healing this break in our family's story.

Kane hands Hailey the pen from his pocket and pulls several napkins from the dispenser. "How about you draw some pictures for Daddy?"

Hailey nods and gives her full attention to the task.

"You guys don't have to stay," I say.

He takes my hand. "I'm here for you, and I'm not going anywhere."

I hold on tight like I'm readying myself for a ride on a coaster. I turn back to May. "Okay, tell me everything."

I settle in, listening as May starts the tragic tale of a college girl who fell in love with the wrong man—my father.

"He was charismatic," May begins, her voice trembling slightly. "Your mother met him during her first year away at college. He swept her off her feet, promising her the world. When she brought him back here, he had all these grand ideas for the town. Said he could bring power and running water, modernize everything. People believed him. He was so convincing."

I lean forward, hanging on her every word, the pieces of my past slowly coming together. There's a flutter of joy in my chest at learning about my father, something I've always wondered about.

"But it was all a lie," May continues, her face hardening. "He took everyone's money and vanished. Left the town in ruins, and your mother ... she was devastated. The shame of it all was too much for her. She couldn't bear to stay."

My breath catches. Joy is replaced by a sinking sensation in my stomach. "And no one ever saw him again?"

May shakes her head. "No. Once he found out Sarah was pregnant, he disappeared without a trace. Your mother tried to find him, but it was as if he never existed. She was left to pick up the pieces on her own."

Tears well up in my eyes. "Why didn't she come back to you?"

May hangs her head. "She didn't come back because she knew everyone would see her differently, see her as the person who brought the man who stole everything from them. She didn't want you to have to live with that legacy either. She thought it was the only way to protect you."

Kane's hand on my shoulder grounds me, a reassurance that I'm not alone in this. He squeezes gently, and then his voice breaks the silence. "I've heard the stories," he says. "I never knew if they were true or not."

May nods. "Oh, they were true. It's funny how one

man's actions altered so many lives. I lost my daughter. Many of the townsfolk lost their life savings. It changed everything."

"Who is my father?" My voice shakes as I ask.

"His name is Erik Anders."

"So, my father was a crook?" As if seeing my mind whirl around, she takes my hand and squeezes it.

"I see you thinking about how that might influence who you are. You are your mother's child. You have her heart."

"That's about all I have. She was slim and dark-haired, and I'm sturdy and blonde. Her eyes were like yours, nearly black, and her hair was long and soft as silk." As I see the pain in her expression, I realize I'm not the only one affected. May now knows the daughter she loved is gone. "I'm sorry she never came back. I don't understand that."

May's eyes glisten with unshed tears. "She did what she thought was best." She rises. "Let me get a pot of coffee and you can tell me everything I missed." She looks down at Hailey, who's stopped drawing and has fallen asleep on the napkins. "This one is plain tuckered out."

Kane nods. "I don't know how she crashed. I've found the entire conversation riveting."

While I love that he's been here to support me, it's time he takes Hailey home. "I'll be all right. You should get her home."

He looks as if he may argue, but as he sees May coming back with a pot of coffee and two cups, he nods, as if he understands we need time alone.

Kane picks up a sleeping Hailey and says, "Call me, and I'll come and get you." He kisses me before he leaves. It isn't a passionate kiss, but one that says, I'm here if and when you need me.

Over a cup of coffee, I catch May up on the years she didn't spend with my mother, and she reveals more about the past.

"I wish my mom would have come back."

"People here have long memories. It appears so did your mom."

Her words resonate with me. I've heard of grudges held for generations. "Kane once told me about an outsider who caused a lot of pain in the community. It was a long time ago, but the resentment still lingers."

"That's the story. It's become a legend told from generation to generation."

"What if I'm just a reminder of those bad times? Eventually, people will know who I am and maybe resent me."

"Timber, you are not responsible for the past. You are here to create your own story, not relive Sarah's."

The comfort in her words gives me a break from my worries. Curiosity tugs at me, drawing me back to the lighter details. "Why do you think she chose the name Aspen Moore?"

May smiles. "It makes sense," she says. "Aspens were her favorite tree. She always said they stood together, strong and resilient. And she always wanted more than what Alaska could offer her."

That image of aspen trees, standing tall and interconnected, resonates with me, and I experience a connection to the mother I never really knew. Then another thought strikes me. "What about my name—Timber?"

May chuckles, the sound rich with affection. "I think she was holding on to a little of her roots after all. Timber—strong, essential, and part of the forest that surrounds us."

As I hear this, calmness overcomes me. Despite her fears and the drastic steps she took, there was a part of my mother that remained tethered to her beginnings. It gives me a newfound sense of connection, not just to my mother, but to May, and to the land that shaped them both. I found out my father was Scandinavian, and my mother was part Tlingit, a Native Alaskan tribe. Mom always said she was a native, but I assumed she meant Cherokee or Navajo. I sit here filled with pride for a heritage I never knew.

I think about her herbal remedies and ask, "Did my mother learn to heal from you?"

May nods. "I'm glad she passed that on to you. Now it makes sense. You knew about Devil's Claw, and then there's the potato salad."

"Capers and bacon. It's the only way," I say. "You know, I have her book. It's a journal with handwritten remedies and such."

May's mouth opens. "My sweet granddaughter. That's my book. I always wondered about you and where you went. Your mother, when she changed her name, didn't leave a trace, but I have never stopped looking and hoping." She squeezes my hands. "It warms me to know

I've been a part of your life, anyway." After several hours of talking, it's time to wrap it up. I stand and hug my grandmother.

"You should let me take you home," she says.

I shake my head. "I need the walk and the time to process."

"At least call Kane."

"I'll be okay. It's still light, and I don't want him to have to get Hailey out of bed."

"He won't mind. I see how he looks at you. I think that boy might be in love."

"A girl can dream."

I step outside, and the cool evening air brushes against my face as the door shuts behind me. I came here searching for my father, clutching a postcard and a handful of fragmented memories. But in this place, among these people, I found so much more.

I think about Kane, his warm, earnest gaze that seems to pierce right through me, understanding parts of me I haven't yet figured out myself. And Hailey, with her bright, curious eyes—how she leans into my side when we watch TV, as if I always belonged there.

As I walk the familiar path, my thoughts drift back to May. The revelation of her being my grandmother has left a tender ache in my heart, a mixture of sorrow for all the lost years and a budding hope for what's to come. I never imagined that my journey would intertwine my past and future so deeply.

I arrived here seeking answers about where I came from, but I wonder if this is where I belong.

Chapter Twenty-Five

KANE

I CHECK THE CLOCK AGAIN. It's been an hour since May called and said Timber was on her way. I can't shake the worry about her walking home alone after such a heavy day.

Hailey's asleep, totally unaware of everything going on outside her dreams. She insisted I read *Cinderella* before bed and then asked again if I'd marry Timber and if so, would there be a pumpkin carriage and a glass slipper. If only life were like fairytales and all stories had a happy ending.

That got me thinking about Timber and me, and if we'd get a happy ending. The only way that happens is if she decides to stay.

I continue looking out the window, wishing I could see her walking up the path. Is this what she did when I was stuck at sea? Was she worried sick about me, too? Did her gut twist and turn when every sound and shadow didn't turn out to be me? Did she want to rush out and search but held back because she knew Hailey would need her? All these thoughts drift through my mind as I do several more passes in front of the living room window.

Each minute that ticks by seems like an eternity. After learning about her mother, what is she thinking? I know the story and the distrust it bred in town. Amanda's actions didn't help either. For me, it only intensified the suspicion that outsiders can't be trusted. But Timber isn't her father. She isn't Amanda. She's proven herself different, repeatedly, with her kindness and genuine efforts to fit into this community. She's one of the good ones.

I'm at the window again, just staring out, when I finally see it—a shadow moving up the path. It's slight and slow, but it's there. Adrenaline surges through me, and without thinking, I'm out the door, racing across the yard toward her.

She looks exhausted. Her steps are slow, but there's no sadness in her eyes, just a weariness that speaks more of physical tiredness than anything else.

"What were you thinking?" I blurt as I reach her.

She gives me a small, tired smile and says, "I was thinking it wouldn't take me as long. In my mind, it was half as far because we always take the ATV."

I'm half-amused despite my concern. "You had me worried, walking all by yourself this late after such a day."

She lets out a soft laugh. "Sorry, I didn't mean to concern you. A lot happened today, and I needed some time to clear my head."

We walk back toward the house together. "You don't have to process this all alone. I'm here for you."

She stops and turns to look at me, her eyes searching mine. "Can you believe it? May is my grandmother. I woke up this morning thinking I was Timber Moore, orphan and alone, and now I'm not sure who I am."

I pull her into my arms, feeling a rush of emotion. "I know exactly who you are. You're a teacher, a friend, a wonderful person, and you're mine."

"Yes," she whispers, as if testing the word. "I'm yours."

Hearing her say it, a rush of emotion hits me hard. It's more than just a word. It's a future. I tighten my hold on her, not wanting to let go. "You have no idea how much that means to me," I say, my voice rough with emotion.

I guide her inside and straight to my room. She stops at the door. "Oh no. I'm not sneaking out of your bed every morning before Hailey wakes."

I can see how that might be a problem, so I take her hand, and walk her to her room, and close the door behind us. "Then I'll sneak out of yours."

In the quiet of her room, the weight of the day's events seems to lift. I hold her close, and experience the rise and fall of her breath, grounding myself in the simple reality of having her here, now. "What are your future plans?" I ask, brushing a strand of hair from her face.

She sighs and looks away. "I can't plan for forever until I process what happened today. There's so much to take in."

I help her sit on the edge of the bed and start removing her shoes. I take one foot in my hands, touching the delicate bones and soft skin with my fingers. Slowly, I begin to massage her, my thumbs pressing into the arch of her foot, working in small circles to ease the tension.

She closes her eyes and lets out a soft moan, her body relaxing under my touch. As I continue, I move to her toes, gently pulling them, then back to her heel, kneading firmly but gently. Her head falls back, and she sinks into the mattress, a look of pure contentment on her face.

"I understand," I say quietly. "I figured with May being your grandmother and all, you might stay."

"I'd love to, but I can't make that decision right now."

"What's holding you back?"

She opens her eyes and takes a deep breath. "There are so many reasons. My new job … I made a commitment, and I can't leave it now. And my mother's house—there's so much that needs to be done there."

Hearing her uncertainty, a mix of emotions rushes through me. I understand her hesitations, but the thought of her leaving is a punch to the gut. I keep massaging her foot, trying to focus on the present moment. "I wish things were different."

She looks at me. "I do too. But I have commitments I need to take care of."

I want to ask her to stay, but inwardly, my thoughts swirl. If she's not going to stay for her grandma, she definitely won't stay for me. The realization hits hard, but I push it aside. For now.

I lift her feet, placing them gently on the bed and move beside her, bringing my face level with hers. Our eyes meet, and I lean in, kissing her. She responds, the tension between us shifting. It's the start of something more intimate, more immediate. As we begin to undress, I close the door on the world outside, on all the worries and the future uncertainties.

In the dim light of her room, I focus on the present. She's here, in bed with me, and I'm not wasting a minute of time thinking about the future when what we have is now. The problems of the world, the weight of our decisions, can wait for another day. For now, the simple truth is that I have her in my arms, and that's enough.

Chapter Twenty-Six

TIMBER

THE MORNING SUN glints off the water as Hank's floatplane approaches the dock, its engine's hum growing louder as it nears. Hailey and I stand there, the crisp breeze tugging at our hair.

"Daddy, you be careful," Hailey says. She hugs him tightly, her small frame dwarfed by his large body.

"Always am," Kane says, ruffling Hailey's hair before turning to me.

I give him a side-eye because his "always am" doesn't ring true.

"Okay, I usually am. But I'll be double careful today."

I step forward with a knot tightening in my stomach. "Don't forget to call when you get there," I say, trying to keep my voice steady, but this is the first time Kane will be on his new boat alone, and visions of when he got lost at sea are still fresh in my mind.

He looks at me. "I will." He pulls me into an

embrace that is far too short. As he moves away, I reach up to kiss him, a brief but intense kiss that says more than words ever could. "I'll see you tonight," I whisper.

He nods, his eyes lingering on mine for a moment before he turns and climbs into the plane. I stand there with Hailey, watching as the floatplane roars to life and lifts off the water, soaring into the clear blue sky. It disappears from sight, leaving an unsettling silence in its wake. I take a deep breath, turning to Hailey. "Ready to head to the community center?"

She nods, slipping her hand into mine. Together, we walk up the dock while Hailey chatters about the day's activities. My mind keeps drifting back to Kane. Each week folds into the next, a subtle countdown reminding me of how temporary this all is.

The relationship with Kane and Hailey has grown unexpectedly strong, entwining our lives in ways I hadn't anticipated. Mornings spent with Hailey and the kids at the community center, playing games and exploring local spots, have become the norm. Evenings with Kane are a mix of cooking dinners, talking long into the night, and sharing quiet, intimate moments in my bed. Love, though undeclared, wraps around us like a warm down comforter.

Yet, each day reminds me that my time here is almost over. I can't shake the sense that I'm setting myself up for heartbreak, building a life I can't keep—a life based on a single, fleeting summer.

This realization sits heavy in my chest as we arrive at the community center to find Tommy and Lucas waiting by the door. I force a smile, determined to make the most of the time I have left.

"Alright, team," I rally the kids. "Today, we're on a mission to find the mother lode of blueberries. May swears they're out there, just waiting for us." I smile, thinking about my grandmother, who has tried to squeeze three decades of memories into the last few weeks. I love watching her talk, especially how she uses her hands to express herself. She always rolls her eyes with a tilt of her head to the right whenever she's exasperated or amused by some small absurdity. Now I see where my mother got so many of her mannerisms. It's proof that the apple doesn't fall far from the tree.

Tommy, ever the skeptic, says, "What if we get lost like Kane on that boat? Do we need one of those beacon things, too?"

Hailey giggles, punching Tommy lightly on the arm. "Silly, we're not going that far!"

"Yeah," Lucas chimes in. "Besides, Timber will take care of us, right?" His voice tilts up at the end, making it clear he's looking for reassurance.

I laugh, nodding. "Absolutely! I'll make sure we all stay safe. No getting lost on my watch. And who knows? Maybe we'll find more than blueberries—like a treasure or something."

With a map that May sketched out, a packed lunch, and enough enthusiasm to power a small town, we set out toward the nearby hiking trail she described. The path winds through the lush forest to a place called Misty

Meadows. Outside, the air is crisp and filled with the scent of pine and earth.

As we walk, I experience a mixture of excitement and peace. The laughter of the kids and the beauty of our surroundings make it easy to forget the worries about Kane's boat trip. Now and then, I pull out my phone, checking for any updates from him, but I also remind myself that he's an experienced and capable sailor despite the last mishap. He knows what he's doing.

The blueberry spot turns out to be a hidden gem, just as May described. The bushes are heavy with fruit, clusters of blueberries hanging like little sapphire jewels. The children dive in with delight, their earlier banter turning into a friendly competition of who can gather the most.

"Remember, we're sharing whatever we find, so every berry counts toward our treasure trove," I remind them.

As they stuff their faces and baskets with blueberries, the inevitable happens—nature calls. Tommy and Lucas look at me with urgent eyes. "Can we go behind a tree?" Tommy asks, hopping from one foot to the other.

"Sure, just over there." I point to a thick bush close to where we are. I stand guard, looking away to give them a bit of privacy while keeping them in earshot. Within a couple of minutes, they're back, grinning and relieved.

"Me too, Timber," Hailey says, tugging at my hand.

"Okay, let's hurry. We don't want to fall behind in the berry competition, do we?" I guide her to another bush, and soon she's scampering back, ready to resume our adventure.

A few moments later, it's my turn. "Okay, you three, stay by that bush," I instruct. "Don't move. I'll be quick."

As I step behind the shrub, a wave of reality washes over me. This simple act—taking a moment in nature—reminds me of how uncomplicated life is here. In a few weeks, I'll be in Arizona, far away from this carefree world. No more berry-picking adventures or impromptu outdoor bathroom breaks. My life will shift from these simple joys to something much more structured and predictable.

Just as I'm about to squat, I hear a rustle. "I thought I told you to stay put!" I yell, assuming one of them is sneaking up to scare me.

Their little voices call back from where I left them. "We are at the bush!"

Confused, I pause and turn toward the rustling noise. I stop in my tracks. There, just a few feet away, is a massive golden bear, its fur shimmering in the dappled sunlight. It's the largest bear I've ever seen, and it's so close.

Adrenaline surges through me, my initial shock morphing into frantic action. I yank up my pants and bolt back to the kids. I can hear the bear following me, getting closer. When it chuffs, I swear the heat of its breath glides across my neck. Kane's stories about bear encounters fill my brain, but the golden fur throws me off. Is this the infamous Grizzletoe? Nothing makes sense anymore, except the need to keep the kids safe.

Charging toward the group, I place myself in front of

them. They cling to each other, eyes wide with fear as the bear approaches. Confusion spirals inside of me, but it's pushed aside by a visceral urge to protect the kids at all costs. I spread my arms wide, attempting to appear larger. With all the bravado I can muster, I let out a series of ear-piercing screams and exaggerated animal noises. "Leave us alone, bear! Ca caw ca caw. Moooooo. Ruff, ruff. Meow." My voice echoes through the trees as I continue my performance, hoping to intimidate the beast and protect those behind me.

The bear pauses, tilting its head as if bewildered by the crazy lady shouting and flailing in front of it. It gives us one long, considering look—almost like it's questioning my sanity—then, with a snort that could be bear laughter, it turns and ambles back into the woods.

We watch in stunned silence until it disappears. Then I turn to the kids, trying to laugh it off. "Well, that's one way to pick blueberries and make friends with wildlife, huh?"

Tommy looks like he may cry, and I think it's a real possibility until he bursts out laughing. "Timber, you looked so funny! Like a big, scary ... bird or something!"

"Scary enough to save us from old Grizzletoe," Lucas adds, grinning.

I gather them close, relief washing over me. "I think it's time to go." I don't want to be here if he comes back with his friends. Do bears have friends? I realize there's so much I haven't learned about the wild here.

The kids gather their buckets, and we rush back to the community center where we divide the berries into four containers. One for each child and some for May for sending us to her secret garden.

Tommy and Lucas are picked up promptly by their parents, their laughter and stories about the day's adventure still echoing as they depart. Hailey, still brimming with excitement, clings to my side as we make our way to the dock to wait for Kane.

The sun is just beginning to dip below the horizon, painting the sky in streaks of orange and purple, when Kane finally arrives. He's apologetic for his lateness. "Sorry I'm late," he says as he ties off the boat and jumps onto the dock with a grin. "I wanted to make sure everything was running smoothly on the new troller."

"It's okay," I respond, watching Hailey get excited at the sight of her dad and the new boat. "It's important to be thorough." I reflect on how detailed this man is with everything he does from the way he treats his boat to how he pleasures his woman.

"You want to take a ride?" Kane asks, his eyes twinkling with a mixture of excitement and pride as he nods toward the gleaming Seas the Day. "Just a quick trip."

"Absolutely," I reply, looking forward to the adventure. We help Hailey aboard, securing her life vest snugly before casting off into the increasingly vibrant hues of the sunset.

Once we're a safe distance from the shore, Kane passes the wheel to me, and the boat moves with a gentle sway. The sun dips lower, streaking the sky with fiery oranges and deep purples, the sea mirroring the sight with every cresting wave. Hailey climbs onto a chair and presses her forehead to the glass, her breath fogging up the window as she peers out at the horizon.

"It's beautiful out here," I say, the vastness making the troller seem like a tiny speck in the endless ocean. "I can see why you love it so much. It seems like you're really in control of your destiny."

Kane nods, leaning against the side of the cabin as he watches me navigate. "Out here, it's just you and the sea. If things go right, it's because you made the right calls. If they don't, well, that's on you too."

I glance at him, considering his words. "It must be nice, having that kind of control. In my job, so many decisions are out of my hands. I'm constantly at the mercy of someone else's choices."

"You might have more control than you think." Kane's hand brushes against mine as he moves to stand beside me. I glance up at him, our eyes meeting for a brief, charged moment. "You can always make different choices, Timber."

Hailey's small voice breaks through the tension. "Look! The sky is all orange and purple!" she says.

I smile at her observation. "It's beautiful, isn't it, sweetie?" I steer the boat around a gentle curve of coastline before turning my attention back to Kane. "You're right, but I have responsibilities—a job that pays the bills, a house that's more of a money pit than a home. I can't just leave all that behind." Part of me wants to leave all that and stay here, but the thought of giving up everything for a man again scares me. I did that once for David and look where that got me. It's too much, too soon.

Kane frowns, the light of the setting sun casting shadows across his face. "I understand," he says, his voice low. "But it's also important to think about what makes you happy."

His words linger in the air between us, heavy with unsaid truths. Sadness fills me, knowing that soon, I'll have to leave this place and the possibilities it represents. The freedom of the sea, the life with Kane and Hailey—it's a stark contrast to the world waiting for me back home.

As we turn the boat back toward the harbor, I let the wheel under my hands imprint on my memory, a reminder of what it's like to steer your own course, if only for a little while. The thought of leaving this behind, of saying goodbye to Kane and the life I've imagined here, is as daunting as the open sea.

"Let's enjoy the ride while we can," I say as I meet Kane's gaze. He nods, and together we watch the shore approach, the reality of our lives waiting to reclaim us.

Chapter Twenty-Seven

KANE

I STAND ON THE DOCK, watching the sun bleed into the ocean. The salt air mixes with a bitter dread inside me. Timber and I have crossed lines I hadn't expected to redraw in my life. Her laughter, her presence on quiet nights—she's burrowed not just into my home but deep into my heart. I hadn't meant to let anyone in that close again, yet here I am, facing a gaping void with her about to leave.

The closeness we share isn't just physical. It's in every shared silence, every look that lingers too long, every honest word spoken in the dark. These moments hint at possibilities my rational mind knows we can't keep.

How has she become so important so fast? The thought of her absence is like imagining a part of me ripped away, leaving a raw, open wound.

I shuffle my feet, hands buried deep in my pockets as I try to sort out my thoughts. Can I really ask her to stay?

To leave everything behind for a love that has no guarantees? The boldness of it makes my pulse quicken.

"What are you thinking about?" Eliza asks, appearing from nowhere but somehow finding her way next to me.

Caught off guard, I glance at my sister, noticing the heaviness in her eyes—a reflection of her own looming goodbye. Her husband is set to return to the oil rig, a cycle of departures and reunions that never seems to get easier. "Just thinking about how quickly things change, how fast time slips away," I admit, kicking lightly at a loose board on the dock.

Eliza nods, understanding the fleeting nature of moments we wish could last forever. "I know," she says. "It never gets easier ... the goodbyes."

Her voice cracks slightly, revealing the strain of repeated separations. It makes me think of Timber, about the agonizing countdown to her departure, and how every moment seems dipped in farewell.

"You could avoid one goodbye, you know," Eliza continues, her gaze steady on mine. "Tell Timber how you feel. You don't have to let her go without knowing what could be. Tell her you love her."

The idea hangs in the air between us, simple yet colossal. "What if love isn't enough?" I ask.

Eliza steps closer, her presence comforting. "What if it is? Maybe it'll turn into something wonderful. You'll never know unless you open up. Don't let fear decide the future for you. I've watched you over these past several weeks and she's good for you. She's good for all of us."

Her words strike a chord. Eliza has always seen through me, knowing when I'm holding back. As much as I try to be a realist, I can't ignore the hope Eliza carries. Maybe I'm afraid of the same gamble she's talking about. But if she, who knows the pain of repeated separations, can still believe in the possibility of something beautiful, maybe I can too.

"I'll think about it," I say, the decision still daunting.

Eliza's expression is a mixture of encouragement and sympathy. "Come on," she urges, breaking the heavy mood. "Everyone's gathered for Matt's goodbye lunch. Let's not keep them waiting. These moments—good or bad—are better shared."

As we walk back toward the gathering, the notion of sharing—not just moments, but life itself—with Timber plays over in my mind. Eliza is right. I need to decide not out of fear, but out of the chance for something greater. I've always played it safe, keeping my emotions guarded, avoiding risks. But Timber has changed that. She makes me want to be different, to take a chance I've never dared to take before.

Maybe it's time to take that leap. Tonight, I'll tell her what's in my heart, and I'll ask her to stay.

At May's Cafe, the laughter and chatter fill the air, bouncing off the old wooden walls and brightening the room. We're all gathered around a few pushed-together tables, making space for everyone. Dad is at the head, his booming voice recounting a hunting trip gone hilariously wrong last fall. My brothers, rowdy and relentless, tease each other over missed shots and forgotten gear.

I sit back for a moment, watching Timber as she interacts with my family. She's seated between Eliza and me, laughing at something my brother Finn said. Hailey is standing next to her, glued to Timber's side, her small hand clutching Timber's like she's the only anchor in a swirling sea. There's a naturalness to her presence, a way she fits into the gaps we didn't even know existed.

"Remember that giant bass Rhys claimed was 'this big?'" Nash waves his arms wide, and the table erupts in laughter.

"Yeah, right, more like this big!" I chime in, holding my hands much closer together, drawing another round of chuckles.

Timber joins in the teasing, her eyes sparkling. "Oh, come on, guys. Us girls know that size matters, especially when it comes to … fish."

Her comment sends us into another round of laughter, and even Dad chuckles, giving her a nod of approval. "Girl's got wit," he says, and something warm spreads in my chest. It's pride mixed with a deeper, more tender emotion.

I drape my arm across the back of Timber's chair, my fingers just barely brushing her shoulder. Watching her, I think of my mother, whose gentle spirit seems mirrored in Timber. Mom would have adored her, would have been overjoyed at the circle of family widening to embrace someone who seems to have always been meant to be part of us.

May moves around to refill half-empty mugs of coffee. When she gets to Timber, she says, "I'm so glad you're here."

"Me too," Timber replies.

The evening winds down, and it's time to walk Matt down to the dock. He stands up, stretching and yawning, and the rest of us follow suit, gathering our things and saying our goodbyes. The air outside is cool, the sun now a fading glow on the horizon.

As we stroll toward the dock, I walk beside Matt, our footsteps echoing on the wooden planks. There's a bittersweet feeling in the air, a sense of closure and new beginnings. Matt's heading back to his job on the oil rig, leaving Eliza and their life here behind for a while. I think about the possibility of having to do this with Timber soon, if she chooses to leave. The thought tightens my chest, but I push it away, focusing on the present moment.

"Gonna miss you, bro," Matt says, clapping me on the back.

"Same here," I reply, my voice thick with emotion. "Don't worry about Eliza. We'll look after her until you get back."

Matt nods, gratitude and trust in his eyes. "Thanks, Kane. That means a lot."

The dock is quiet, mostly empty except for a few

locals who nod in greeting as they pass. We gather, waiting. A few moments later, the distant drone of the plane grows louder.

Eliza holds baby Cody a little tighter, her other hand clasped by Matt. Their goodbyes are filled with whispered vows and fleeting kisses, a poignant scene that makes me wonder how they do it without falling apart.

As the plane touches down smoothly on the water and taxis toward us, the pilot expertly maneuvers it to the dock. The door swings open, and as Matt readies himself to board, another figure steps out first. I freeze for a moment—Amanda.

A shock runs through me, freezing me in place. I blink, hoping my eyes are playing tricks, but there she is, unmistakably Amanda. My stomach knots and a cold sweat prickles at the back of my neck.

"You've got to be kidding," Rhys says.

"Who's that?" Timber asks.

Eliza groans. "That's Amanda."

I look around, searching for Hailey, afraid of her reaction, and spot her beside Timber, holding her hand.

"Why is she here?" Timber whispers. Her hand tightens around mine.

"I don't know," I say. All I can think about is how this complicates everything. The hope I'd been nurturing all day now seems overshadowed by this unexpected challenge.

Amanda waves, her smile strained. Rhys nods, barely acknowledging her. Eliza forces a small, tight-lipped smile before turning her gaze away. The rest of my family ignores her presence. Beside me, Timber tenses, her grip on my hand growing firmer.

As Amanda draws closer, reality sinks in. Her arrival isn't just a visit. It's a disruption that threatens the delicate balance of the life I'm trying to build. A life that, I hope, includes Timber, not just for now, but forever.

Chapter Twenty-Eight
TIMBER

AMANDA STANDS there with effortless grace, somehow making old jeans and a man's suit shirt, tied neatly at her waist, look like they belong on a runway. The casual outfit, meant to be simple, on her looks intentionally stylish, her sandy blonde hair perfectly tousled as if she's just stepped out of a fashion magazine's "effortlessly chic" spread.

I catch myself stealing a glance down at my own attire—comfortable, practical clothes that now seem plain next to her curated casual look. My curves, which I usually embrace, are overly pronounced, and so different from her lithe figure. I'm suddenly self-conscious, the familiar weight of insecurity settling in my stomach like stones.

"Hailey, sweetie, come to Mommy!" Amanda calls out with a tone that seems both heartfelt and rehearsed.

But Hailey doesn't move toward her. Instead, she tightens her grip on my hand and ducks behind my legs.

Her little body pressed against mine sends a wave of protective affection through me, mingled with a spike of anxiety. I wonder, will Hailey's reluctance reflect badly on me in Amanda's eyes? Does she see me as an obstacle?

I glance down at Hailey, whose eyes are wide with a mix of confusion and caution. I try to offer her reassurance, but my nerves are frayed.

"It's okay," I whisper down to her, as her fingers clutch at me. Her response is to cling even tighter, seeking comfort in the familiar.

Amanda's smile wavers as she watches this interaction, then quickly recovers. She straightens and, with a quick, confident step, approaches Kane.

She kisses his cheek as if she had never been away, treating it like the most natural thing in the world to do. The others pause, but Amanda doesn't seem to notice their reaction. She greets Kane warmly, lingering just a moment with her hand on his arm, showing how comfortable she is with him.

"It's good to see you," she says cheerfully, her demeanor relaxed and familiar. Watching them, I'm uncomfortable. They have a past that doesn't include me. The others look on, exchanging glances, clearly sensing the change in the air but saying nothing. Amanda's friendly manner, however, leaves an undertone of tension.

"You could have called," Kane says.

"I never do. You always liked my unpredictability."

"That was before you gifted me with a child and left."

Amanda rolls her eyes. "It's been years, Kane. Let it go."

He shakes his head. "I can't and I won't."

Amanda then turns her attention to me, her gaze curious yet measured. "And you are?" she asks, her tone friendly but with a hint of surprise. The way her eyes scan me makes it clear she's trying to place me in the context of her daughter's life—a puzzle piece she hadn't expected to find.

"I'm Timber," I say. My voice is steady despite the churn of emotions inside me. "I've been ... helping out with Hailey."

"Helping out?" Amanda echoes, a slight tilt of her head suggesting she's piecing together the information. Her look is not unkind, but it's analytical, as if she's reassessing the scene before her based on this new data.

"Yes," I continue. Hailey's grip tightens further, a plea for security in the midst of uncertainty. "I've been filling in temporarily for Eliza since she had Cody."

The mention of Eliza's baby doesn't seem to register with Amanda. She doesn't even look to see the baby Eliza is holding.

"Timber belongs here," Kane says. His tone is brusque yet protective, leaving little room for doubt. He glances my way, trying to reassure me. Despite his efforts, a sudden mix of emotions—jealousy and insecurity—unsettles me.

Kane clears his throat, gently pulling away from Amanda's lingering touch. "You've actually walked into a family send-off," he informs her, his voice carrying a hint of firmness.

Amanda's brows lift in mild surprise. "Oh, I see. Then, I'll catch up with you at home later," she responds casually, assuming that the familiarity of their past gives her the same privileges as before.

Kane shakes his head, the lines of his face hardening. "You can't stay there, Amanda. It's not just my place anymore."

"Why not?" Amanda's voice sharpens. "Hailey is there, and I'm her mother. I need to be by my daughter."

From the side, I watch the exchange, a knot tightening in my stomach. The way Amanda asserts her role strikes a nerve, reminding me of the temporary nature of my own position within this new family dynamic. How much I'll miss being part of this household tugs at my thoughts. Even though Kane is not welcoming her with open arms, I wonder if in my absence they will bridge this gap between them. Maybe it would be good for Hailey, I tell myself, trying to find consolation in the possibility.

Kane looks visibly conflicted, his eyes flicking toward me briefly before returning to Amanda. "Things have changed, Amanda. We need to talk about arrangements that work for everyone. You can't assume things will go back to how they were."

The tension between them hangs in the air, and I'm both protective of our shared life with Hailey and deeply anxious about the impact of Amanda's return.

Kane turns to Finn. "You got any space in your cabins?" he asks.

Finn rubs the back of his neck, looking apologetic. "Not for a few weeks," he responds, his tone indicating he wishes he could do more.

Kane scans the faces of his family, pleading for help. It's Eliza who speaks up, her voice gentle but firm. "Amanda, you could stay with us for a few days. We've got the room."

A wave of relief washes over me at Eliza's offer. The thought of Amanda staying with us makes my stomach roil but knowing there's another option eases some of the tension.

Amanda's face contorts. "Thanks, but I really don't like ki—" She cuts herself off abruptly. "I mean, babies." The words hang awkwardly in the air, and she quickly waves off the offer. "But thank you."

I glance down at Hailey, who has stayed unusually close during the exchange, her small hand clutching my sleeve.

Bending slightly, I whisper, "You okay, Hailey?"

Hailey nods, but she doesn't let go of my sleeve.

Amanda, seemingly oblivious to her child's discomfort, brightens considerably as she turns back to Hailey. "Hey, sweetie, when you get home, I've got presents for you," she says, her voice lifting in a cheerful lilt.

At the mention of presents, Hailey peeks out from behind my legs, her earlier apprehension replaced by the gleam of curiosity typical of a five-year-old. "Presents?" she asks.

"Yes, lots of fun stuff!" Amanda assures her, then turns to the rest of us. "I'm just exhausted from the trip. I really need a nap," she announces and walks away as if it's all settled. And maybe it is because no one stops her. But if Amanda is staying at the house, where does that leave me?

I'm compelled to offer a solution. "Eliza, maybe I should stay with you," I suggest, trying to sound as helpful as possible. "I can help with the baby. It might make things easier for everyone." I glance at Kane who is shaking his head.

"No, Timber, you belong with me," he says, leaving no room for argument. "We'll figure it out."

A whirlwind of thoughts races through my mind. What does "figuring it out" really mean? I know he's in a tough spot, caught between past commitments and current realities, and I don't want to add to his stress. I nod, happy for his decision, but I feel a heaviness with the implications of what lies ahead. Amanda's return has stirred up a storm of uncertainty, and I question the universe's intentions.

I see the road ahead, fraught with challenges and tension.

As the time comes to say goodbye to Matt, the farewells are filled with hugs and well-wishes, but also a sense of loss. Eliza, teary-eyed after hugging Matt, turns to me with an open, earnest expression. "If things get to be too much, you're welcome at my place, anytime," she whispers, giving me a tight squeeze.

I'm touched by her kindness and the safety net she

offers is like a ray of hope in a suddenly uncertain future. "Thank you, Eliza. That means a lot," I say, my voice thick with gratitude.

I find myself reflecting on the life I've come to cherish at Kane's. The joy of our days together, the laughter of Hailey that fills the rooms, the peace of knowing I belong somewhere—it's been close to perfect. But with Amanda's return, the perfect little world we've built is about to change. I'm left wondering how much of that tranquility we can preserve, or if I'll need to consider taking Eliza up on her offer sooner than I'd like.

We wait until the plane is a mere speck on the horizon and we know Eliza will be okay.

In the ATV, Kane, Hailey, and I make our way along the path that leads back home, with Hailey blissfully unaware of the grown-up complexities swirling around her.

Hailey sits in the back. She chatters away about everything from the bumpy ride to the butterflies she spotted earlier.

Kane's knuckles are white as he grips the steering wheel, his eyes fixed ahead. He leans in close to me, his voice low. "Operation Home Front might encounter some ... unexpected weather," he says.

"You think?" I stifle a chuckle, appreciating his attempt to lighten the mood. "Do we have a storm shelter prepared?" I ask, playing along with our coded conversation.

Kane nods solemnly. "We might need to reinforce the walls. Maybe build a new addition," he says, implying the need to accommodate Amanda without disrupting our current family dynamics too much.

"What about the chicken coop?" I suggest.

Kane laughs. "It would never work. Animal rights activist. She'd set them free."

Hailey, catching only bits of our conversation, looks at us with a puzzled frown. "Are we getting a new room? Can it be purple?"

I exchange a quick, amused glance with Kane. "Well, we might consider some new paint," I tell her, grateful for her innocent interruption.

"And maybe some sparkles?" Hailey suggests enthusiastically, completely oblivious to the actual topic at hand.

"Definitely sparkles," Kane agrees, his tone serious, but his eyes laughing.

"Sparkles that can withstand all kinds of weather," I add, ensuring our "code" remains intact.

Hailey nods, satisfied with our plans for hypothetical renovations.

As we pull into the driveway, Hailey unbuckles and jumps off the ATV first, excited and bursting with energy, racing toward the house. Kane and I follow more slowly. I steel myself for what lies ahead.

"I'm sorry," Kane says. "I should have set boundaries, but I didn't expect this."

I'm not sure what he means by "this." Is it Amanda showing up, or the emotions between us? We enter the house, and everything looks normal, but the air is different—heavier. Hailey calls out, "Mommy?" and we hear movement from down the hallway.

"Stay here," Kane says quietly as he walks away. I listen, hearing muffled voices.

After a few minutes, Kane comes back, looking tense. "She's in my bed like she belongs there."

A cold wave of shock washes over me, but I force myself to stay calm. I think about Amanda being in his bed. The image stabs at my heart. I want to scream, to demand she leave, to make it clear that she no longer belongs here. But I know I can't give in to those emotions. Instead, I steel myself, taking a deep breath and clenching my fists at my sides.

What does this mean for us? The questions swirl in my mind. I fear this will complicate everything, that Amanda's presence will resurrect old feelings and create a rift between Kane and me. But I also fear looking weak, like I'm not strong enough to stand my ground.

I meet Kane's eyes, trying to mask my turmoil. "Let her stay there. You aren't sleeping there, anyway." My voice comes out steadier than I expect. Inside, I'm imagining the worst—Amanda trying to reclaim her place in Kane's life.

As Kane walks away, the weight of the situation presses down on me. My mind is a storm of conflicting emotions. I know I was supposed to leave after the summer, that this was meant to be temporary. But somewhere inside, I want to stay. Kane said I belonged here with him, but was that just a statement for now, or did it mean something more? Was he thinking of a future with me, or was he simply trying to manage the chaos of the moment?

My thoughts spiral back to my past. My husband left me, and the wound is still fresh. Now, faced with Amanda's unexpected return, old insecurities resurface.

I fear history repeating itself, losing Kane to someone who fits better into his past and maybe his future.

But then it hits me, like a bolt of lightning—I've spent so much time trying to be enough for others, to be wanted and needed. All I ever wanted was for someone to want me and only me. To choose me, not because of what I could give them, but because of who I am.

The tears well up, but I blink them away. I can't show weakness, not now.

A few minutes later, Amanda arrives wearing nothing but my favorite flannel shirt of Kane's. The sight of her in his shirt is like a punch to the gut. Seeing her in it, so casually claiming something so personal, stirs a storm of emotions within me.

My mind races, anger and jealousy bubbling up, battling with my resolve to stay calm. I clench my fists at my sides, struggling to maintain my composure. Amanda's audacity is infuriating, and the way she flaunts her presence is like a deliberate challenge. My chest tightens. This isn't just about a shirt—it's about territory, about boundaries that are blurred and violated. And yet, this isn't my house. It's Kane's job to set those boundaries. And Kane, is he mine?

Before anyone responds, Amanda calls Hailey from the living room where she was watching cartoons. "Hailey, sweetie, look what I brought you!" she says, holding out a package for Hailey to see.

Hailey's eyes widen with excitement as she looks at the present, but her excitement quickly fades when she sees what's inside—a set of jumbo building blocks. She frowns. "Those are for babies," she says, her disappointment evident.

Amanda's smile tightens. "But I thought you'd like them."

Hailey looks up at me, seeking my reaction. "Why don't you thank your mom, Hailey? It was very nice of her to bring you a present."

Hailey hesitates but then mutters, "Thank you, Mommy," before turning back to me. "Can we go play with the sparkles now?"

I shake my head. "In a few minutes. Why don't you finish your cartoons first." Hailey happily skips away.

Kane shakes his head. "Amanda, we need to set some boundaries," he says. "You don't belong in my bed or my clothes."

Relief floods through me, mingling with an unexpected sense of validation. Kane is choosing me, asserting our relationship in front of Amanda. But almost immediately, doubt creeps in. Is this just a passing defense, or does it signal something deeper?

She sighs and brushes her hair back. "I didn't think it would be such a big deal." She looks at me. "Aren't you temporary?"

I stand there, speechless. Amanda's words pierce the fragile bubble of relief, bringing back the nagging uncertainty about my place here. I am like a ping pong ball, bouncing between moments of clarity and confusion, security and doubt.

Kane claimed I'm more than just help, but what does that even mean? More than help but less than a partner? His words felt comforting in the moment, yet they lack a clear definition.

I hate being at the mercy of someone else's decisions. The fear of losing Kane is gnawing at me, growing with each passing moment. Seeing Amanda here, so comfortable and confident, makes that fear seem more real than ever. What if Kane realizes he still cares for her? What if I'm just a temporary distraction in his life?

The thought of losing him to Amanda, of being pushed aside again, is almost unbearable.

Needing to escape the tension, I get Hailey and lead her out of the room. "Let's find those sparkles now," I say.

Walking down the hall to my room, I replay Amanda's words in my mind. "Aren't you temporary?" It's not what I want, but the truth is I am temporary.

Chapter Twenty-Nine

KANE

As soon as Timber walks away with Hailey, I set some boundaries with Amanda. Her expression is smug, and it grates on me.

"Since there's no other place to stay, you can stay here for now, but as soon as there's another option, you need to take it. This is not a permanent solution."

"But I always stay here," she counters, her voice laced with entitlement.

"That was before Timber. This isn't your home," I say firmly, my gaze hardening as I make it clear I won't tolerate her attempts to manipulate the situation.

I walk away, needing a moment to clear my head. I find Timber reading a book to Hailey and I tell her I'll be in the chicken coop. I head there, a place where life's only concerns are pecking and preening. I unlatch the door and step inside, greeted by the familiar clucking and fluttering of the chickens.

I run my hand through my hair. "How did it come to this?" Before, when Amanda showed up, it was just a thing. She was here and she was gone. It didn't matter to me, but this time it matters because it affects Timber.

The chickens scatter as I move toward the feeder, filling it with grain. The rhythmic action brings a semblance of calm, but my mind remains restless. What if Timber decides she can't wait any longer? The thought of losing her to the uncertainty I've imposed is unbearable.

"Alright, ladies," I say, leaning against the wooden frame, watching them scurry about. "I've got a serious question for you." They continue their pecking, oblivious to my human problems. "What do you do when your past decides to barge in uninvited, threatening everything you've started to build?" I chuckle, despite the bitterness of the situation. "Not much for advice, huh?"

I watch a hen chase a stray bug across the coop. "You've got it easy," I tell them. "No exes, no emotional turmoil—just bugs and feed." Their simple existence makes me envy them, if just for a moment.

Lost in my thoughts, I barely catch the soft sound of footsteps approaching until I turn to see Timber standing at the entrance.

"Hey," she calls out, stepping closer. "Hailey is watching TV with Amanda." She looks at the chickens. "Do they give good advice?"

"The best," I answer. "They recommend more pecking and less thinking."

As Timber comes closer, I break the news. "It's only for a week or so, and then she's out of here." I paint a clear end to the upheaval. "Honestly, she probably won't last that long." Amanda's impulsive nature and our strained history suggest she might cut her visit short once the novelty wears off and the reality of daily life sets in.

Timber looks at me with a mix of hope and skepticism. "You really think so?" she asks.

"Yeah, I do," I affirm, squeezing her shoulders gently. "Amanda's never been one for sticking things out, especially not when they get uncomfortable. And it's going to get uncomfortable if she keeps trying to stir things up."

Timber nods, her expression brightening as she considers my words. "Then we just need to hold on for a bit, weather the storm together." Her use of our earlier metaphor makes us laugh.

"Exactly," I say, with a renewed sense of partnership. "We've got this, as long as we stick together." The resolve in my voice isn't just for her reassurance—it strengthens my own determination to protect what we've built here, no matter the challenges.

"It's none of my business, but I have to ask." Her voice trembles, and she frowns deeply, avoiding my eyes. "Does she always sleep in your bed, with you?"

She twists her hands together, knuckles white, then lets them drop to her sides, her fingers curling and uncurling restlessly. "You don't have to answer. It's just ... she seems very comfortable here and I got the feeling that—"

"Nope," I cut in, shaking my head firmly. My chest tightens, and I force myself to keep my voice steady. "We don't sleep together. She tries, but that ship sailed the day she did."

I glance away, memories flashing briefly in my mind, a painful reminder. "It was never a love match," I continue, swallowing hard. "It was an oops that I tried to make right. She'll never be anything more to me than Hailey's mom."

Timber's shoulders relax, and a small sigh escapes her lips. She takes a hesitant step forward, searching my face for any sign of doubt.

"I'm sorry," she whispers, her voice barely audible. "I didn't mean to—" She stops, her words faltering as she reaches out, her fingers brushing against my arm. "Thank you for being honest with me."

Before I can respond, she steps closer, wrapping her arms around me in a gentle hug. The weight of our unspoken words melts away. She holds on for a moment longer, then pulls back slightly, looking up at me with a mixture of relief and something else—something hopeful.

"I just needed to know," she murmurs, her breath warm against my neck. "Because I care about you, Kane. More than you realize."

"You have nothing to worry about. I'm with you. I was never really with her."

"Really?" She lifts a brow and smirks. "Then how do you explain Hailey? The stork?"

"You know what I mean." I look at the house. "Maybe we should go back inside. Who knows what damage those two can do."

Timber and I leave the chicken coop more fortified against the chaos Amanda has brought into our home. As we step back inside, the atmosphere shifts. The house seems quiet. We walk toward the living room, unsure of what we'll find.

Peeking around the corner, I see Hailey sitting on Amanda's lap. A pang of unease twists my gut. Hailey's body is tense, her small shoulders stiff and her hands fidgeting. I want what's best for her, but is that really Amanda?

The moment Hailey spots Timber in the doorway, her face lights up with unmistakable joy. She wriggles off Amanda's lap without a second thought and rushes toward Timber, throwing her arms around her legs.

I watch Amanda's reaction. Her smile falters, a hint of frustration crosses her face before she masks it and picks up the remote control. "I missed you," Hailey says, her voice muffled against Timber's jeans. Timber bends down, lifting Hailey into a warm embrace.

"I missed you too, honey. Are you ready to help me make dinner?" Timber asks, smoothing back Hailey's hair.

Hailey nods enthusiastically. "Yes! Can we make spaghetti? I wanna help stir the sauce!"

"Actually, how about we mix it up tonight? Let's make some homemade pizza. You can help me knead the dough and choose the toppings."

Hailey gets excited at the suggestion. "Pizza! Can we put on pepperoni and lots of cheese?" she asks eagerly, her energy infectious.

"Of course, and maybe some veggies too? You can pick them out," Timber leads Hailey by the hand into the kitchen.

I follow them, watching as Timber lifts Hailey onto a stool by the kitchen counter. They start gathering ingredients, and the kitchen soon fills with the sounds of laughter and the pleasant aroma of cooking.

While Timber and Hailey immerse themselves in pizza-making, I keep an eye on Amanda, who remains in the living room, her presence somewhat distant from the warm activity in the kitchen. She sits on the couch, her fingers idly scrolling through the channels on the remote, her expression reflecting a mix of fatigue and disinterest.

I glance her way occasionally, noting the lack of connection. After a few moments, she seems to notice the aroma and makes her way over. She leans against the doorway, watching Timber and Hailey laughing and spreading sauce on the pizza dough.

Her eyes follow their movements, and I catch a brief glimmer of something—perhaps longing, perhaps regret—before her usual mask of indifference slips back into place.

"Is there going to be a vegan option?" She crosses her arms, surveying the array of toppings laid out on the counter.

I glance over from where I'm setting the table and

meet her gaze. "This isn't a restaurant. If you want something different, you'll have to make it yourself."

Timber smiles. "We've got extra dough. I'm happy to help you figure it out."

Timber steps up as Amanda surveys the toppings, clearly not thrilled with the choices.

I watch as Timber smooths things over, grabbing the extra dough. "Let's fix you up with something nice," she says, her tone light and friendly. "We've got plenty of veggies here, like bell peppers, olives, artichokes. Do any of those sound good?"

Amanda seems taken aback by Timber's kindness, but she nods. "Yeah, that sounds fine. Thanks," she replies, and steps up to the counter. They start putting together a pizza, Timber showing Amanda where everything is.

Hailey joins in, giggling as she places olives on the dough. "We're making a smiley face!" she declares. The kitchen lightens up a bit with their laughter.

I lean back, watching them work. Timber's got a way of making things smooth. She turned what could have been a standoff into something normal—just making dinner. She's transformed this place into a true home, not just a house.

As we all sit down to eat, the mood is way better than I expected. Amanda even cracks a few jokes. Watching Timber, I'm struck by how naturally she brings everyone together. Makes me grateful, not just for the peace she brings, but for her. Everything is right when she's around.

Suddenly, in the midst of her excitement, Hailey, with a slice of pizza in one hand, declares loudly, "I have two mommies!" Her innocent comment, meant to express her joy at having two important women in her life together, hangs in the air.

The room goes quiet. Amanda's face freezes, the smile fading as she processes Hailey's words. There's a palpable shift in her demeanor. What was meant as a sweet observation from Hailey cuts deep.

"She is not your mother. I am. She's ... I don't know what she is." Amanda pushes back from the table, her chair scraping loudly against the floor. She stands, her expression clouded with a mix of hurt and anger. She turns and rushes out of the room, heading toward my bedroom. The sound of the door slamming echoes through the house.

The sudden departure leaves me stunned. Hailey looks confused and ready to cry, not fully understanding the impact of her words. Timber quickly tries to console her, while I'm left trying to figure out how to handle the situation.

"How about we go for a walk? We can pick some wildflowers for your mommy." Timber shoots me a look, her eyes conveying a mix of concern and a need for action.

I nod, pushing back my chair to head for my bedroom. As I leave the kitchen, I'm torn. Hailey meant no harm with her simple declaration.

I pause in front of my door, my hand raised to knock. A moment of irritation flashes through me. *This is my house, my door. Why should I have to knock?* But the sound of muffled sobs from the other side reminds me of the delicate situation at hand.

I fear what Amanda might do next. Will she lash out further? Say something to Hailey that she can't take back? My mind races as I stand there, torn between anger and empathy, hoping I can diffuse the situation without making things worse.

Taking a breath, I tap lightly on the door. "Amanda?" I call.

The crying stops momentarily, then resumes, softer now. I take that as an invitation, pushing the door open to find Amanda curled up on the bed, her face buried in my pillow. She's shaking with sobs, her body racked with the weight of her emotions.

I step inside, closing the door quietly behind me. Approaching the bed, I sit down cautiously at the edge, giving her space yet offering my presence as comfort.

"She hates me," Amanda gasps out between sobs. "My own daughter hates me."

I shake my head, feeling a mix of annoyance and sympathy. Amanda often reacts like this, and it always frustrates me. Her dramatic, emotional outbursts seem to demand a response I'm never quite sure how to give.

"Hailey doesn't hate you. She doesn't know you," I say, trying to keep my voice calm and steady. "You can't expect a few phone calls and random visits to fill the gap of several years. She's spent more time with Timber these last few weeks than she has with you her entire life."

Amanda turns, her eyes red and swollen. "So, what am I supposed to do?"

Inside, there is a familiar pang of helplessness. I know she wants me to offer a solution, to tell her what to do, but I don't have all the answers.

"We start by taking it slow," I suggest, trying to be as supportive as possible while suppressing my own unhappiness. "Spend more time with her. Be there consistently. Show her that you care. You can't walk in here and expect it to be all rainbows and butterflies. It's going to take time. She doesn't trust you."

"She doesn't or you don't?" Amanda shoots back, her voice sharp.

Her question cuts deeper than I want to admit. I've never said a bad word about her in front of Hailey, always hoping she'd shape her own opinions. But Amanda's erratic presence has always left scars. "I guess we both don't. You always have an angle, Amanda. Do you truly want to get to know Hailey, or are you just killing time between assignments?"

She shakes her head, her expression turning weary. "I'm getting too old to flit between continents. It's time I settled down. But it looks like I'm too late."

Her words hang heavy in the air, and a surge of bitterness wells up inside me. "Do you know how many times she's asked why you're not around? You've missed most of her life events like birthdays and Christmases. It's not just about being late, Amanda. It's about the damage already done."

Amanda wipes her face, the anger giving way to

despair. "I just ... I thought it would be easier. That she'd be happy to see me."

"She was happy to see you," I admit. "But building a relationship, especially with a kid, takes more than just showing up with presents. It takes time, effort, consistency. It's not too late, but it won't be easy."

"What about Timber? Who is she to you?" Amanda's voice is almost a whisper, but it carries a weight that makes me pause.

I think about it for a minute, the answer clear as day. "She's everything." My voice cracks slightly, the emotion too strong to hide.

Amanda's eyes flash with something I can't quite read—regret, jealousy, maybe both. Then she drops the bombshell. "I'm planning to stay, Kane. I want to be here for Hailey. For us."

A mix of shock and anger surges through me. "There is no us, Amanda. There never was. I tried to do the right thing once, and you left. You don't get to mess up your life and then come back and screw up mine. You think you can just waltz back to town, and everything will be fine? After all this time? You think there's still a chance for us?"

Her eyes well up again, and I can see she's struggling to hold it together. "I know I've made mistakes. But I want to make things right. I want to be part of Hailey's life. And ... maybe yours too."

I stand up abruptly. "Amanda, you can't just decide this now. It's not fair to Hailey, and it's not fair to Timber. Or me." I glance back at her, my emotions a turbulent mix of anger, regret, and confusion. "Get your shit together."

As I leave the room, the weight of Amanda's presence presses down on me, making it impossible to focus on anything else. The conversation with Timber will have to wait. Right now, I need to navigate the storm Amanda has brought into our lives.

Chapter Thirty
TIMBER

I LIE awake with Kane next to me. His breaths are even, and deep, and comforting. Tonight, he came to me, desperate, loving me as though he might lose me tomorrow. Yet, when morning broke, words of love or invitations to stay remained unsaid. He comforts and confounds me.

I understand Kane's struggle to open up. The wounds of his past are not easily healed, and his protective instincts are heightened now with Amanda in the house. Perhaps it's on me to make the first move, to voice the deeper emotions and commitments we've shied away from. Do my own fears keep me quiet?

Amanda had slept in Kane's room alone, a constant, uncomfortable reminder of their shared past. The thought of her presence just a few rooms away had created a sense of urgency, a desperate need to affirm our connection despite the shadow of his ex.

Facing Amanda the next morning is awkward. She

steps into the kitchen, fully dressed but wearing one of Kane's old shirts, making the scene even more surreal. She looks tired, her eyes red-rimmed, yet there's a determination in her stance as if she's gearing up for a battle.

Kane and I prepare to leave for the day, him to the docks and me to the community center. Getting ready brings a comforting routine. As I help Hailey gather her small backpack, filled with snacks and her favorite coloring books, Amanda says, "I'm going to keep Hailey home today." Hailey pauses and looks up at her, then over at me.

The words hit like a sharp stab to my heart. My eyes shift to Kane, searching for support or perhaps a challenge to Amanda's plan, but he only nods. "Okay," he says, his voice neutral.

The response leaves me stunned. As we step outside, leaving Amanda and Hailey behind, Kane asks, "Is it wrong to leave them together? I mean, I don't know what to do."

I nod, experiencing the same conflicting emotions. But Amanda is Hailey's mom, and if she's truly trying to establish a relationship, they need time. "I think it will be good for both of them." Despite my words, my insides coil. I'm not sure if it's jealousy, fear, uncertainty, or simply a fierce protectiveness over Hailey. I worry about the disruption Amanda could cause and the potential pain for Hailey if things don't work out. Yet, I understand the importance of Hailey knowing her mother.

Kane looks at me, his eyes searching for reassurance. "I just don't want Hailey to get hurt."

"I know," I say, squeezing his hand. "But Hailey deserves the chance to know her mom. We'll be here for her, no matter what happens."

The rest of the trip is met with silence until we get to town. Kane kisses me. "See you around four," he says.

"Be safe out there."

As we walk our separate ways, a sense of isolation wraps around me. The logical part of me understands and even champions Amanda's need to reconnect with her daughter, knowing it's healthy and right for Hailey. Yet, emotionally, it's as if I'm watching a small part of my world shift out of reach, a space where I once stood now being reshaped without me.

Inside, it hurts—more than I expected. Hailey's bright laughter, her endless questions, and the way she'd hold my hand—a sudden absence of these small joys creates a hollow space in my day. It's a personal loss, quiet and deep, and I find myself grappling with the realization that my role in Hailey's life has boundaries I hadn't felt so acutely before.

I focus on the tasks ahead, telling myself that adapting to this new dynamic is part of loving and caring for Hailey—it's about what she needs more than what I feel. I throw myself into the morning for Lucas and Tommy.

Around noon, the door swings open and Amanda steps in, her face etched with aggravation. Her shoulders are tensed, and there's a slight quiver in her voice as she speaks. "She's been crying and complaining all morning," she says, almost thrusting Hailey toward me.

For a moment, a surge of worry and confusion grips me. Did something happen? Is Hailey okay? But as Hailey steps forward, I see Hailey's eyes are red from crying. The moment she sees me, her face lights up, and she rushes into my embrace, a clear refuge from her distress.

This immediate reaction—Hailey clinging to me—fills me with a mix of emotions. Relief that she finds comfort in me, annoyance at Amanda for causing this situation, and a deeper worry about the fragile bond between them. Hailey's instant relief at seeing me, while soothing, also confirms the emotional distance between her and Amanda. It shows that their connection isn't just frayed—it's barely there.

As I hold Hailey, I try to push aside my frustration and focus on comforting her. Amanda stands awkwardly at the door, her irritation turning into a resigned weariness. The difficult reality of the situation settles over us—Hailey prefers me, and that preference is driving an even bigger wedge between her and Amanda.

"Amanda, maybe it's best if Hailey stays with me for the rest of the day," I suggest gently, not wanting to escalate the tension. Amanda nods, her shoulders slumping as she steps back.

"Fine," she says, her voice filled with resignation. "I just ... I wanted to try."

I nod, understanding but still bearing the weight of the complicated dynamics. "We'll figure this out," I say, more for Hailey's sake than Amanda's.

As Amanda leaves, Hailey stays nestled in my arms,

and a pang of sadness for the strained mother-daughter relationship fills me.

That evening, the tension lingers in the air. Amanda avoids making eye contact with me, and I can sense the unspoken words hovering between us. Hailey seems more at ease, playing with her toys in the living room, but the atmosphere is anything but relaxed.

After dinner, I find a quiet moment with Kane in the kitchen. He leans against the counter, his expression weary but determined.

"We need to talk about Hailey," I say, keeping my voice low.

He nods, his concern evident. "Yeah, today was rough."

I take a deep breath. "I'm worried about her. She was so upset today."

Kane sighs. "I think we should just let it play out for the rest of the week. Anything new is going to be hard on her, but she will adjust."

I bite my lip, unsure. A part of me agrees—we do need to give Hailey time to adapt. But another part of me is anxious, worried that letting things play out might just make everything worse. I am torn between supporting Kane's plan and my instinct to step in and protect Hailey from any more distress.

The next day unfolds similarly, and by the third day, it's clear that Amanda is struggling. She starts each day eager to try again, but her determination seems to wane as the hours pass. Hailey, on the other hand, is visibly upset every morning when we leave her with Amanda.

She clings to me, her eyes pleading, and it takes all my strength to gently pry her off and encourage her to stay.

This time, though, after dropping Hailey off, Amanda pulls me aside. Her eyes are weary, her voice strained. "Timber, can't you see? Your presence—it's making it impossible for me to connect with my daughter. If you care about Hailey, you'd see that she can't get to know me with you always around."

Her words hit hard, a mix of guilt and resistance spinning inside me. I look over at Hailey, who's hanging her coat and joining the boys at the art table, her earlier distress already fading. Amanda's right in a way—I am a barrier, however unintentional, between her and Hailey. In that moment, filled with conflicting emotions, I realize the gravity of our situation. This isn't just about coexisting or adjusting—it's about making real, painful decisions that affect a little girl who doesn't understand why the adults in her life can't be happy.

I need to talk to Kane. As I nod to Amanda, my phone rings. It's the school district I transferred to. I step away and take the call.

"Hello, this is Timber."

"Hi, Timber, this is Mr. Bromley from the school district. We've had a development and were wondering if you might be able to start a week early," he says, his voice carrying a mix of hope and urgency.

I pause, filled with a rush of conflicting emotions. A part of me wants to cling to every extra moment here, to resolve the situation with Hailey and Amanda, to find a way to solidify the fragile peace we've been building. But another part, the part that came here searching for growth and new beginnings, knows this call might be my cue to leave. And then there's Kane. The thought of saying goodbye him tugs at my heart. How will my departure affect him, and what will it mean for us?

"Mr. Bromley, I need to arrange a few things, but I'll be there," I reply, my voice steady, a decision made in the heartbeats between his question and my answer.

As I hang up, a sense of resolve settles over me. This isn't just about leaving a place. It's about embracing the next chapter. Maybe, coming here was never about finding someone else—it was about finding myself. And in finding myself, I've also discovered the strength to make tough choices, not just for my own good but for others, too.

Turning back to the room, I find Amanda watching me closely, her expression unreadable. The kids are busy with their activities, oblivious to what's going on.

"It looks like I'll be starting my new job a week early," I say to Amanda, my voice calm despite the storm of emotions inside. "So, I'll be out of your way soon."

Amanda's expression changes. Am I seeing relief or regret in her eyes? "Thank you," she replies, her tone more subdued than before. "Maybe it will help to have some space to figure things out with Hailey."

The acknowledgment that my departure might ease her path to a relationship with her daughter is bittersweet. It confirms the painful reality that my presence has become an obstacle rather than a support system. It also reassures me that stepping back is the right choice, not just for me, but for everyone.

The weight of my decision settles in my heart. I glance at Hailey, who is happily drawing at the table, and a pang of sorrow grips me. The thought of leaving her—leaving what we've forged—is almost unbearable. I know, deep down, that I'll never truly get over her. She has woven herself into the very fabric of my being in ways I hadn't anticipated.

As for Kane, he has irrevocably captured my heart. It belongs to him now, and I could never dream of reclaiming it. How will I ever manage to live without him, without the heart he holds?

Chapter Thirty-One
KANE

Timber takes my hand and leads me out for a walk, leaving Hailey with Amanda back at the house. We don't talk much as we walk down the familiar path that leads to the pond. It's quiet, except for the sound of the birds and the breeze rustling through the pines. The longest days of summer have passed, taking with them the endless hours of daylight.

I've been grappling with Amanda being back, trying to support her attempt to reconnect with Hailey while managing the strain it's putting on everyone else. With Timber's departure date getting closer, I've been thinking about how to ask her to stay, hoping we could talk tonight and finally clear the air.

Timber stops by the creek that feeds the pond and faces me. There's a serious look in her eyes that tells me something's up before she even speaks.

"Kane, I've been called to start my job early," she says. "I'm leaving next week."

The words knock the wind out of me. Panic surges through me, gripping my chest with a vise-like pressure. "What do you mean, you're leaving? I thought you'd stay."

"You never asked," she replies, her voice soft.

Desperation claws at me, making it hard to breathe. "I'm asking now. Stay."

She shakes her head. The decision is already made. "Everything's set up. I talked to Eliza, and she's coming back early to teach. My job is waiting. I need to go."

I scrub my palm over my face, my mind reeling. "This is because of Amanda, isn't it?" My voice is sharper than I intend.

"Yes, but not like you think." She kicks at a stone under her foot. "If I stay, Amanda won't ever get to really know Hailey. Do you remember when you and I talked about how much we'd give to have more time with our moms? Amanda is here, and she's trying. I can't get in the way of that. I don't want to be the reason Amanda isn't close to Hailey."

I shake my head vehemently. "*She's* the reason she doesn't have a relationship. It's because she leaves." Anguish wells up inside me, choking my words. How can Timber not see that Amanda will just leave again, hurting Hailey all over?

She cups my face with her palm, her touch both soothing and tormenting. "I know, but she's here now. You once told me you wouldn't take her back for you, but you'd give her another chance for Hailey. So, this is for Hailey."

"But Hailey loves you," I say, my voice breaking. The thought of Hailey losing Timber is unbearable, knowing it will hurt her as much as it's hurting me.

"I love her too, Kane. I'm not saying goodbye forever. I'm saying goodbye for now. I'll be back," she says, her eyes shimmering with tears. "I love you," she adds.

Her words pierce through my heart, bringing both comfort and pain. I want to believe her, to trust that she'll come back, but everyone goes. They always leave. How can she do this to me, to Hailey? How can she think getting out of the way is the solution when Amanda is just going to leave again?

I pull her close, holding her tight as if I can keep her from slipping away. "I just..." My voice trails off, overwhelmed by the turmoil inside me. All the women in my life except Eliza leave, one way or another, and it seems Timber is no different. But this time, it's supposed to be for the right reasons. That thought doesn't comfort me —it just hollows out the ache even more. "What about us?" I know I should be the bigger person here, but all I feel is abandoned, even if it's her love for Hailey that's pushing her away. How do you hold on to someone who believes letting go is for the best?

I think about my daughter, and how she'll react to Timber leaving. The confusion and hurt she'll experience The thought makes my stomach ache.

"How am I supposed to do this without you?" I whisper, my voice raw with emotion. "How is Hailey supposed to?"

Timber's tears spill over as she holds me. "You're stronger than you think, Kane. And Hailey will be okay because she has you. She needs you."

The weight of her words settles heavily on my heart. I know she believes this is the right thing, but the fear of losing her and the uncertainty of the future make it almost impossible to accept. Yet, deep down, I know I have to let her go. For now.

She holds my hands and looks into my eyes. "I need you to hear me. It's important for you to know some things. I came here looking for a place where I could belong, and I found it. I found it with you and Hailey," she says.

Her raw honesty hits me hard. "Then why is it so easy for you to leave?" I ask.

"It's not easy," she answers. "Leaving is the hardest decision I've ever had to make. But it's not about what's easy. It's about what's right—for Hailey, for Amanda, and even for us."

I shake my head, struggling to reconcile her intentions with the pain of her departure. "How can it be right for us if you're not here?"

"Because sometimes love means doing what's best for the other person, even if it tears you apart," she says. "And right now, Hailey needs to know her mother, to have the opportunity to create something. We've both felt the void of not having ours. We know what it's like to miss that piece of our hearts."

I look away, the tree line blurred by the mist in my

eyes. "And what about my heart?" I ask. "Who fills that void when you're gone?"

She squeezes my hands, pulling me back to meet her gaze. "This isn't forever, Kane. I'm not closing the door on us. I'm asking you to hold on to the hope that there's more to our story than just this goodbye."

The idea of hope seems distant. Yet, as I stare into her eyes, filled with genuine love and pain, I find myself clinging to it. "And if it's too hard? If the distance is too much?" I whisper.

"Then you decide. You give up or you fight for us." She leans into me. "We'll find a way because that's what you do when you love someone—you fight. And I do love you, Kane. I'm not walking away from that."

Her words, so fierce and certain, give me strength. I pull her into an embrace, my broken expectations shifting into something new and hopeful. Maybe this isn't the end but a step toward a new beginning. As we hold each other, I let myself believe, just for a moment, that this goodbye might one day lead to a joyful reunion.

"I love you too, Timber. So much."

She smiles through her tears, and I see the resolve in her eyes. "This space ... it's not to divide us. It's to prove if what we have is made of the tough stuff that lasts."

I nod, understanding now what she's saying, even if it doesn't make the goodbye any easier. "We'll fight for it," I say, my voice steady. "We'll fight for us."

We turn and walk back to the house, the silence between us now filled with a new understanding. The path seems shorter on the way back, each step a mix of bittersweet acceptance and a fragile hope for the future. I hold her hand tightly, not wanting to let go, even for a second.

Back at the house, we find Amanda and Hailey engaged in a game, the sight of them together offering a small reassurance that this painful decision might just be the right one. Timber squeezes my hand before letting go and joining them, her smile genuine despite the turmoil I know she carries inside.

That night, as the house settles into quiet, Timber and I find ourselves alone in her room. As I look at her, the need to make this moment unforgettable swells within me. I want her to carry this night with her, a solid reminder of what we have, what we're fighting for.

I pull her close, my hands brushing her skin with deliberate care, as if I'm trying to imprint my touch, my love, into her being. We make love slowly, passionately, each movement filled with a desperate intensity. It's as if I'm imprinting my very being onto her, ensuring that she'll never forget me, never forget us.

Every kiss, every caress, is a vow. Her fingers dig into my back, conveying the same urgency, the same need to hold on to this moment, to hold on to us.

Our bodies move together in a rhythm that's both familiar and frantic.

When it's over, we lie tangled in each other's arms, our breaths mingling in the darkness. I hold her tightly. She rests her head on my chest, her fingers tracing lazy patterns over my skin. Her tears seep into my heart.

"I'll come back," she says. "No matter what, Kane. I'll come back to you."

I press a kiss to her forehead, emotions heavy and full. "I'll be here. I'll be waiting."

We fall asleep like that, holding each other as if the sheer force of our hug could keep the world at bay. And for that night, it does.

Chapter Thirty-Two

TIMBER

A WEEK LATER, my departure day arrives. The dock bustles with townsfolk who have come to see me off. Hailey clings to me, her small frame trembling with sobs, her grip so tight it seems like she's trying to fuse us together.

"I'll be back," I say, my voice cracking.

Hailey looks up, her tear-streaked face twisted in anguish. "You're just like my mommy," she cries, her voice breaking into a desperate wail. "You're leaving me too!"

Her words cut through me like a knife. I try to soothe her, but her sobs only grow louder, her small body shaking with each heartbreaking cry.

I reach into my bag and take out Cubby the Bear. I've never left it behind. Where I go, it goes—until today. It was one of the first things I grabbed when the cabin caught fire. Handing it to Hailey, I say, "This is a very special bear. Hold on to it until I come back."

Her eyes widen as she clutches it. "Do you promise to come back?" she asks, her voice filled with desperate hope.

"I do," I whisper, trying to hold back my tears. "I love you."

Those words only add fuel to the fire, and her cries grow louder as she tightly holds the bear to her heart.

Guilt washes over me. Leaving Hailey feels like abandoning her, but I know it's a necessity. It hurts me as much as it hurts her, but we all need time. You can't jump into forever headfirst. That stupid saying about setting something free and it coming back if it's yours echoes in my mind. As I walk away, I feel the weight of every step.

May moves forward, her frail arms pulling me into a tight hug. "I just got you, and now I have to give you up," she whispers. "Are you sure about this?"

Tears stream down my face as I hold my grandmother. "No, but I have commitments," I say. "You should come to Arizona and visit me."

May shakes her head, her eyes filled with a lifetime of wisdom. "My place is here, child."

Next is Eliza, who hugs me fiercely and whispers in my ear, "You know he loves you. Don't be an idiot."

I nod, tears blurring my vision. I turn to the rest of the family and friends, each goodbye making the weight in my chest heavier.

Lucas and Tommy hug me, their faces solemn. "Thank you, Miss Moore," they say in unison.

Kane steps forward, his eyes red and puffy. He pulls

me into a tight embrace, his voice a choked whisper. "I'll wait for you. Please come back."

The intensity of his hug, the desperate need in his voice, makes my chest tighten with emotion. The strength of his arms around me etches this moment into my memory. I pull back slightly, just enough to look into his eyes, then lean in for a kiss. It's not a simple goodbye kiss, but one filled with all the love and longing that words can't convey. It's as if we're trying to store up enough of each other to last until we're together again.

When we finally break apart, my lips tingle with the memory of his touch. "I love you," I whisper, my voice barely holding together. "I'll be back for school breaks, holidays. As often as I can."

His eyes search mine, as if trying to etch this moment into his soul. "I love you. Always."

I nod, unable to speak, my emotions too overwhelming. As I step onto the floatplane, I glance back one last time. Hailey chases me to the edge of the plane, still crying. She hands me her quartz rock. "It's my favorite. Hold on to it for me," she says.

I take the rock, feeling an ache deep within. Kane stands there, his shoulders heavy with the weight of this goodbye.

As the plane takes off, I clutch the rock and stare out the window, feeling my chest splinter with each moment that takes me farther from them.

Hailey's cries still echo in my ears, and the realization of what I'm leaving behind hits me like a tidal wave. I wonder if I've made the biggest mistake of my life.

Tears stream down my face while my mind replays the painful goodbye. Did I make the right choice? What if Amanda leaves again and Hailey gets hurt by both of us? What if Kane can't forgive me for the choices I made? What if I can't forgive myself?

I close my eyes, trying to calm the storm of doubts raging inside me. I think of the promise I made to Kane, to Hailey. I think of coming back for school breaks, holidays, and whenever I can. I have to believe this is just a temporary separation, a painful step toward a better future.

The plane rises higher, and the town below becomes smaller. I close my eyes, praying that one day, the pain of this goodbye will be replaced by the joy of a new hello. Until then, I have to hold onto the hope that love will be enough to bring me back to them.

My return to Arizona is stark and unforgiving. The sun beats down relentlessly, turning the air into a suffocating blanket of heat. Sweat trickles down my back as I sit in my mother's old house, the broken air conditioner doing nothing to alleviate the oppressive temperature. The house needs a lot of repairs—peeling paint, creaky floors, and plumbing that's seen better days—but it's all I have right now.

I glance at the clock. The seconds tick by slowly, each one a reminder of how far I am from Alaska, from Kane and Hailey.

My new job as a testing coordinator is a far cry from what I imagined. Instead of the vibrant, chaotic energy of a classroom filled with children, I'm stuck in a sterile office, surrounded by stacks of paperwork and spreadsheets. The daily grind of administering and coordinating standardized tests is empty of the joy that teaching once brought me. I miss the laughter, the curiosity, the moments of connection that made every day worthwhile. I don't miss the gross things like boogers and farts, but I'd take them just to hear a student giggle or stand tall because they are proud of their accomplishments.

I miss Hailey's bright eyes and endless questions. I miss Kane's steady presence, his touch, his love. The distance between us seems like an unbridgeable abyss, each day apart stretching it further.

Every evening, we have Zoom calls. Seeing their faces on the screen is a bittersweet comfort. Hailey's giggles and Kane's reassuring voice bring some solace, but it's not the same. The screen creates a barrier that their voices and images can't fully penetrate. I hate to admit it, but the calls aren't enough. They can't replace Hailey's small arms around my neck or the strength of Kane's embrace.

The nights are the hardest—the quiet moments when my thoughts drift back to Kane and the evenings we spent together, his touch lingering on my skin like a ghost. I lie in bed, staring at the ceiling, thinking about when I'll be able to visit. Until then, I hold onto the hope that love will be enough to bridge the distance.

For now, I distract myself by tackling the endless list of repairs the house needs. I paint, fix the creaky floors, and attempt to wrangle the ancient plumbing into working order. But the effort is hollow. Each day is a struggle, each moment a reminder of what I left behind. The decision to come here, to give Amanda and Hailey space to build their relationship, seems more like a sacrifice than ever.

One evening, as the heat of the day begins to fade, I sit by my open window, hoping for a breeze. I close my eyes, imagining the cool, salty air, the sound of the waves, the feel of Kane's arms around me. A tear slips down my cheek, quickly followed by another, and before I know it, I'm sobbing uncontrollably. I question everything I've done—every decision I made, but I believe in fate, in the universe guiding us to where we need to be. The call to come back early was another sign, a nudge telling me it was time to go. If I'm meant to return, the universe will show me the way.

The phone rings, startling me out of my daydream. I scramble to answer it, excitement leaping within me at the possibility of hearing his voice.

"Hello?"

"Timber?" Kane's voice soothes my aching heart.

"Kane," I whisper, my throat tight with emotion. "I miss you so much."

"I miss you too," he replies. "How's Arizona?"

"It's about six degrees cooler than Hades," I say, trying to keep my voice light.

"Been there, have you?"

"I'm living it daily. Every day without you is hell. My heart aches for you."

"Only your heart?"

My face heats, and I know he's brought a blush to my cheeks. "No. I miss every inch of you."

"Now you're torturing me."

We could spend hours reminding each other about what was shared in that bed in his house, but it only makes us miss each other more. The distance between us seems sharper with every word, every memory.

"I think about you every night," I admit, my voice filled with longing. "I imagine you are here with me, and it helps, but it's not the same."

"I know," Kane says. "I do the same."

"How's Hailey?"

"She's doing okay but asks when you're coming home all the time."

I don't want to ask about her mother, but I do. "And Amanda?"

"She's got the attention span of a stone and the patience of a yellow jacket. I think she'd be gone if she didn't meet a logger at the bar. She's living in one of Finn's cabins and hardly visits. You should come back. We need you."

A fresh wave of tears threatens to spill over, but I blink them back. "Let's give it some time. We'll know when the time is right."

Kane lets out a growl. It's the kind I'd expect from Old Grizzletoe. "Stop waiting for a sign and start deciding. You either want us or you don't."

"I want you both."

"Then come back." There was no small talk tonight.

No sharing about our day, just a quick I love you and a hang-up.

I sit staring at the blank screen. What makes me hesitate to go back? My motivation for staying in Arizona is clear. I have a stable job and responsibilities to rebuild my mother's house. But deeper than that is a fear—if I go back now, I won't have a job. What would I do if I gave up everything for him and it didn't work out?

My past haunts me, too. I'm terrified of history repeating itself. What if I uproot my life and it ends in heartbreak? What if everything falls apart, and I've sacrificed everything for nothing?

During times like these, I really miss my mother. Then I realize I've got the second-best thing ... my grandmother. I dial her number and as soon as she answers, I sob.

"Timber, what's wrong, honey?"

"I miss them so much, May. It's so hard being here."

"Oh, sweetheart, I'm sorry. Why are you staying there when your family is in Alaska?"

I take a deep breath, trying to gather my thoughts. "This house ... it's all I have left of Mom. I can't just leave it. And my job here ... I'm waiting for the right moment to come back."

"Or are you waiting for a sign?"

Her words hit home. "Maybe. I guess I'm afraid of making the wrong decision. What if I go back and things fall apart?"

May sighs. "Your mother was the same way, always looking for signs, always waiting for the perfect moment.

But life doesn't work like that. Sometimes, you have to make your own signs. You have to take risks."

"But what if it's the wrong choice?"

"Staying in a place that makes you miserable, waiting for some cosmic intervention. Is that the right choice? Honey, that's just a house. Your mom isn't in it. And the job, it's just a job," she says. "Your soul is telling you what you want. Sometimes, the universe doesn't give you a sign because it wants you to take control, to make your own destiny."

I sit with her words for a moment, letting them sink in. "You're right. I'm scared."

"Don't give up everything out of fear, Timber. Your mother did the same thing."

"And she died alone and lonely," I say, the truth of it settling heavily in the silence that follows.

"Exactly," May says. "Don't let that be your story, too. You've got a chance to build a life with people who love you. Don't waste it waiting for a moment that might never come."

After we hang up, I sit in the quiet house, her words echoing in my mind. I think about my mother's decisions, how she was always waiting for the right sign, and how that led her to a life of unfulfilled dreams and loneliness. I look around at the house, the peeling paint and creaky floors, the physical remnants of her unfinished plans.

My life in Arizona is like a half-existence. The job brings no joy. The empty house holds more ghosts than comfort. I have a chance to build a different life, a life with Kane and Hailey, a life filled with love and purpose. But that means taking a risk, stepping into the unknown without waiting for a sign.

I think about Amanda and the time she's had to build a relationship with Hailey. I gave them space, but enough is enough. If it's not working now, it never will. Hailey needs me, and so does Kane.

I have an opportunity to write a different story, to choose love and connection over fear and solitude. The decision isn't easy, but May's wisdom lingers, guiding me. Slowly, I begin to see that the time to act is now, not when some elusive perfect moment arrives.

Chapter Thirty-Three

KANE

THE PAST FEW days have been a blur. I've let Timber's calls go to voicemail, listening to her messages that never say she's coming back, only that she misses me. I meant it when I said she needed to make up her mind, but the uncertainty is like a heavy burden pressing down on me. I'm miserable without her. Her absence haunts every corner of the house, every quiet moment. Hailey keeps asking about her, and each time I tell her we'll talk to Timber soon, it feels like a lie. I'm just waiting for Amanda to leave so I can pick up the pieces of that as well. I can't force Timber to come back, and I wouldn't want to. She needs to choose this life, choose us, on her own. But the waiting is tearing me apart.

Amanda visits late one night after a date, her eyes brighter than I've seen in weeks. She looks at me and points to the couch. "Take a seat, Kane. I've got something to tell you."

I sigh, bracing myself for the inevitable. She's leaving. It's been written all over her face for days now. "When will you go?"

"I truly came back hoping to make a go of it, Kane," she says in an uncharacteristically soft voice. "But I squandered too much time chasing my dreams. Honestly, I'm not cut out to be a mother. I don't like babies. I don't like toddlers. Kids from four to twenty are tolerable, but still not my favorite."

As her words sink in, a swirl of emotions overtakes me. Relief floods my chest, knowing the chaos she's brought into our lives will finally end. But there's a sharp edge of bitterness too—she showed up just long enough to destroy everything I'd built with Timber. I can't shake the fear that she'll return again someday, bringing more upheaval.

But for now, I focus on the immediate reprieve. At least now, we can start to move forward again, pick up the pieces, and rebuild what was lost. The path ahead won't be easy, but it's a path we can finally begin to walk.

"You came back because you said Hailey needed a mother—her mother," I argue, my anger bubbling to the surface.

Amanda shakes her head. "Not a mother like me. I'm selfish and shallow. She's got a mother—her name is Timber, and she's perfect. And if you don't do everything it takes to get her back, then you're a knucklehead."

"You're the reason she left."

"I know, and I'm sorry about that, but this was good.

With her here making it easy, I might have muddled through motherhood for a few more months, but that wouldn't have been fair to Timber or Hailey. She left so I could sink or swim. I sank like a boat full of holes. I mean, how many times can Hailey watch that show *Frigid*?"

"It's *Frozen*, and it's endless, but I'm not sure that's why Timber left."

"It doesn't matter. What matters is that you get her back. You two are perfect for each other."

I blink, taken aback by her blunt honesty. Amanda, the one who messed everything up, is now telling me to go after Timber. A mix of anger and hope churns inside me.

"It's not that easy. Timber believes in signs," I mutter, more to myself than to Amanda.

"Then send her one," Amanda says. "Maybe I can stop by from time to time and be the aunt who gave birth to Hailey or some shit like that, but I'll never step into the mother role."

I stare at her, the bitterness I've been carrying suddenly shifting. Her words, unexpected and raw, resonate with a truth I can't ignore. Despite everything, she's right. Timber is perfect for Hailey, and she's perfect for me. And if Amanda, of all people, can see that, then maybe it's time to act.

"Send her a sign," Amanda repeats, softer this time, and for the first time in weeks, I experience a spark of hope.

She kisses my cheek and heads for the door. There's guilt and sadness, but also a strange sense of relief. "What about Hailey?" I call after her.

Amanda laughs lightly. "I told her that I was leaving for good earlier today, and she waved and told me goodbye. She's a smart little girl. She knows who her real mother is."

With that, Amanda walks out, leaving a silence that seems almost peaceful in its finality. I sit there for a moment, letting her words sink in. Timber is Hailey's mother in every way that counts. And if I don't do something, I might lose her.

I look around the quiet house. The emptiness left by Timber's absence presses down on me. Amanda is right. I need to send Timber a sign, something undeniable, something that shows her she's meant to be here with us.

An idea starts to form, and for the first time in days, a spark of hope ignites. I need to act, to make my intentions clear. I need to bring Timber back home where she belongs. And I'll do whatever it takes to make that happen. It's time to stop waiting for the universe and start creating our own signs. Timber needs to know she's missed, needed, and loved. And I'll make sure she gets that message loud and clear.

I wake up early and hurry to get Hailey to class. There's so much to do and so little time. I rush in fifteen minutes early with a grin on my face.

My sister walks over and touches my forehead. "Are you sick?"

"No, I'm motivated." I lean in and whisper because I don't want to wake Cody, who's sleeping in a bassinet nearby, and I refuse to get Hailey's hopes up if my plan doesn't work. "Timber is coming back."

"Really?" my sister squeals, but I shush her. "She doesn't know it yet."

Eliza gives me a confused look, but I can see the excitement in her eyes. "What do you mean she doesn't know?"

"I have a plan to bring her back, but I need a couple of days."

She frowns, clearly puzzled. "Kane, just tell me when she gets here. I've been talking to Matt, and I think we can make it just fine without me working. It would be great if Timber could come back and take over. They say a woman can have it all—a job and a family—but I don't want it all. I'm too damn exhausted to enjoy any of it."

Her honesty hits me hard. I knew Eliza was struggling but hearing her say it out loud brings a new urgency to my plan. "Are you sure?"

"Yes, I'm sure. I love my job, but I love my family more. And right now, I need to focus on Cody."

I nod, a swell of gratitude rising within me. "In two days, I need you to post the job again."

She nods, still looking a bit confused. "Okay, I'll do it. But you better make sure Timber comes back. We all need her."

"I will," I say. "I'm not letting her go this time."

"Alright, let's do this," she says.

With my sister on board, I am more confident than ever. It's time to set my plan in motion and send Timber the sign she's been waiting for.

Chapter Thirty-Four

TIMBER

Today is officially the worst day of my life.

The district I work for assigned me an additional role overnight, doubling my workload without any increase in pay. My responsibilities now include absorbing the tasks of a reassigned diagnostician, leaving me buried under paperwork and overwhelmed by the demands. Quitting on the spot isn't an option. I'm under contract, and breaking it means I'd be barred from working in the state for at least a year. Who knows what other consequences would come of it. The thought of losing my job security is terrifying, but so is the idea of staying in this untenable situation.

As I sit at my desk, I start to think through my options. If I quit, I'd have to find a teaching position in another district, which might be difficult. The uncertainty of starting over again is daunting. But on the other hand, quitting would free me from this suffocating job and give me the opportunity to go back to Kane and Hailey.

My mind races as I weigh the risks and benefits. If I stay, I'll be miserable, trapped in a job that's draining the life out of me. If I leave, I'll have to navigate the challenges of finding a new job, but I'd have the chance to rebuild my life with people I love.

Overwhelmed, I push away from my desk and throw up my arms. "Okay, universe, give me a sign!" I say out loud, the desperation clear in my voice. I need guidance, something to point me in the right direction.

I wait, half-expecting some magical solution for what I should do, but the room remains silent, the weight of my decision still pressing down on me.

The drive home is unbearable. It's the hottest day on record in Phoenix, and my car's air conditioner chooses today to give out. By the time I get to my mother's old house, I'm drenched in sweat, and my patience is wearing thin.

The air conditioner in the house is still broken, of course. The heat inside is suffocating, and the only relief is a lukewarm glass of water from the tap. I collapse onto the old, creaky couch, the weight of everything bearing down on me.

I miss Kane so much it hurts. We haven't talked since he told me to decide. Today, I'm deciding without a sign. I'll call a real estate agent and set the ball in motion to sell the house. It's time to move on.

As I drag myself up to check the mail that's come through the slot, I notice a single piece lying on the floor.

It catches my eye immediately—a postcard. I pick it up, the memories flooding back. This postcard looks like the one that brought me to Alaska in the first place, but there's something different about it.

I turn it over, and my breath catches. The handwriting is different, but the message is similar.

"Timber, please come back. We love you. We need you. We can work anything out when we're together."

It's signed by Kane, with a little stick-figure drawing of three people smiling—him, me, and Hailey.

Tears spring to my eyes as I clutch the postcard to my chest. I realize I didn't need a sign because I had already decided. But the universe gave me one anyway.

I glance at the clock. It's early enough to arrange for a flight out and to dial a real estate agent.

I call an agent first. "Hi, my name is Timber Moore. I need to sell my house. I'll take whatever you can get. I'm leaving for Alaska." We work on the logistics, and once it's all settled, I hang up.

Immediately, a weight lifts from my shoulders. I start packing, feeling lighter with every box I fill. The oppressive heat seems to fade into the background as the excitement of returning takes over.

I call Kane, but when I do, I get a message saying he's out of range until Thursday and to leave a message. I debate whether to tell him or not, my finger hovering over the end call button. Finally, I decide to show up and surprise him.

As I gaze around the house, a swirl of nostalgia and relief washes over me. This place is filled with moments of laughter and tears. Yet, it's time to step forward, to craft new memories with the people I cherish.

At the airport, I sit at my laptop, unable to resist the urge to look up Port Promise again. I'm reliving everything from before—searching for images, reading about the town. It's a comfort, a way to reconnect with what I left behind.

As I scroll through the town's website, something catches my eye. A job posting.

Job Posting: Schoolteacher Wanted

Position: Schoolteacher (Not a Camp Counselor)
Requirements:
- Must be named Timber
- Must love my brother Kane
- Must love my niece Hailey

Application Process:
- Apply in person

Joy fills me, a laugh bubbling up from deep inside. Tears of happiness blur my vision as I stare at the screen, rereading the post over and over.

I hear the announcement for boarding, and excitement surges through me. This is it. I'm going back to where I belong, to the people who love me and need me. I stand up, clutching the postcard tightly in my hand, and make my way to the boarding line.

It's time to go home.

About twelve hours later, I'm back in the tiny plane,

while Hank scrapes the peak with the pontoon floats. The plane bucks wildly, but this time, instead of gripping the seat in terror, I laugh. The roar of the engine is the same, the turbulence just as jarring, but I feel steady.

"Back for more? Couldn't get enough of us, huh?" Hank shouts over the engine's roar, offering me his familiar grin.

"You bet! This time, I'm ready for anything!" I shout back, my excitement rising as I see the port come into view.

Hank's hands are steady on the controls, and instead of praying, I marvel at how far I've come.

"Alright, brace yourself!" His tone is still casual, but now it seems like an old friend's reassurance.

"If you get me there in one piece, I'll let you officiate at my future wedding!" I shout.

"Challenge accepted." The plane splashes down and skitters across the water, and I ride the bumps like a pro. We glide to a stop, and I step out with a confidence I never had before. This time, I'm not just following breadcrumbs. I'm blazing my own trail. And I can't wait to see where it leads.

Chapter Thirty-Five

KANE

It's been days since I sent the postcard, and I haven't heard a word from Timber. Did she change her mind? Did my silence drive her away? These thoughts swirl in my head as I haul in the biggest catch of my career. The nets are heavy with fish, and the excitement of such a successful day is dampened by not sharing it with Timber.

Did she call and get my message—the one stating I'd be out of town until Thursday? Did that contribute to her silence? The uncertainty gnaws at me, making it hard to fully appreciate the moment.

The sea is calm, the sky a clear blue, but my mind is a mess. I pull in the lines with methodical precision, each movement a distraction from the uncertainty that's been eating at me. The new boat has been a game-changer. I haven't been late to port once since I got it. There's pride in that, a small comfort knowing I've kept things running smoothly despite everything.

As I steer the boat back toward town, the dock is filled with tourists snapping photos of the whales that like to come into the port. It's a bittersweet sight—beautiful, yet a reminder of the emptiness her absence leaves behind.

The boat glides smoothly into its berth, and a woman with her head down and wearing a puffy blue jacket approaches. I gruffly tell her to step back.

But she raises her head, and I nearly jump out of my skin. My breath catches, and for a moment, I think I'm imagining things. It's Timber. Every emotion I've been holding back crashes over me—relief, joy, and a love so fierce it nearly brings me to my knees.

"Are you Kane Hollister?" she asks.

I realize she's reliving her first day here. Deciding to play along, I respond, "I am," my voice trembling with the effort to stay calm. "Timber Moore?"

"For now. I'm setting my sights on becoming a Hollister."

I can't hold back anymore. I jump from the boat and pull her into my arms, holding her tight as if she might disappear again. "I can make that happen."

She laughs, the sound like music to my ears. "Good, because I told Hank if he got me here in one piece, he could officiate."

I lean in and kiss her deeply, pouring all the love and longing of the past weeks into that one moment. It's a kiss full of meaning, and when we finally pull apart, I rest my forehead against hers, savoring the connection.

"Can I help unload?" she asks, a mischievous twinkle in her eye.

I chuckle, still holding her close. "Have you got experience with that?"

She grins. "I've picked blueberries and faced down a bear. How hard can it be?"

I laugh, feeling lighter than I have in weeks. "Alright then, let's get to it."

Together, we unload the catch. I toss the salmon, and she catches them and places them in the bins effortlessly. It's natural, like she's always been a part of this life.

As we work side by side, a profound sense of gratitude fills me. She's back, and this time, I'm not letting her go. When the last of the fish is on ice, I pull Timber close.

"I missed you so much," I say.

"I missed you too." Her eyes shine with unshed tears.

"Hailey is going to lose her little mind." I can't imagine the joy my daughter will feel when she sees that Timber has returned.

"She's already seen me. I got in about eight hours ago."

I stare at her, stunned. "Eight hours? You've been here that long, and I didn't know?"

She nods. "When I called, I got your message saying you'd be back on Thursday. I decided to surprise you."

A mix of surprise and a twinge of guilt washes over me. "You got the postcard?"

"I did, but I was already coming home anyway."

Her words hit me, and I reel with a surge of emotion.

Alaska, Hailey, and I—this is home for her. "Then let's go get our daughter and head to the house."

Timber looks at me and sighs. "I love you."

"I love you more." I pull her into a tight embrace, the weight of her presence sinking in.

She lifts on tiptoes and whispers, "Eliza is taking Hailey home for the night. The price to get me alone and naked is chocolate chip pancakes for breakfast at May's tomorrow morning."

"Wait, we have the house to ourselves?" A grin spreads across my face.

"Just you and me," she confirms.

I scoop her up and throw her over my shoulder, making her squeal with surprise and delight. As we walk toward the ATV, she giggles and tells me to put her down.

"I let you go once. I won't make that mistake again." My grip is firm but gentle.

May sticks her head outside the café door and grins. "I'll see you tomorrow!"

Timber laughs. "Kane, all my things are in the storage closet on the dock! If I don't get them, I won't have anything to wear!"

"For the rest of the night, you'll be wearing me," I say, making her blush and laugh harder.

We drive toward the ridge, and Timber glances at something. "Go back, I want to see that sign," she says.

I turn the ATV around, and we stop in front of the new sign I installed days ago. It reads "Timber Ridge."

"You named it after me?" Her eyes are wide with

surprise. "Didn't you tell me sentimental names were unnecessary?"

I shrug. "Some things change. Baby, you needed signs, so I put them everywhere." I pull her close for another kiss.

As we head back home, the excitement of being together fills the air. With Timber by my side, everything feels real, everything seems right. Never in my wildest dreams did I imagine that I'd fall in love with a city girl who once was a stranger and quickly became my everything.

Chapter Thirty-Six

KANE - ONE YEAR LATER...

The pier is packed with friends and family, all here for our wedding. The decorations are perfect. The sky is clear. And everyone is present—except for Hank. I want to throttle the man, but I keep my cool. This is important to Timber. Hank delivered her safely to the port, and she wants him to deliver us into marriage.

I hear the drone of a plane engine and look up to see Hank's floatplane descending toward the water. Finally. The plane skims across the surface, and I watch as Hank expertly maneuvers it to the dock.

He steps out, straightens his bowtie, and flashes an apologetic grin. "Sorry I'm late, folks!" He starts tossing fancy suitcases onto the dock, each one thudding heavily. "But I had to deal with this one." He points to a woman teetering on her heels as she exits the plane.

She's wearing a tight, black leather dress that barely covers anything and some kind of shiny wrap that looks more suited for a Hollywood gala than the Alaskan wilderness. She's clearly struggling to keep her balance on the uneven dock. Her over-the-top wave and bright smile make it obvious she thinks all these people are here to see her.

"Hello, everyone!" she calls out, waving like a beauty queen on parade. "Thank you for the warm welcome!"

She turns to me. "Are you my driver?"

I shake my head. "You've got the wrong guy."

Finn steps forward, already gathering the suitcases to clear the dock. "You're two days late."

"I had a medical procedure."

"You mean Botox and a facial?" my brother asks.

She leans in and whispers, "How did you know?"

"Your agent called," Finn says.

At the mention of her agent, I know exactly who this is. Business is slow for Finn, and when a Hollywood agent wanted to rent out Finn's cabin and put Lena Kensington in the wild to up her ratings, Finn took the gig.

"Do you mind?" I ask. "You're holding up my wedding, and I'd like to get to the forever part of my life." I point to an empty chair at the back. "Have a seat."

"Oh, so these people..."

Finn sighs. "Aren't here for you, sweetheart."

Lena struts down the dock like it's a runway, but one of her heels gets caught between the boards. She pulls and tugs, but she's good and stuck. I laugh to myself because that is exactly who I thought Timber would be

—a city girl without a clue. I'm one lucky bastard that she wasn't.

Finn bends over and tugs, but the heel won't budge. Finally, he pulls her foot from the shoe and snaps the heel straight off from the sole. "You won't be needing those here." He kicks at the heel until it loosens from the crevice and falls into the water.

She looks at him in horror. "These are Louboutins!"

Finn shrugs. "Well, you'll have to buy Lou another pair."

As soon as Lena is seated, the wedding music starts. My heart skips a beat as I turn to watch Timber walking down the dock. She's a vision in her white dress, catching the sunlight with each step. The dress hugs her figure perfectly, flowing gracefully around her legs. Her hair is in soft waves, cascading down her shoulders, with a daisy-chain crown on top. She looks like a woodland goddess, ethereal and stunning.

Her eyes lock onto mine, and in that moment, the world narrows down to just the two of us. Her eyes sparkle with unshed tears, and her smile is radiant, more beautiful than anything I've ever seen. She holds a bouquet of wildflowers she picked from our yard this morning.

My dad walks beside her, smiling proudly as he escorts her down the makeshift aisle. The love and approval in his eyes mirror everything inside me. Behind them, Hailey skips with a basket, joyfully tossing daisies, her laughter a sweet song that fills the air.

As Timber gets closer, I notice the little details. The delicate curve of her lip that I've kissed so many times. The way a strand of hair has escaped and brushes against her cheek. The slight tremble in her hands as she grips the bouquet. She glances down, almost shyly, then looks back up at me with a look that says she's exactly where she wants to be.

A lump forms in my throat as emotions swell within me.

This is the woman I love, the woman I'm going to spend the rest of my life with. The thought fills me with a profound sense of joy.

May sits in the front row, wiping tears from her eyes. The guests are all captivated, and it's not because of the diva sitting in the back row. It's all because of my future bride.

When she finally reaches me, we take each other's hands. Her touch is warm and reassuring, an electric connection sparking as if our souls are aligning perfectly in that moment.

"I love you," I whisper, my voice thick with emotion.

"I love you too," she replies, her voice steady and full of conviction.

We turn to face Hank, our officiant, ready to begin. I know, without a doubt, that this is the beginning of something extraordinary.

Hank clears his throat and begins the ceremony. "Ladies and gentlemen, we are gathered here today to witness the union of Timber and Kane. But first, let's all acknowledge that I got her here safely—twice now—and that deserves a round of applause." The guests laugh and clap.

"We're here to celebrate love, the kind that weathers storms, both literal and metaphorical," Hank continues, a mischievous look in his eye. "So, without further ado, let's get to the fun part. Kane and Timber have prepared their own vows."

I turn to Timber, taking a deep breath. "Timber, when you first arrived here, I thought you were just another city girl out of her element. But you proved me wrong every single day. You showed me what love, strength, and determination look like. I promise to stand by you, to laugh with you, and to love you with everything I have, even when the seas get rough. You're my compass, my safe harbor, and I love you more than words can say."

Timber's eyes shimmer with tears as she squeezes my hands. "Kane, when I came to town, I was searching for something—my place, my purpose. I found all of that and more with you. You are my anchor and my adventure all at once. I'll support you, laugh at your jokes even when they're terrible, and love you fiercely every day. You've taught me what it means to truly be home, and I love you with all my heart."

Every word she says is a reminder of how much we've been through and how much I love her. Tears sting my eyes, but I hold them back, focusing on her face. She's everything I've ever wanted, and her vows reaffirm that I'm the luckiest man in the world.

Hank grins, wiping a fake tear from his eye. "Beautiful, just beautiful. Now, before we wrap this up, there's someone else who wants to say a few words."

Hailey steps forward. She looks up at us with wide eyes. "Timber, I promise to share my toys, to help you bake cookies, and to always give you lots of hugs. And Daddy, I will be good and not kiss anyone until I'm thirty-five. I love you both."

The crowd melts, a collective "aww" sweeping through them. Timber bends down to hug Hailey, and I join in, wrapping them both in my arms.

Hank continues. "Now, by the power vested in me by the great state of Alaska, I now pronounce you husband and wife. Kane, you may kiss your bride."

I straighten and pull Timber close and kiss her deeply, the cheers of our friends and family ringing in my ears. When we finally pull apart, Hank is there, grinning like a fool.

"Ladies and gentlemen, I present to you, for the first time, Mr. and Mrs. Hollister! Now, let's get to the part where we eat and drink!"

The guests laugh and applaud, and Timber and I turn to face them, hands clasped tightly together. This is it. Our forever starts now, surrounded by the people we love, in the place that brought us together.

"I love you," she whispers again.

"I love you more."

As the ceremony ends, Timber walks down the dock toward the community center, her hand tightly in mine. At the end, she pauses and turns, tossing her bouquet over her shoulder. It sails through the air and lands right in Lena's hands.

"Oh, hell no," Lena exclaims, holding the bouquet like it's a live grenade.

Need more Port Promise? Finn and Lena are next.

Other Books by Kelly Collins

A Port Promise Series

Timber Ridge

Crystal Creek

An Aspen Cove Romance Series

One Hundred Reasons

One Hundred Heartbeats

One Hundred Wishes

One Hundred Promises

One Hundred Excuses

About the Author

International bestselling author of more than fifty novels, Kelly Collins writes with the intention of keeping love alive. Always a romantic, she blends real-life events with her vivid imagination to create characters and stories that lovers of contemporary romance, new adult, and romantic suspensewill return to again and again. Kelly has sold half a million books worldwide, and in 2021 she was awarded a Readers' Favorite Award Gold Medal in the Contemporary Romance category.

For More Information
www.authorkellycollins.com
kelly@authorkellycollins.com

Printed in Great Britain
by Amazon